their support I would never have been lucky enough to meet other authors, interact with people who love books and reading, and get involved with the fantastic events the library hold. As a local Dagenham gal, the Dagenham Library holds a special place in my heart -- and always will -- because of its welcoming, comfortable, homey feeling. A big, big thank you to Lisa Roullier, Heather Pope, Angelica Gedviliene, Lena Smith, Vince Thomas, David Wheaton, David Golland and James Botchway the resident security aka DJ. I'm proud to know them!

D0807455

To my readers:

Without you lovely lot, my dream would never have come true. You've been there by my side through it all -- at book signings, on Facebook, on Twitter, emails, Amazon reviews and on my blog. As we've gone on this journey together, I've been lucky enough to make new friends and found old friends. A big, big "thank you" to you all for your encouragement and support. Your messages and comments make me so happy, a smile is on my face instantly. You're my daily motivation to keep writing, writing, writing. I wouldn't be Sandra Prior Author without each and every one of you. I've been called a lot worse . . . lol and told I have to get 'a proper job'

I hope you enjoy reading Mickey's War as much as I enjoyed writing and getting it out there to you!

"You ask, what is our aim? I can answer in one word. It is victory, victory at all costs, victory in spite of all terror, victory, however long and hard the road may be; for without victory, there is no survival."

Winston Churchill

Mickey
Dagenham, July 2005

"Mornin' Mickey!"

"All right, Guv'nor?"

"Told you he'd be here!"

Mickey Taylor strolled across the floor of the boxing club – his boxing club – eyes taking everything in, acknowledging the greetings with a nod. Despite the grey hair at his temples, he still had the build, the gait of a fighter. Powerful shoulders, a firm jaw, a cocky "get out of my fucking way!" walk.

He loved it, fucking loved it here. "Mickey's", that was what the place was called, and for anyone in the Dagenham area who knew anything at all about the Taylors, or had any interest in boxing, that was the only name it needed. "Mickey's." His club. His manor. His name.

He glanced around. The club was busy, even for a Wednesday, a mix of young and not so young, talented and no hopers, fit, fat and everything in between, pounding on punchbags, skipping rope, lifting weights.

Mickey inhaled deeply as he crossed the floor. The smell reminded him of the first time he stepped into a boxing gym, barely ten years old at the time. It was the smell of sweat and rusting metal, of old leather and liniment, the smell of hard work and strength, of fear and hope, joy and despair. He'd had plenty of all of them, inside the ring and out on the streets, but now he had finally reached a place in his life where he felt settled, like he'd arrived.

Mickey allowed himself a half smile as he reached his office. It was not like you could ever sit back on your laurels in this business, there was always some cocky cunt waiting to snatch everything away from you, but he no longer lived on a knife edge – and that was mostly down to Martin.

Martin was already in the office, had probably been there since the crack of dawn, the little fucker – that was still the way Mickey thought of his younger brother. Martin never seemed to sleep, never seemed to do anything much except work. Not that Mickey was complaining. They complemented each other perfectly. While Mickey was the face, the presence of the Taylors out in the street, in the pubs and bars and seedy restaurants where their deals were made, Martin was the respectable face of the Taylors. He fronted up all their legitimate businesses, laundered all the money, made sure there was nothing that the Old Bill – or the tax man – could pin on them.

Mickey pushed open the office door. Martin was on the phone, suited and booted as ever, looking immaculate. The unimpeachable businessman, able to mix and mingle and charm, most people oblivious to the fact that he was brother to the notorious Mickey Taylor, "Dangerous," convicted murderer, the hardest, most vicious crook to come out of Dagenham.

Martin gave Mickey a nod as he saw him come in, continued his conversation. "If the deliveries continue to be late, we will find ourselves another supplier," said Martin in an even tone. He grinned at Mickey, pointed to a stack of messages on the desk for Mickey. Mickey picked them up, leafed through them half-heartedly as Martin continued his conversation.

"Effective tomorrow, I'm discounting all your invoices by five percent."

Mickey grinned. He loved watching Martin work – someone pissed Mickey off, he'd go round and break their nose. But Martin was a businessman through and through, worked the angles, used more subtle means.

"Well, if you prefer we can cancel your contract right now?" The voice of reason. Power through control, through certainty. "That's what I thought," continued Martin. "So we're agreed. Five percent off all invoices from this point on and any late deliveries will be discounted ten percent." There was a short pause. "I hope so too."

Martin hung up the phone, looked up at Mickey.

"Problem?"

Martin grinned. "Opportunity. Make someone depend on you to keep their business afloat and you've got them by the balls. I'm quite certain that these clowns will keep fucking up."

"So why don't you cut them loose? You don't need the hassle."

Martin smiled. "Now why would I want to do that? They'll keep stumbling along in their usual inefficient way, I'll keep squeezing them, and in six months they'll be so broke we'll be able to buy them out for a song."

Mickey shook his head. "You're an evil bastard, you are."

"I learned from the best." Martin glanced out towards the floor of the gym. "You working with Kenny today?"

Mickey nodded as he headed through to his own office. "Yeah. He's fighting Saturday night. A couple more bouts and he'll be ready for the ABA championships."

"You be done by lunchtime? There's a few things we need to catch up on."

"Yeah, about one?"

Martin nodded. "I can be free by then."

Mickey's office was very different from Martin's. It had a big window that looked out over the gym so Mickey could keep an eye on what was going on in the club. He loved watching people train, whoever they were. From middle-aged punters hoping a bit of the Mickey magic would rub off on their tubby frames through to hungry young fighters scrapping and clawing to try and make something of themselves. But of all of those, the best was Kenny.

Kenny Jackson, sixteen years old, with dancing feet, fists like anvils, and a jaw that could take a big punch. Mickey had been training him for three years now, and the kid had really come on. He never said much – hardly said anything at all, really – but he looked at Mickey with fierce intensity, listened to every word he said, did exactly what he was told. Mickey had been one of Britain's best up and coming boxers as a teenager, might have made it to the very top if his cunt of a Dad hadn't had him knocked down in a hit and run. Anything to stop his son from outshining him. But that was life, things happened, you couldn't dwell on it, just got on with it. Being fucked up and miserable about it wouldn't change a thing.

Mickey peeled off his jacket, his shirt, pulled some clothes from a locker in the corner of his office. Mickey's body was still hard, muscular. He'd lost some of the speed he had when he was younger, but made up for it in power, street smarts, and sheer viciousness. The metal rod in his arm still stopped him from training as much as he'd like – it would ache for days after a session on the heavy bag – but he was still in incredible shape for his age, definitely not someone you'd want to fuck with.

As Mickey changed into tracksuit bottoms and a T-shirt, his eyes sought out Kenny. He was unmistakable, a shock of black hair, eyes like coals, moving with startling speed as he worked the bag under the careful gaze of Mickey's son, Tommy. Tommy knew his stuff too, had a lot of his dad's fighting talent, but like Mickey had knocked a girl up, got married early, and like Mickey he had never got to fulfill his dreams as a fighter. They made a right pair, father and son, both of them passing on their knowledge and intensity to a new generation of local fighters.

Mickey checked his reflection one more time – "You're a good looking fucker, Mickey Taylor!" he grinned to himself very aware that he was more than averagely good looking for a man of his age. He kept himself in excellent shape, every morning he was up at five, shorts, vest top and trainers on, ready to start his day with a five mile run. Then he went back to his gym for a workout and finished off with a few lengths in the pool. Whatever the weather, Mickey stuck to his daily rigid routine.

He strolled out onto the floor of the gym. Music blasted from a boom box in the corner of the room, but it could barely be heard over the sound of clanking metal, fists slamming into punchbags, the grunts and groans of the fighters as they strained and sweated. Time to go to work.

By the time he was done working with Kenny, Mickey was covered in sweat. He grabbed a towel and a bottle of water, was about to start his own workout when Martin called out to him. "They're about to make the announcement!"

Fuck, he'd almost forgotten! Mickey turned and headed to Martin's office, Tommy at his side, the other fighters following along. Within seconds, only Kenny was still out on the floor, his hands a blur as he worked the speed bag, the rattle echoing across the now empty gym floor.

Everyone else crowded into Martin's office, filling it with chatter and sweat, jokes and laughter, all peering at a small TV that was on one end of Martin's desk.

"All right!" Mickey ordered. "Shut the fuck up and listen!"

Instantly the room fell silent, the only sound the announcer on the TV, the rattle of Kenny on the speed bag in the background.

A man in a dark suit stood at a podium, a host of microphones in his face. He cleared his throat, looked up at the cameras. "The International Olympic Committee has the honor of announcing that the games of the Thirtieth Olympiad in 2012 are awarded to the city of ..." the announcer paused for a brief second, "London!"

For just a moment there was silence as the word sank in, then the small office erupted into a cacophony of cheers and excitement.

"Fuck me, the Olympics in London!" was the most commonly expressed sentiment.

Tommy poked his head out of the office, shouted across to Kenny. "Oi! Kenny!"

The youngster paused for a moment, caught the speed bag between his taped hands to silence it, looked across at Tommy.

"We won! You're going to be fighting on home soil in 2012!"

Kenny said nothing, just gave one brief nod, then immediately resumed his abuse of the speed bag.

Tommy shook his head, grinned to himself, stepped back into Martin's office to join the celebration.

It was a good ten minutes before Martin was finally able to clear his office. He waved a hand under his nose, scowled. "It's going to fucking stink in here for the rest of the day!" he grumbled.

Mickey was still grinning. "Stop moaning you fucking big tart!" He headed into his own office, his voice coming back to Martin as he rummaged around for something. "I've got something that will get rid of the smell!"

Mickey reappeared seconds later, a bottle of champagne and two glasses in one hand, a pair of thick cigars in the other.

Martin looked surprised, annoyed. "That's a bit much, isn't it, Mickey! I'm sure we'll make a few bob off the Olympics, but fuck me this is a bit OTT –"

Mickey kicked Martin's door shut, set the glasses on the table, a huge grin on his face.

Martin gave him a curious look. "All right, come on, tell me, there's more, isn't there? This isn't just about London winning the Olympics, is it?"

But Mickey was giving nothing away. Still grinning, he popped the champagne, poured two glasses, held one up, ready for a toast. Martin had no choice but to follow along, see where this was heading. He picked up his glass, looked at Mickey expectantly.

"Here's to the Olympics making us fucking millionaires!" Mickey announced.

Still puzzled, Martin clinked his glass against Mickey's, took a sip. "I'll drink to that, even though I ain't got a fucking clue what you're going on about …"

Mickey downed his glass in one, quickly refilled it, the annoying grin never leaving his face.

"Martin, my son," he announced, handing him a cigar, "that is the best fucking news we've had in a long time."

Mickey lit his cigar, leaned over and lit Martin's.

Still Martin said nothing, just drew on his cigar and waited for Mickey to explain things in his own good time. The phone started to ring, but Martin ignored it, sipped his champagne and waited.

"A long time ago," said Mickey finally, "before you were even born, our old man – I hope he's rotting in hell, the fucking prick. Well, he won a chunk of land in a card game. It was nothing, a piece of shit you wouldn't even build your fucking outhouse on it back then. Bobby had no use for it, so he let the gypsies camp on it. He and Big Frankie knew each other from the old days when they went hop picking; Big Frankie had helped him out of a scrape or two, so he was happy for them to set up on it."

Mickey paused, sucked on his cigar, exhaled slowly, a cloud of smoke settling round his head.

"So anyway, time goes on, Frankie sets up a scrap metal business there, it's still a shit piece of land, but everyone's happy." Mickey paused again for dramatic effect, then leaned in close to Martin. "But the thing is, that plot of land, that shitty, dirty, stinking fucking plot of land, is smack in the middle of where they want to build the Olympic Park!"

Mickey's eyes were shining. "Who knows how much it's now worth?"

Martin leaned forward, narrowed his eyes. "And you still have the deeds to it?"

Mickey grinned. "Tucked away in my safe at home!"

Martin sat back, twirled his cigar in his fingers. "When something like that hits – the Olympics I mean – land prices go up ten times, a hundred times …"

Mickey nodded.

Martin suddenly looked serious. "What about Frankie, the gypsies? They've must have been there almost forty years?"

Mickey scowled. "Right. Forty years. Forty years rent fucking free! They can't have no complaints if we want to sell the land."

"But they've got a good business there," Martin pointed out. "And they've built a couple of buildings there, haven't they?"

"All without planning permission." Mickey sucked on his cigar. "No, I reckon Big Frankie will be good with this. Whatever Bobby owed him has been paid off a hundred times over. They'll leave when we ask them."

Martin didn't look so certain. "And if they don't?"

Mickey's eyes narrowed, he glared at Martin through a haze of smoke. "Then I'll fucking deal with it!"

Tommy watched as Kenny continued to work on the speed bag, but he had one eye on his Uncle Martin's office the whole time. He could see the cigars and the champagne, knew his dad and Martin too well to believe that they were simply celebrating London winning the Olympics.

They would be pleased, of course, especially as they had Kenny and a couple of other young lads who should be in their prime by 2012, but Tommy knew it was more than that. If Mickey had pulled out the champagne and cigars – and it would certainly have been him to do it, it wasn't Martin's style – then it was something personal, something that impacted the Taylors.

But desperate as he was to know what was going on, what they were celebrating, Tommy knew better than to go ask. When it came to Taylor family business, there were two sides – what you needed to know, and what you didn't need to know, and Mickey had always kept his kids out of the dodgy side of things.

Of course, Tommy knew who his dad was, what he did, but he was never a part of it, never had been. Instead, Tommy ran a couple of dry cleaning shops that Martin had bought, made a nice living at it too but the other side of the business, the violence, the drugs, the guns, Tommy had never been brought into that. Tommy understood why, knew his dad was protecting him, and was grateful for what he had, but at the same time, he couldn't help but feel shut out, excluded. His dad's world, Martin's world, was so much more exciting and glamorous than his. Mickey was the man, a man of substance and significance, everyone knew who Mickey Taylor was, royalty virtually, but Tommy rarely got to share that. Tommy had to be squeaky clean, Tommy had to keep his nose out of anything dodgy, Tommy had to do what he was told and not ask any questions.

Fuck that! Tommy was pissed off for still being treated like a kid, an outsider. He was twenty eight years old, not a fucking big baby like his dad treated him, he could more than handle himself. And he had his own secrets, things his dad didn't know about. If they wanted to shut him out, fine. He'd just do things his own way, without their help.

He turned his attention back to Kenny. The kid was good, with a dedication that was scary. He'd train all day if you let him, pound the heavy bag till his hands bled, but he did at least listen to what he was told to do.

"All right Kenny, that's enough!" Tommy had to shout to make himself heard over the noise.

Kenny glanced at him, then reluctantly stopped. The bag still shook as Kenny grabbed a towel, wiped his face. There was a pool of sweat on the floor at his feet. He looked to Tommy for further instruction.

Sharon

Sharon raised the whip, brought it down hard across the man's back. He grunted in pain, gasped for breath. Angry red stripes already marked his skin, but once more Sharon raised the whip, once more she brought it down with a crack across his back.

His gasp was louder this time, his arms pulling against the chains that bound him to the wall as he squirmed in pain, panting like a dog to catch his breath before the next blow came. The man was in his fifties, with a soft, pale body, thinning hair. Right now, he was shaking from the abuse he was receiving.

Sharon raised her arm once more, but before she could deliver another blow, the man forced out a single word. "Amber!"

Sharon paused, looked at him curiously. "Already?" There was a sneer on her lip, disdain in her voice.

"I'm sorry, Mistress!" he moaned.

"What are you?"

"I'm a pathetic, mewling little shit!" he gasped.

Sharon cracked the whip against the wall beside him. "Truly pathetic!"

"Yes, Mistress. Truly pathetic!"

She watched him for a moment more, then stepped forward, placed the whip on a small table alongside a collection of other whips, canes, paddles and crops. She stepped up close behind him, whispered in his ear. "Who do you belong to?"

"To you, Mistress!" he gasped.

She looked down at his pale body, the welts still glowing red across his back, down to his buttocks. A strap that passed around his waist held a dildo firmly in place between his cheeks. "You are my bitch, aren't you?"

"Yes, Mistress!"

She pushed against the dildo, forcing it deeper inside him. "What are you?"

"Your bitch, Mistress!"

She surveyed the table, a wicked smile on her face. "I think it's time for the paddle, don't you?"

The man's eyes opened wider, a mix of fear and ecstasy. "Do you think I'm ready?"

Sharon glared at him, lifted a heavy wooden paddle. "You question my judgement?"

The man trembled, licked his lips. "No Mistress, you always know exactly what I need!"

"But you questioned me? And for that there is a price to pay!"

The man trembled, making his pale, flabby flesh jiggle. Whether it was from fear or anticipation was hard to say. "Whatever you say, Mistress!"

Sharon stood back, weighing the paddle in her hand as she lined it up with his exposed buttocks, the dildo strapped in place. "Right! And what I say is it's time for the paddle!" She pulled her arm back, then swung hard and true.

Sharon slumped on the couch, sucked on a cigarette. She was still in the PVC basque she had worn for the last session, still wearing black stockings and high heels, but she had pulled off her wig – long, dark tresses that hung down her back – to reveal her own hair, short, stylishly cut, bleached blonde as always.

As she drew in the nicotine, she began to relax. It had been a long day, three sessions. Sometimes it wore her out, all the spanking and caning and whipping, but fuck me, she thought, if that's what the punter wants, that's what he gets. And at three hundred quid a session, who was she to complain?

It had taken her a while to adjust to her changing role with clients. For a long time, she had been top totty, able to keep a steady stream of customers just on her looks. But time had caught up with Sharon as it did with everyone, and she had had to reinvent herself. First she had become a MILF. It was amazing how many blokes wanted to fuck an older woman, especially when she kept herself in shape, dressed the part. Some kind of mummy fantasy, she supposed, but as long as they were paying, she didn't care.

But even that could only work for so long. And that's when she had stumbled across the whole dominatrix thing. It started with a customer, Roger, asking if she would spank him. Nothing new in that and she was happy to oblige – it was better than sucking another cock – and it had taken off from there. Roger was hardcore, wanted more and more and more, and the more she abused him, the more he paid her. Soon, she had started a collection of whips and shit, and was wondering what to do with it, if there other men out there who liked it as much as Roger.

Sharon had always had a good eye for business, so it didn't take long before she did some research and realised that she was on to a winner. She bought all the gear, dressed the part, even put up a website. Before she knew it, she was making more money not fucking guys than she had been for fucking them!

Some of them still wanted her to jerk them off or suck them, but most of them got off on the abuse, which was fine by Sharon. "I mean," she had told her best mate, Della, another hooker, "who really wants to still be shagging and swallowing for a living when before you know it we will be in the queue at the post office waiting to collect our pension.?"

Being a hooker had been a natural progression for Sharon. She had learned from an early age that men liked good looks and big tits, and she had both. Sex was power, and power was a feeling she loved.

Sharon had always been pretty, was one of the taller girls in her class at school, with lovely long legs and a slender body. To top it off she had long blonde hair, long lashes, chestnut eyes and wide full lips.

By her late teens she was living a life of partying, into drugs and men, sleeping with whoever she wanted too, whenever she wanted to, having fun snorting cocaine and clubbing the night away.

Being smart, she soon realised that the best way to continue to enjoy her wild lifestyle was to have affairs with older men. They had the money to support her decadent lifestyle.

But the affairs were unreliable, she never knew when one might end and she would be cast adrift, scratching for money and trying to live like a normal person. And although there were times in her life where she felt she belonged nowhere, she could never imagine her life ever resembling normal.

And so, little by little, she had gone on the game. It wasn't a conscious decision, more something she drifted into – a tip here, some cash there, and before she knew it, her rich boyfriends had turned into rich customers, with Sharon doing anything and everything as long as she got paid at the end of it.

She shuddered to think of how many cocks she had sucked and fucked. There were times when she felt like she was selling her soul, and of course, she had to keep it a secret from her family. Mickey would have flipped, and her mum, well, Lizzie would have shrivelled up and died on the spot if she had ever found out what Sharon did.

As far as they were all concerned, Sharon had a top job in the city, as a PA. It was true, actually, at first anyway. She worked at a law firm during the day, then plied her trade in a top west end bar at night. The only person who ever knew the truth was Miranda.

The funny thing was that despite what people might think, you didn't need any expert sex skills to become a whore; there were no classes on sex. Anybody could do the job. What's skillful about opening your legs and bending over?

The trick, as Sharon soon learned, was all about erotic appeal. Your eyes, your smile, your body language. If you just went with the flow, let the bloke think it was all about them and their desires, then you'd pretty much cracked it.

In fact, Sharon found that most blokes were turned on just by meeting her, talking, touching, kissing, caressing. They worshipped her body, and if she was smart, the kissing and caressing would get them so fucking horny and excited that by the time they actually got around to the sex it didn't take long before they came, and it was all over. Some even exploded before the sex! The trick was to understand that when they were with her, they could relax. There was no social pressure, no obligations or expectations.

And every client was different. Some men just wanted straight sex, some nice, some naughty. Some wanted to be in control, others to be controlled. Some loved dressing up as schoolboys, or babies, some liked bondage and others wanted to use toys while others enjoyed sadomasochistic sex. With so much variety, it was never boring!

And in return, Sharon got taken to flash restaurants, clubs, casinos, parties, got to travel all around the world. Class A drugs were always available, the cocaine flowing as freely as the obligatory champagne.

It didn't take long for Sharon to become addicted to cocaine and alcohol. She got herself into a proper mess, spunked all her money on drugs and drink. She didn't see the big crash coming until finally it all came tumbling down around her.

Just like when she was a kid, it was her big brother Mickey who came to the rescue, dragged her out of her house one day, kicking and screaming like a banshee. She called him a few choice words. She had been spiteful and vicious, told him how much she hated him; that he wasn't her brother, that he was evil, a dirty whore, even slagged him off for getting involved with Miranda Her mouth was worse than a fish wife. She really gave it to him. How he didn't give her a slap she would never know.

Mickey paid for her to go to the Priory, where she spent six torturous months. It was hell, but it gave her the chance to take a long hard look at her life and what would truly make her happy. Mickey had saved her life and her sanity, and for that she would always be grateful. When she came out, she was clean and sober for a while, but the demons had never really left her, and though she understood herself better, she still couldn't stay away from the booze and the cocaine. They were just such a part of her job, her world.

Sharon stood up, stepped out of her high heels, peeled her stockings off, dragged herself to her bedroom. The basque was easy to get out of, a big zipper down the front. She set it carefully on the end of the bed as it would need a rinse before tomorrow. She sweated like a pig in the damned PVC, but for some reason her submissives loved the look of it.

A long, hot soak in the tub was what she needed, but she was too tired to wait for the bath to run, so she turned on the shower, stepped under the fierce jet of water. That was an essential in any place

Sharon lived – a really good shower. After a long day on the game, the most important thing was to be able to get clean, wash away the sweat and spunk and saliva and feel fresh again, even if it was only for a few hours until it started all over again.

It wasn't all bad, wasn't all gross. There were odd occasions where the bloke was gentle, wanted soft, loving sex, the kind they used to get from their wives. She had seen it so many times, filthy rich men who got married to some hot looking girl half their age, but within a year the girl seemed to have forgotten what a blow job was, and claimed to have gone off sex. Getting it from some young bloke, more like it, thought Sharon.

She had asked quite a few of these men, "How would you feel if your wife was sleeping with another man?" They all said the same. They wouldn't tolerate it, but their wife wouldn't do that to them, they were certain of that.

And it helped that Sharon had always enjoyed sex, right from the first knee trembler up against the wall behind The Railway pub, so she figured she might as well get paid for it. One night stands, a score and a cab wasn't going to make her rich.

And once the money started rolling in, she was in a continued fantasy of her own that she needed to prove to everyone that she was successful and independent; that she had made it. The lies and deceit that Sharon had used had quickly built a mask that she wore when she was with friends and family, and over the years the mask had just got thicker and thicker.

The booze and drugs were inevitable, the only way to block how she was feeling, the devastation, the guilt, the pain, but most of all the shame.

Quite simply, Sharon was a good Catholic girl who was on the game. What she did was against everything she had been brought up to believe. Christ, she thought as she stepped out of the shower and toweled herself off, if God was real, he would be very angry with her, ready to smash a hammer down on her head at any moment.

Sharon looked at her tattoo of Dad on the in sole of her right foot; she traced the tattoo of DAD with her finger. God how she hated him. Many people had asked her 'why on earth have you had that done on the bottom of your foot, didn't it hurt? Yes it bloody hurt but the pain was all worth it. Every day she could walk all over that man she called Dad, the man that had destroyed her, broke her into a million pieces.

Still, what did she expect? As long as she could remember, men had used and abused her. She had been heartbroken when she had an abortion years ago; Paul was her first love, and it shattered her when he wanted her to get rid of their baby. Her self-worth had been destroyed, and she had never recovered. She had spent a lifetime looking for love in the wrong places, with the wrong people. Why was she always attracted to people with issues like her, promiscuity, nightclubs, drinking, drugs, parties? She was chasing to belong, hungry for acceptance, just wanted to be loved.

She curled up under the covers, turned out the light, lay very still, fighting back the tears, the overwhelming urge. She had put on her mask at an early age, and now she had to wear it continually, pretending everything was OK. Put on that pretty smile and everything would be all right; that was what she had been taught as a young girl when her dad was fumbling around under the covers, raping and abusing her. Her shameful secrets she tried running away from and denying. And all the time she lied to everyone about how she really felt inside, striving for success and love in order to stay strong, always burying her pain deep inside.

Over the years, she had done it all. Street and high-class hooker, exotic strip dancing, bisexuality, drugs, binge drinking, smoking. Sharon had been on the game since she was eighteen, had even fucked a Saudi prince for a while. He flew her to Paris to a five star hotel; the bed covered with red roses and the finest champagne on ice, then sat and watched while she took on five, six, seven men at once, more cocks than she could count. They had a contract, she went there once a month for six months, earned thirty grand.

But now Sharon was worn out, fucked up and ready for a fresh start, but what else could she do? She knew her vocation, knew what she was good at, and it was being a dirty whore.

She wiped her eyes on the soft, cotton pillowcase, sat up, turned on the bedside light. Why did she even bother fighting it? It was the same thing every night.

She slid open the drawer, pulled out the mirror, the little bag of white powder. Charlie was her friend, always there for her, Charlie would make her feel better, help her to get through another miserable fucking day.

She opened the bag, gently tipped a small pile of powder onto the mirror, cut it into two neat lines, leaned over and snorted, once, twice.

The buzz was instant, erasing the shitty day, the memories of fat, ugly blokes with nasty bodies and demeaning requests, erasing all the self-loathing, the hatred, the misery, the pain.

Sharon slid the mirror back into the drawer, lay back down on the pillow. Now she could relax. Now she could finally unwind and know she would make it through to tomorrow …

Charlie and Del
Harwich Docks

The battered white van pulled up outside the dark warehouse. The driver cut the motor, and the only sound to break the silence was the slow swish of the van's wipers as they fought a vain battle against the relentless rain. From inside the van, two red pinpricks of light could be seen as the driver and his passenger sucked on their cigarettes.

"Where are they?" Charlie Groves, the passenger, leaned forward to peer out into the downpour. In his early twenties, Charlie had short cropped hair, a lean muscular body, arms covered in tattoos.

"Relax. We're five minutes early." Del Watson slumped in his seat, closed his eyes as he pulled the smoke into his lungs. In his early forties, Del was starting to run to fat, but was still a big bloke with a boxer's flattened nose and dark eyes that took in everything.

But still Charlie peered outwards. "What if this isn't the right bleedin' place? It looks dead as a fucking morgue!"

"It's the right place."

"How can you be so sure?"

"Because I've been here a hundred fucking times before, that's how!"

"So where are they?"

Del sat up with a sigh, gave Charlie a weary look. "Unlike some of us, these blokes are professionals. They are always, always on time."

"But what if they aren't? What if this is some kind of set-up?"

Del looked at him. "A set up? Really?"

Charlie looked back at him defiantly. "Why not? I mean it happens, doesn't it? Geezers get jacked, or whatever."

Del shook his head. "You've been watching way too many dodgy films, Charlie. We work for the Taylors. That means we don't get jacked, we don't get shot. We pick up the goods, we drive them back to the manor, we deliver them, we get our money, we go home. No fucking fuss, no fucking drama, no fucking geezers leaping out of the dark with guns blazing." He shook his head. "Jesus Christ, this is Harwich, not Los fucking Angeles!"

Charlie started to reply, but before he could speak a metal door cracked open, and light blazed out onto the van.

Del took one last drag on his cigarette. "Let's go."

He climbed out into the rain, throwing his cigarette down as he did, hurried towards the open door, Charlie right behind him. Although it was just a few feet, they were both wet by the time they scurried inside.

The door led into the scruffy corridor of a nameless, faceless warehouse, one of hundreds that clustered around the port. Filling the corridor was a massive man, six four and twenty stone, glaring at them through a bushy beard. His face relaxed when he recognized Del. "I hope you're going to clean up my carpet, bringing all that fucking rain in with you!"

For a moment, Charlie thought he was serious, then his eyes looked down at the stained concrete floor, he saw the laughter in the man's eyes.

"All right, Del?" The big man turned and headed back along the corridor.

"Apart from this fucking rain!" grumbled Del. "I was supposed to take my little ones to the bleedin' circus tomorrow. Now it'll be like a fucking swamp!" They turned through a side door into the warehouse, metal racking floor to ceiling stacked with boxes, crates and barrels of industrial cleaning supplies. "How about you, Sam?"

Sam, the big man, led them back towards the entrance, where a dozen big boxes were stacked on the loading ramp. "Can't complain." He nodded to the boxes. "Handcart's there."

As Del grabbed the handcart and wrangled it under the first of the boxes, Sam pressed a button to open the metal roller door. With a grind of gears, the door slid upwards, revealing the van parked outside in the rain.

"Open the doors," Del ordered Charlie.

Charlie grimaced, then trotted out into the rain, threw open the double doors on the rear of the van.

Del rolled the cart down the ramp, and he and Charlie hauled the big box into the back of the van. They repeated it for each of the boxes, hurrying as much as they could, but despite their best efforts, by the time the six boxes were loaded they were both soaked to the skin, water running down their faces and into their eyes.

Sam stood inside, warm and dry, watched them with a grin on his face. "You two look like a pair of drowned rats!" he laughed as Del slammed the doors shut.

Del wiped his sodden hair back from his face, peered at Sam. "Fuck you!"

Sam just laughed.

Del turned and headed towards the front of the van. "Tell your boss to get a fucking awning!"

Sam's reply was drowned out by the sound of the van door slamming. He peered out into the darkness, then pushed the button to close the roller door, turned and rumbled back into the warehouse.

"Fuck me, I've been drier in the fucking bath!" moaned Del as he cranked the key. The engine roared into life, and Del immediately turned on the blowers to clear the front window. It was already thick with steam from their hot, wet bodies.

The blower was making little impact, so Del leaned forward, wiped it with his hand, clearing enough of the screen to be able to start driving.

Charlie grabbed two cigarettes, lit them both, handed one to Del, who sucked greedily on it. "I hate the fucking rain!" he moaned.

Del shrugged. "It ain't so bad. Miserable night like this, Old Bill doesn't want to be out and about. They'll all be tucked up tight at the station or hiding out in a motorway caff."

He drove slowly through the quiet roads of the industrial estate, sticking to the speed limit, doing nothing to attract attention.

"You never told me about that girl you were going to see last night?" said Del suddenly. "Did she show up?"

Charlie grinned, put his feet up on the dashboard of the van. "Fuck me, did she!"

"Tell me about it, then. I'm married. Your exploits are the closest I get to actually having sex these days!"

Charlie sucked on his cigarette, blew the smoke out. "So we met at the The Bull. I'm thinking she probably won't show because she's hot, a proper class bird. I mean she's really fucking stacked, know what I mean?" He gestured a huge pair of breasts with his hands.

Del smiled. "Yeah, I get the picture!"

"So anyway, she doesn't show, I get another pint, then another one. I'm getting more pissed off, then just when I'm about to go home, she turns up, wearing this low-cut figure hugging dress, half her fucking tits hanging out. She's all over me, all apologetic, so sorry I kept you waiting, blah, blah, blah. I got a hard on just looking at her"

The van slowed as Del approached a red light.

"So anyway, cut a long story short, we have a couple of drinks, decide to go for a dance somewhere. So we head to my car, we're barely in the car before she's all over me. Before I fucking knew it she was giving me head!"

"In the car park of The Bull?" Del stopped at the red light, glanced around. A big black 4X4 had pulled up at the light across from them. "All I've ever done in that car park is take a piss and throw up a few times!"

"She fucking went to town on me, mate!"

"Was she any good?"

Charlie had a huge smile on his face. "Good? I reckon she could suck a golf ball though a fucking hosepipe!"

Del looked over at him, started to say something, froze as the headlights of the 4X4 suddenly blinded him, the truck engine roaring as it ran the red light to smash into them, nose to nose.

Del and Charlie were thrown forward against the dashboard, their bodies flopping like rag dolls from the sudden impact, all the rubbish from the van flying around them.

Del's face hit the steering wheel, splitting his forehead wide open.

Charlie smashed into the windscreen, shattering it, crushing his nose.

Both of them slumped back in their seats stunned, didn't even notice as a large black van pulled up next to them; three hooded men jumped out.

The first thing Del was aware of was blood running down his face from a cut on his forehead, a gun pressed to the side window of the van.

Blinking from the blood in his eyes, Del slowly raised his hands. He could hear the rear doors of the van being opened, the boxes being unloaded.

He licked his lips, managed to force some words out. "You are making a big fucking mistake!" he snarled.

His door was suddenly pulled open, and Del tumbled out onto the wet tarmac, landing on his hands and knees.

The rain was still falling in thick sheets as Del peered up into the dark night, into the barrel of the gun.

But rather than feeling fear, he found that it was surprise, outrage that he felt. This simply wasn't supposed to happen, not to him, not someone working for the Taylors. "Do you have any idea who you're messing with?" he shouted, struggling to be heard above the torrential rain that fell in sheets on his upturned face.

On the other side of the van, another masked man grabbed Charlie, hauled him out and threw him on the ground.

Del tried to see his attacker, but all he could see was a black mask, two dark eyes above it. His eyes strayed to the black barrel of the gun, a dark hole against a dark background, seeming to stare at him.

"When Mickey Taylor finds out –"

Crack!

The single gunshot was dulled by the heavy rain, but it still startled Del, who glanced across to the other side of the van. There was no sign of Charlie.

"Charlie!" Del's voice was no longer so self-assured. "Charlie!" He sounded frantic, felt himself coming apart, tried to pull it back together.

He stared back up at the man standing over him. "You are so fucking dead!" he croaked. "I can't believe –"

The gun whipped across his face, busting his cheek open and sending him sprawling flat on his back on the wet ground.

His assailant stood directly over him, the gun still pointing at him. "I have a message for Mickey Taylor," said the man. He had a thick accent that Del couldn't quite place.

For a second, Del thought he was going to live, was going to make it home that night to his wife, would get to take his kids to the circus the next day, stomp through a muddy field to see a bunch of tired acrobats and bored animals perform their stunts.

No chance.

The man raised his arm, the gun pointed directly at Del's head.

The blood and rain filled Del's eyes. He tried to blink them back, but he was still half blinded. He didn't see the short muzzle flash, didn't hear the crack of the gun, didn't feel the bullet as it smashed through his skull, ploughed through his brain, before burying itself in the soft tarmac behind him.

The man looked down at Del for a brief moment, the rain pouring down his arm to drip off the end of the gun. "I think Dangerous will understand the message, don't you?"

Terri

"Oi! Where's me fucking dinner!"

Terri cringed at the sound of his voice. Jimmy.
Her husband. The one who was supposed to love
and cherish her. Till death us do part. Now there was
a nice thought.

Terri took one last pull on her joint, stubbed it
out on the marble bathroom countertop, threw the
stub into the toilet and flushed it. She checked her
reflection in the mirror – not bad for an old girl, she
thought – then ran a brush through her hair.

She needed the hairdresser to keep her hair
dark these days, and there were tired bags under her
eyes, but other than that she wasn't doing too badly.
She still had the delicate features that made her so
pretty as a young girl. Looked like Lizzie she did –
that's what Mickey said. Loved to look at her because
she reminded him of their mum, and that always
made him happy.

"Where the fuck are you?" He shouted clicking his fingers "Get your fat lazy arse down here and sort my fucking dinner out." Jimmy's voice was getting even angrier, if that were possible. Terri still couldn't believe that she just naturally responded and obeyed when Jimmy clicked his fingers at her or whistled at her like a dog.

Terri hurried out of the bathroom and headed for the stairs. "Just in the loo, on me way down!" she replied quickly, not wanting to rile him up anymore. Jimmy had a hair trigger temper and spent most of his life on the verge of losing it. The last thing she wanted to do was piss him off tonight, get into another of their flaming rows. She was sure he was born to moan, everything that came out of his mouth was a put down, he never had anything nice to say about anyone or anything. Christ knows what the neighbours must think when they went at it, they would have needed two foot thick castle walls not to hear the screaming matches that Terri and Jimmy had. And their rows usually ended in one of three ways: Terri storming out to escape his anger; Jimmy storming out to get drunk and shag some slapper he met at the pub – again; or him hitting her, and Terri locking herself in their bedroom.

Terri tried to fix a sweet smile on her face as she hurried into the kitchen. Jimmy was standing by the sink, a can of beer already in his hand, glaring out at their tiny garden. He'd peeled off his work shirt, so the first sight Terri saw was his hairy shoulders, his fat belly rolling over the top of his trousers. Christ, how had she ever found him attractive? His hands were constantly stained from his work at the garage, his nails chipped and blackened. The thought of those hands on her made her shudder.

"All right, sweetheart!" she said breezily as she headed towards the oven.

Jimmy turned, glared at her. "What the fuck you all done up for?"

Terri reached for the oven gloves, pulled a plate out of the oven and set it on the table. "I told you, I'm going to see Georgie tonight."

Jimmy glared at the plate. "And I get this pile of shit, the dried up leftovers!"

"It's not leftovers, Jimmy! I cooked it fresh tonight!"

"What you need to see that fucking fruitcake for anyway?" Jimmy hated Georgie, hated that she had a brother who had been in Rampton. "Runs in the fucking family," he said. All the Taylors are fucking mad, just Georgie was the only one who had ever been locked up for it. He was always mouthing off about her family, he hated that she was close to Sharon and her brothers, missed no opportunity to slag them off. The only one he ever had a kind word for was Sharon. "All right, she is," he had said on more than one occasion. "Well worth a fuck, is Sharon. I wouldn't mind given her a good seeing too, having her lovely long legs wrapped round my neck!" He would grin and leer, seemed to think it was funny. Then he'd give Terri a dismissive look. "Think I married the wrong fucking Taylor girl!"

But he reserved his worst ire for Mickey. Jimmy fucking hated Mickey, called him an evil murderer of the lowest level, a psycho, a cunt. He went on and on about how he'd heard that Mickey used to take it up the arse from anyone and everyone when he was inside. Of course, that was only when Terri and Jimmy were alone. When he met Mickey it was an entirely different story, Jimmy was all, "All right, Mickey, how are you, mate?"

Not that he ever got a word out of Mickey. Mickey loathed him, thought he was beneath contempt, like a piece of dog shit that you scraped off your shoe. More than once Mickey had offered to take care of him when he'd seen Terri with a shiner, and she'd had to beg her brother not to batter Jimmy senseless or worse, kill him. Why? Why did she bother? Why didn't she let Mickey loose on him? It was what the nasty fuck needed. Truth was Jimmy was shit scared of Mickey, would crap his pants as soon as Mickey came near him.

But something always held her back, always made her tell Mickey it wasn't that bad, Jimmy made her happy, whatever bollocks she could come up with to stop Mickey from tearing Jimmy apart.

She grabbed another beer from the fridge, the ketchup, set it beside the plate with his knife and fork. "There you go, all ready for you." She gave him a sweet smile, wanting nothing more than to just get out of the house.

"In the kitchen! You think I want to eat by myself in the fucking kitchen!" His big, dirty hand swiped the ketchup across the room. It hit the wall, burst open, spraying deep red sauce up the wall. "Put me food on a fucking tray and bring it to me in the fucking living room!" He turned and stomped out the room. "And clear up that fucking mess before you go!"

Terri glared at Jimmy's retreating back for a moment, her eyes full of pure hatred, then glanced back at the red streaked wall. The ketchup had splattered onto the kitchen counter, a few drops on the kettle, the knife block. Her eyes strayed to the knife block. Six long, sharp knives sitting right there. How easy would it be to grab one, march into the living room, and plunge it into his fat, white belly as he sat watching TV or wait till he feel asleep on the armchair snoring and farting ? She could stab him three or four times before he even had time to react, and then, as he tumbled from his chair, clutching at his bleeding belly, wrap her fingers in his thin, greasy hair, lift his head up, and slice his throat ...

"But you didn't, did you?"

Terri shook her head, looked up into Georgie's soft brown eyes.

Georgie reached out an immaculately manicured hand, gently ran his fingers through her hair. Terri felt a little shiver. How long had it been since a man had caressed her tenderly? "You told me that Mickey had offered to get rid of him for you. Why don't you take him up on that?"

Terri nodded, sipped her tea. It was always such a relief to come and visit Georgie. His flat was, as ever, pristine. Not as blank as it had been before he went to Rampton – that place had scared her, white from floor to ceiling and everywhere in between – but still minimalist, with pale wooden floors, just the barest minimum of furniture. But whereas his previous place was cold and clinical, felt like a hospital, she liked Georgie's new flat. It was calming, relaxing, made her feel as though she could think clearly, something she never felt like doing at home. That was why she smoked the weed, it was the only way she could relax in her own home.

Terri smiled despite herself. "You know what Mickey is like. Says Martin has bought them some farm out in Essex that they use for whatever it is they get up to. Says there are some very hungry pigs out there who will eat whatever you feed them. Reckons they love a bit of human flesh …"

Georgie shook his head. "You shouldn't have to put up with him, Terri. No man should ever hit a woman."

She shrugged. "He doesn't do it much. Mostly he just shouts."

"What was that song," mused Georgie. "She doesn't mind the language, it's the beatings she don't need?"

Terri laughed despite herself. "I'd forgotten that one. Squeeze, wasn't it?"

Georgie's eyes stayed on her. "You look pretty when you laugh."

"And the rest of the time?"

"You look tired, worn down."

Terri sighed. "That's how I feel. It's every fucking day, Georgie. It never stops, picking at me, nagging, shouting. I can't do anything right. I'm fat, I smoke too much weed, the house is a mess, my cooking's crap, I'm a lousy shag, there's nothing I can get right, nothing I can ever do to stop him shouting at me, cutting me down.

"What you allow Terri, is what will continue"

"I know Georgie, I know what I have got to do and what I should have done years ago. I just want all this pain and hurt to go away."

"I know that feeling Terri." Georgie took a sip of his wine "I've always preferred physical pain over emotional pain. At least when you cut your finger or break an ankle, you know when it's over, when it gets better. When your hearts been broken you never know when the pain will end."

"Oh Georgie I feel lost."

"You're not lost Terri, you're on your way, you're on the road of your destination, you will find a place you like and you'll stay there."

"Oh Georgie, I feel like I want to run away and die."

"Eccedentesiast!"

Terri smiled at Georgie "Now stop using all those big words on me, talk to me in proper English not double Dutch."

Georgie smiled back "Eccedentesiast is a person who hides their pain behind their smile."

"Very philosophical Georgie"

"So why don't you do someth . . ."

Terri cut him off. "Can we talk about something else? Talk about you."

Georgie fluttered his eyelids. "My favourite subject!"

Again Terri laughed. That was why she liked coming over to see him. It was the only place she ever seemed to feel happy these days.

"So, have you thought about it?" she asked him.

For a moment, Georgie looked serious. He was a handsome man, with intelligent features, soft, curly brown hair. Even the years in Rampton seemed to have barely aged him. He could easily pass for mid-forties, twenty years younger than he actually was. "It's given me such pleasure," he murmured, giving her a sly smile. "We've had a lot of adventures together."

"But the doctor said it would . . ."

Georgie stood up, looked impatient, irritated. "He's a quack, Terri. I only go to see him because that was a condition of my release." He wore a pair of elegantly cut wool trousers, a soft alpaca sweater. "I tell him these things because I know that secretly they turn him on, he loves to hear me talk about cross-dressing, my sexual fantasies."

"So you're not going to have the operation?"

Georgie turned, gave her a look that was pure Georgie. "Heavens no! Get my dick cut off?" He looked down at the front of his trousers. "Don't worry fella," he cooed, "you're quite safe."

Terri still looked concerned. She loved Georgie so much, they had been through so much together. Georgie was an abused child in the dark and he had been in the darkness ever since "You are being safe, aren't you?"

The humour disappeared from Georgie's face like shutters suddenly slamming shut. "I don't know what you mean."

Terri looked up at him, tried to catch his eyes, but he turned and gazed at a large modernist oil painting that filled one wall of his living room. "You know exactly what I mean! It's a whole different world out there from when you went inside, Georgie. AIDS and everything? I just don't want you getting ill."

Still Georgie gazed at the painting, as though he had discovered something fascinating hidden in its abstract lines, something so fascinating that it rendered everything else irrelevant.

Terri watched him for a moment, then slowly climbed to her feet, set her teacup on the floor, walked over to stand behind him, gazing past him at the painting, then looking up at the side of his face.

Still he didn't move.

Terri reached up and wrapped her arms around him, nestled her head into his shoulder. At first he didn't relent, she could feel him stiff, unyielding, then suddenly he relaxed, his body softened, he reached up and held her arms to his chest.

"I just worry about you, Georgie. We lost you for so long, I couldn't stand it if anything happened to you again."

Georgie turned, allowed her to rest her head on his chest while he stroked her soft hair. "It's OK, I'm careful, love," he murmured. He lifted her face, used his thumbs to wipe away the tears that trickled down her cheeks. "And you, you sort out that husband of yours, agreed?"

Terri met his concerned gaze, nodded. "Yeah. I've got an idea, something that I've been thinking about for a while."

Georgie grinned. "Ooh, do tell!"

Terri shook her head. "Not yet. But I'll tell you when the time comes, trust me …"

Mandy

How had they come to this place? wondered Mandy. Mickey was stood in front of the fireplace, straining and groaning while Mandy was on her knees in front of him, his cock in her mouth, his hands wrapped tight in her hair. Faster and faster she stroked, harder and harder she sucked, deeper and deeper he thrust until he finally came. With a deep sigh, he pressed himself against her mouth, then just as quickly withdrew, zipped his cock back into his pants.

As Mandy climbed to her feet, he reached inside his jacket, pulled out a bundle of twenties, shoved them in her hand. "There you go, girl."

Mandy took the money, crammed it in the pocket of her dressing gown, took a sip of her Scotch and coke, which had been sitting on the mantelpiece.

That had become their weekly ritual. Mickey lived with the whore, Miranda while Mandy was still living in their old house. Once a week, Mickey would come over, let himself in – he still had a key – get a blowjob, a quick shag and bung her some cash, usually about five hundred quid.

Why did Mandy put up with that? She asked herself that every week, usually while she was on her knees sucking him off or later in the bathroom while she feverishly brushed her teeth, trying to make herself feel clean again. But she loved him. She couldn't help it. She didn't want anyone else to have his heart, kiss his lips, or be in his arms. She wanted to be the only one he loved. Mickey was her man, no one else's.

The answer was simple. As long as Mickey was coming to see her every week, as long as he was getting his cock out then Miranda didn't completely own him.

Miranda might be the one living with him, the one he wined and dined, the one he slept with every night, but as long as Mandy gave him his weekly blow job and a fuck she still owned a piece of him, still had something over on the whore.

Mickey headed for the door, then suddenly paused. She could tell by the look on his face that something was bothering him.

"We need to talk," he said suddenly.

Mandy felt her heart sink. She knew straight away what it was, but didn't want to admit it, didn't want to hear it. It was her worst nightmare, and the longer she could postpone it the better. "What about?" She grinned, downed her drink. "What once a week not enough for you, you want a little bit more of me don't you?"

Mickey's face stayed serious. "We have to stop this," he said. "It ain't happening no more."

Mandy moved closer to him, her eyes desperate, pleading. What she did for him was sick, it was demeaning, but it was all she had. "But you like it, don't you, Mickey? Like me sucking you? You always said I gave the best blow job you've ever had?"

"I want a divorce."

There. It was out. The words hung heavy between them for a moment, neither of them saying anything, Mickey wondering how she would react. Would she take it calmly, agree?

"I'll look after you," he added quickly, "regular payments and all that. You won't go without, won't want for anything."

Still she said nothing, but he could tell from her eyes, had known Mandy long enough to know that under the surface she was furious, was building up to an explosion of rage. Mickey just wanted to get out of there, leave her alone to think about it, then get the lawyers to do the rest. "Look, you take a few days to–"

"– Divorce!" she screamed at him. "I will never fucking divorce you!"

Mickey didn't want to argue, but like most couples who had been married a long time, it was hard not to get into it. "You will," he snarled back at her, his voice full of menace.

Mandy didn't care. She'd been around Mickey too long to be afraid of him, and the Scotch she had just finished was her fourth of the night. "You're having a laugh," she sneered. "Do you really think you are going to get rid of me so easy?"

He glared back at her. "If I say we're getting divorced, we're fucking getting divorced!"

Mandy glanced at her empty glass. "I need a drink."

Mickey gave her a look of pure disgust. "You look like you've had enough. Look at the fucking state of you!"

Mandy ignored him, opened the drinks cabinet, refilled her drink, several measures of Scotch and a dribble of coke. "Want one?"

Mickey shook his head.

"Please your fucking self." Glass in hand, she turned back towards him. He was cloaked in his usual aura of certainty. She had a strong urge to kick the smug bastard right in the bollocks.

"It's hard to talk to you when you're pissed, Mandy." She stared at him provocatively, took a long sip of her Scotch. "You might as well fuck off now with your tail between your legs, Mickey. I will never divorce you."

"You don't have a choice!"

Something in his tone infuriated her. She set her glass on the mantelpiece, grabbed an empty flower vase, determined to hurl it at him, but as she turned around he was right there, his strong fingers wrapping around her wrist. He pulled the vase from her hand, set it back on the mantelpiece.

For a moment, they stood like that, their bodies close, rage and hatred radiating from both of them, a toxic stew of dark, destructive feelings.

Mickey noticed the dark rings under her eyes, shook his head, pushed her away. She picked up her glass and took another sip, emboldened by the alcohol. "You should be tarred and feathered for what you've put me through," she slurred.

Mickey shook his head, looked at her sadly. "You're drunk."

The pain was evident in her eyes as she stared at him. "You really don't know me anymore, do you? You think I'll just bend over and take it up the arse?" She snorted. "Bollocks! You are going to suffer for what you've done to me."

She turned to the CD player, fumbled with a pile of discs for a moment, then made her selection. "Remember this, do you?"

The strains of 'When A Man Loves A Woman,' filled the room.

"Leave it out, Mandy!"

"This song used to mean something!" she sobbed.

"I'm leaving." He turned towards the door.

Mandy still couldn't get to grips how it had turned out this way between them after all they had been through together. She hurried after him, her eyes blazing.

"You must be so far up your own arse you can see your tonsils if you think I am going to let you divorce me and let that dirty whore have you!"

Mickey stopped, turned and faced her, still trying to stay calm. "Mandy, let's talk about this like adults." He tried to take her hand, but she pulled it away as though his hand were red hot.

"I hate you so much!" she screamed. "Can't you see that she's just a two minute wonder, a dirty whore? I reckon prison made you go a bit soft. Too many dicks up the jacksie while you were inside, is that what did it?"

Mickey stood by the door, shocked, unable to leave, no answer for Mandy's stream of vitriol. She could see he was torn, piled it on. "You don't even know that the nose job she had was cause she's a fucking cocaine addict! And you, you think that because you've got a few bob and are shagging a dirty rich bitch that you're champagne in a glass. No fucking way. Warm piss in a plastic cup, that's what you are!"

Mandy hated Miranda with a deep burning passion. Mandy felt that Miranda and Mickey had taken her as a Class A mug, insulted her intelligence. Mandy could see that Mickey was still hesitating, maybe she was getting through to him. She delivered her final weapon. "Any more fucking talk about divorce, and I'll go straight to the press, sell our story."

Mickey said nothing, just stared at her.

Mandy sipped her drink, jubilant inside. That had shown him! She couldn't resist one more comment. "That's what I thought," she sneered. "You just needed someone to give you a big cup of shut the fuck up. Now piss off back to your whore!"

But still Mickey stood staring at her. It was starting to unnerve Mandy. What was he thinking? What was he going to do? Finally, he took a step towards her, flicked a hand at her dressing gown, hanging half open to reveal baggy sweats and an old T-shirt underneath.

"Look at the fucking state of you," he sneered. "Smoking, drinking, and fat. You have really let yourself go, girl."

Mandy glared back at him. "I might be fat Mickey, but I can lose weight, stop smoking and knock drinking on the head any time I want. But you, Mickey, you're just a nasty cunt, a bully, a womaniser and that will never change!"

He moved so suddenly it took her by surprise, grabbing her throat and pushing her back across the room. She collapsed into a sagging armchair, Mickey leaning over her, but still found the courage to stare up at him. "Go on, Mickey, hit me! Just like you did years ago when I wanted to divorce you! Fuck, I should have listened to my gut then!"

He stared at her with his cold, dark eyes.

"Hit me," she repeated. "Go on, give me a lovely shiner. You know Tommy will fucking kill you if you ever lay a hand on me!"

Mickey stood up, straightened his jacket. "You're a fucking low life, Mandy," he said softly, his voice tinged with pity. "I'm not going to crawl in the gutter with you."

That hurt. That really hurt. He pitied her. But she knew how to hurt him. "You're just like your dad." She saw the change in his face and eyes, instant, like a light turning off.

"Don't you ever compare me to him! I'm nothing like him!"

He loomed over her again, and for a minute, Mandy thought he really was going to hit her, but then he looked at her in disgust, turned away.

Something about the glimpse of sadness in his eyes got through to Mandy, and like a dam bursting the tears began.

Mickey glared at her. "Why are you crying? Turn it in!"

She looked at him, dabbed her eyes, sniffed. There was that pity in his eyes again. "I've been offered a lot of money by a newspaper for your story," she told him.

"You'd never live to spend it."

"I've been offered a complete new identity," she lied.

"Right. Even you wouldn't give up your kids and grandkids for a few quid."

Mandy had no response to that. Why did he always seem to have an answer?

She should have listened all those years ago when her friends had warned her about marrying into the Taylor family. There's no escape they had said. They will get their hooks into you. Christ, they'd been right. In a few years, she had changed from a vibrant, outgoing young woman into a cowering frightened wreck.

And always in the back of her mind was that horrible night when love had turned to hate, when anger and hopelessness really came to live with Mandy. It was just like a hundred rows before, both of them screaming and shouting, when in the middle of his drunken rant he had pushed her to the floor, gone berserk, beat her so badly she had two black eyes. The unbearable hurt and pain of what he did to her always lingered, a deep pain that never really left her.

Did he ever beat Miranda? Mandy doubted it. Miranda was everything Mandy wasn't. Good looking, clever, articulate, classy. She probably got up in the morning looking wonderful and refreshed. Mandy needed four coffees and half a pack of fags before she could function. When she looked at herself in the mirror these days, she hated what she saw. She looked so old and haggard, felt it too. Her face burned with anger, she didn't know if it was against herself or Mickey.

She looked over at him. "You moan about me smoking and drinking, but when you met me, I smoked and it didn't bother you then. We drunk together all the time, that was OK."

"Things change, girl," he said, that cold pitying look still on his face. "You've changed."

"Me?" She was outraged. "You are such a two-faced bastard! You've never really been in this marriage, always been a fucking passenger! I ain't even a fucking Catholic, but I was the one who took the kids to church every Sunday. Christ, you was banged up for all their communions, their school plays, football, Tommy's boxing tournaments. So don't give me that, 'you've changed' old bollocks!"

She was getting riled up again. "Then when you do show back up after fourteen years, it's one quick shag for old times' sake and then suddenly you're banging that dirty whore! You think I waited fourteen years for that? You think I'm going to just roll over and let her win! Fuck that! You've taught me well, Mickey. Information is power – remember telling me that? Well, I have enough information on you to have you back in prison just like that!" She clicked her fingers at him. "If I spill the beans, you'll die in a stinky dirty prison cell!"

"Grow up, Mandy!" snapped Mickey. "You know you won't do anything like that. The kids would never forgive you. I'm divorcing you and marrying Miranda, so get used to the fucking idea!"

Mandy felt her blood boiling at the thought of him marrying Miranda. Him living with her was bad enough, but marrying the whore? No fucking way. Her eyes narrowed. "If you divorce me, Mickey, I will kill her, I promise you that!"

Once more they were close, eyeball to eyeball. "She is worth ten of you, you fat slag," he hissed. "You touch one hair on her head and I will fucking tear you apart!" He headed out into the hallway. "I'm going. You fucking disgust me!"

She waited until he was almost out the door before delivering her final barb. "That's not what my lover says."

Mickey paused, not wanting to react, trying to calm himself.

"Thought that would get your attention. He loves me, he does, wants me, adores me. Compliments me, makes me feel good, thinks I should tell you to fuck off!"

Mickey laughed. "What a fucking mug you are. If anyone says all that shit, it's just so he can get in your knickers, you ugly slag."

But despite his words, she could see he was angry, his jaw tight, eyes narrowed.

"I've been seeing him for a few months," she added.

His look changed. "Who the fuck is it? One of my mates?"

"Give me some fucking credit. Like I'd want to shag any of your mates!"

He shook his head. "You're a fucking liar, just trying to wind me up. Who the fuck would want to shag you?"

She grinned. "Wouldn't you like to know? Tell you what though, he's good in bed …" She reached down, rubbed between her legs. "I'm getting wet just thinking about him."

"Shut the fuck up, and tell me who it is!"

"I'm getting a blinding fuck," she said, her voice rich with pure pleasure. "Knocks spots off you. I've finally been shown what sex is all about." She gave him a pitying look. "I used to think it was me was the problem, thought maybe I was frigid, but it turns out it wasn't me at all. It's you, you're fucking shit in bed." She laughed raucously. "Best fuck I've ever had, I come every time, over and over again." She turned, gestured towards the rest of the house. "We've done it in every bleeding room, in the garden, on the stairs, the kitchen table, the shower. He's a wicked lover; knows exactly how to please me." She leaned forward, smiling, her face close to his. "Unlike you."

"You're a cunt!" He spat in her face. "You're a lying fucking cunt!"

She laughed at him. "You don't know the half of it!"

Mickey shook his head. "You live in a dream world girl, you could rewrite history with your version of events. You're a fucking nutter, no sane fucker would wanna come near you." He looked at her with disgust, "I won't be round here again. My solicitor will bring the papers." And just like that he was gone, quietly closing the door behind him.

Mandy stared at the door for a long time, a swirl of emotions racing through her head, then suddenly collapsed, sobbing bitterly, her face pressed to the worn carpet. She lay there for hours, crying, wailing, stunned. Mickey was gone. How would she live without him?

Mandy shivered. She couldn't believe it was ten years ago to the day that her divorce from Mickey had come through. Mandy would never give up her fight for Mickey, she would win this war, claim her victory.

Mickey

Mickey steered the gleaming black BMW onto the driveway, turned off the motor, sat for a moment just looking at the house. It was a view he never tired of. A huge, seven bedroom house in the heart of Upminster; his neighbours bankers, stockbrokers, accountants, respectable to the last one. They had an indoor and outdoor swimming pool, a gym, a sauna, a Jacuzzi, and a steam room in his luxury home. It was like Fort Knox with its secure alarm system and surveillance cameras that were on 24/7. No fucker could get in their house unless Mickey opened the door for them. For Mickey it represented everything he had ever wanted, a sure sign that he had arrived, that he had risen above his roots, outdone his dad, the vicious bastard who had made their lives miserable for so long.

What would Lizzie make of it, he wondered? She had thought their council house in Dagenham was the bollocks, she had never wanted to live anywhere else. Her wish had been granted, she had died in that house, surrounded by all the memories, good and bad, that had made up her life.

But not Mickey. He'd always wanted out, and once he'd served his time, got back on his feet, he couldn't escape quick enough. All of them had really, all his brothers and sisters, each of them taking the money they had got from Bobby's diamonds and investing it in property.

Mickey threw the car door open, climbed out. He was in a good mood, a really good fucking mood. The Olympics represented a huge opportunity for them, the chance to take another huge leap up the ladder. If they could sell the land in Stratford for anything like what Mickey thought it was worth, they would all be millionaires. Take that up the arse, Bobby fucking Taylor!

"Miranda, where are you?"

Mickey dropped his keys on the hall table, hung his jacket on the end of the polished oak banister. The house was immaculate as always, fresh flowers in the hallway, not a thing out of place, light flooding in from the huge kitchen at the end of the hallway.

"I'm in the living room, babe."

Mickey headed towards the sound of Miranda's voice, struggling to keep a smile from his face. Christ, how come her voice could make him feel this happy, this sexy, this alive, even after all these years? The divorce from Mandy had been bitter, she had fought tooth and nail, scratching and clawing and making everything as hard as possible, but it had been worth every painful minute to get away from her and spend the rest of his life with Miranda.

Mickey stepped into the living room, stopped short. "Fuck me, girl!"

Miranda smiled at him. "That's what I was planning!" Mickey still had blatant sex appeal, fiery energy and a body to die for. He was great in bed, never left her alone, but she wasn't complaining, she loved every minute of it. Whenever Mickey was ready so was she. He satisfied her needs inside and outside the bedroom. He was still as sexy and horny as he was all those years again when she was a young sixteen year old. He had aged well. What a body he still had, tall and lean, very agile, so handsome. Mickey possessed her in every way, she loved and adored him. He had always been a good lover, he knew how to turn her on, knew what she liked. He knew how to almost get her there and then stop, he was such a tease and a torment.

Mickey stood and stared at her – she was curled up in a big, cream leather chair, wearing just a thin, silky white camisole, tied at the top, open below.

He could see her dark nipples through the thin material, one long tanned leg curled provocatively over the other to hide her crotch.

Miranda smiled, fully aware of what the sight of her body did to Mickey. "You said we were celebrating tonight, so I thought you might like a little hors d'oeuvres to get the evening started off on the right note?"

Mickey tore his clothes off as he marched across the floor towards her, was naked by the time he reached her, stood above her and leaned down to press his hungry mouth to her upturned lips. As their tongues met, her cool hand reached out, and she wrapped her fingers around his hard cock. They kissed passionately, mouths hard together, tongues probing, like lovers still discovering each other, though this was a dance they had done many, many times.

As suddenly as they had started the kiss, Miranda pushed Mickey away, her hand still gripping his cock tightly, then pulled him back in to take his cock in her mouth. Mickey gasped in pleasure and surprise, his hands on her blonde hair as she moved her mouth up and down on him, his cock sliding in and out of her soft, warm mouth.

Jesus Christ, whenever she did this it still felt as good as the first time, in the front of his car all those years ago.

Mickey could feel his passion rising, her tongue driving him crazy as she sucked and pulled on him, but Miranda knew it too, suddenly lifted her head, grinned at him. "Not yet. You have some work to do first!"

Mickey needed no second invitation, knew exactly what Miranda wanted, what she craved from Mickey. He dropped to his knees on the thick, white carpet, spun the chair around so she was directly facing him, and gently opened her legs to reveal her smooth, shaved sex.

Miranda stretched like a cat, arched her back, grabbed Mickey's head and pulled him into her waiting pussy. As his tongue buried itself inside her she groaned and squirmed. "Make me come, baby!"

Mickey lay on the carpet; Miranda still draped across him, both of them half awake, half asleep, his hand gently stroking her back while she buried her fingers in his chest hair, nuzzled against his shoulder.

When he'd first started dating Miranda, everyone had assumed it would soon be over. Mickey was just out of prison, hadn't had sex for fourteen years while Miranda was fulfilling a fantasy she'd had since she was a teenager. It was inevitable, everyone said, just you wait, they'll soon burn themselves out.

When they announced their wedding, everyone had a field day. It will never last, was the prevailing opinion, you can't build a relationship on lust alone. They'll soon get fed up with each other; she'll get fat, he'll get busy with work, they are as different as chalk and cheese, they'll have nothing.

Christ thought Mickey; they should have come on the honeymoon with us! Two weeks in Corfu in a beautiful beachfront villa, but the truth was they had barely gone anywhere. They had fucked in the bedroom, on the kitchen table, on the balcony, on the beach, on the little rocky trail that ran up behind the villa, in the back of their rental car overlooking the ocean. With Mickey and Miranda it was anytime, anyplace, anywhere. They were constantly at it. Love had never felt so good.

But that was just the honeymoon period, they said, wait till reality sets in …

Mickey sighed, happy, contented, glanced over at the clock on the mantelpiece. Seven forty-five. "We need to get going," he said softly. "I made a dinner reservation for eight thirty."

Miranda nuzzled closer, her tongue flicking across his nipple as her hand found his soft cock, slowly began to squeeze and stroke it. "Or we could just stay here, order takeaway …"

Mickey tried to be strong; tried to resist her. "I've booked us into Charlotte's. You know how much you like it there."

Miranda slid her head down across his stomach; flicked the end of his cock with her tongue. "I prefer it here …"

Mickey made one last effort. "But this night calls for a big celebration!"

Again Miranda's tongue flicked against him. "You go if you want. I've got everything I need right here." And with that she enveloped him in her mouth.

Mickey sighed, thrust his cock up into her soft mouth. Takeaway it was ...

Mickey paced back and forwards in front of the stone hearth, the phone clamped to his ear. "Dead? What do you fucking mean, dead?"

It was just after ten, the remains of the Chinese takeaway still spread out across the dining room table. When the phone rang, Miranda had begged him not to answer, wanted him all to herself that night, but it was Mickey's work phone, and she knew by now that when work called, Mickey answered.

"Well, do we know who did it?" he demanded.

The caller was Brick, Mickey's number one enforcer, his nickname earned from his resemblance to a brick shit house. "Nothing yet, guv," Brick told him. "I've got feelers out, but so far it's all quiet."

"Fuck! It could be any of them! The Chinese, the fucking Bangladeshis ..." Mickey ground his teeth, his eyes a dark storm of fury. The drugs trade, the heart of their business these days, was under increasing threat from London's growing immigrant communities. Not just the Chinese and the Bangladeshis, but the Turks and the Vietnamese had muscled in of late, each staking out their own patch of turf. And caught in the middle of them, the old established families like the Taylors, doing it the old way. Martin kept saying they needed to move out of the drug trade, diversify, but Mickey was having none of it, he would never give up, especially to a bunch of foreign cunts..

"Stay on it, Brick. Spread some dosh around, pump everyone you know. Sooner or later some cocky cunt is going to say too much, and when they do we'll be on them like stink on shit!"

Mickey hung up the phone, paused for a moment as he caught a glimpse of his reflection in the huge mirror that hung above the fireplace.

A sudden thought crossed his mind – was this the beginning of the end? Was this where it all started to unravel? The eyes that looked back at him weren't as young as they once had been, there were tiny crows' feet around his eyes, but the eyes themselves were hard chips of granite with the killer instinct.

When Mickey had got out of prison he had been forced to start again at the bottom, fight his way back to a position of prominence. It had been hard, bloody, desperate at times, but he had come through, emerged as the top dog in the area once more. He was fucked if he was going to give up without a fight because some bastards had killed two of his boys.

Mickey's eyes narrowed. They had killed two of his men! Fuck me, who would even think of doing something like that? Surely even the immigrants were smart enough to know that you didn't rattle the hornet's nest, you didn't piss Mickey Taylor off? He wasn't called Dangerous for nothing. They would pay for this. Mickey could feel himself getting very, very angry.

You take two of mine, thought Mickey, I'll take four of yours, six, ten …

The phone rang again. It was Martin. "I just heard."

Mickey slowed his breathing, forced himself to talk calmly to his brother. "This is not some random act, Martin," he growled. "This is an act of war!"

"We don't know that," said Martin, ever the careful one. "It could be –"

"It could be, but it fucking isn't!" barked Mickey. "Whoever did this knew the fucking lot, knew everything, our route, our schedule, what we were moving."

"The stuff's gone too?"

"All of it."

"Yes, all of it"

"Fuck!"

They were both silent for a moment. Mickey saw Miranda standing in the doorway, an elegant cut glass of whisky in her hand. Mickey nodded. She padded across the floor, handed him the glass, retreated. He loved that girl so much, she was simply beautiful.

"Brick said he was on it."

Mickey nodded, sipped his drink. "This won't stay secret for long."

"I've called in all the boys, doubled the watch on all our distribution centres."

That's Martin, thought Mickey. He might not be convinced that it's the start of a war until he has the evidence, but he takes precautions all the same.

"Brick'll find whoever it is, Marty, you know that?"

"And then?"

Mickey drained his glass, crunched the ice between his teeth. "We'll burn them to the fucking ground!"

Martin

Martin slumped back in his office chair and let out a deep sigh. Jesus Christ, why this? Why now? He had been trying to get Mickey out of the drugs trade for fucking years now, felt he was making progress, getting him to see the wisdom in it – then this happened. And whereas with a reasonable person this might serve as a wake-up call, a sign that now was the time to quit while they were ahead, before things got worse, Mickey was the most stubborn man Martin had ever met.

For Mickey, this would be a red flag to a bull. Rather than encouraging him to get out, this would make him burrow in even deeper, like a tick on a warm dog.

He would burn down whoever had started this. But at what cost? Mickey was a bit of a dinosaur, still thought the Taylor name and a bunch of heavies could sort out most situations, but Martin wasn't so sure. These immigrant gangs had deep roots, ties back to their home countries, an endless supply of expendable manpower. If things got really nasty they could easily see themselves wiped out, and Martin was fucked if he was going to see that happen.

Already, their legitimate businesses were making almost as much money as the illegal ones. Martin had invested in a haulage company – he knew that business from his time in Australia – the dry cleaners that Tommy ran, a string of beauty parlours that Mickeys' daughter Jacqui was managing. Christ, even Mickey's gym was a money maker. If Mickey would only agree to it, Martin could have them totally legitimate within the year.

But now this had happened. Now someone had decided to take them on, challenge them. Now someone had got Mickey fired up, thirsting for blood, and there could be only one outcome. Mickey would have his blood, exact his revenge, and the Devil take the hindmost. Martin only hoped that he could keep everything together while Mickey went on his rampage …

A hand stroked Martin's thigh, slid inside his trousers, which were already unzipped. He looked down at the figure kneeling patiently in front of him, was met by a warm smile. "You ready for me to carry on, hun?"

Martin nodded. "Yeah. You're exactly what I need right now."

As Martin settled back in his chair, the hand slid his cock out, and a warm mouth enveloped him. He sighed, closed his eyes, tried to forget the hell that was about to be unleashed as the head began to bob rhythmically up and down on his stiff cock …

Two days passed before they finally got a break. Two days of turning the screw on people, handing out fists full of twenties, pulling in everyone they knew who kept an ear to the ground.

"The Vietnamese?" Mickey looked indignant. It just didn't seem right. They'd only recently started coming over to London, and here they were, already taking on the established local boys? Who the fuck do they think they are coming over here and daring to step on Mickey Taylor's toes? Like, fuck, Mickey was having none of it. Fucking cheek! It was a small, select group that were gathered in Mickey's office. Mickey and Martin, Brick, plus Darren and Scrubs, who handled the drugs shipments.

"Some young kid was mouthing off in a Vietnamese restaurant just off the Mile End Road," Brick told them. "One of our boys happened to be in there getting a takeaway, heard this geezer coming out of the kitchen laughing and taking the piss about how surprised our blokes had been when they jumped the van."

Mickey's eyes narrowed. Killing two of his boys, then laughing about it? That was beyond wrong – that was taking fucking liberties.

Mickey poured himself another glass of Scotch, passed the bottle round the table. A thick haze of smoke filled the room, the light from Mickey's office spilling out into the darkened gym, casting strange shadows from the punchbags and weights.

"What do we know about them?" asked Martin. He sat in a big chair looking cool and aloof, the ice to counter Mickey's fire.

Brick scratched his shaved head, scowled. "Not much. They've got a place near the canal where they seem to hang out. There's the restaurant and a warehouse next door. That seems to be it."

"So they're pretty small time right now?" grinned Mickey. "Perfect!"

Martin looked up, his eyes dark. "Right now."

"So let's keep them that way!" growled Mickey. Make them sorry they messed with the Taylors. Hit 'em hard before they're well established, maybe they'll back off and focus on easier pickings.

All the others nodded agreement – except Martin. He sat quiet, gazing at the photos on the walls. Mickey's office was full of photos of the kids who'd come through the gym in the past ten years. Martin found his eyes drawn to the photos. They all had the same hungry look, serious faces trying to look hard, muscular bodies below frightened eyes, kids just taking their first steps into the harsh world of adults, desperate to make their mark, desperate that no one discovered that underneath their cocky exterior, behind their tough faces and clenched fists, they were just scared kids wondering what would happen to them, where life would lead them …

"Marty?"

Martin shook his head, blinked, looked round. Everyone was looking at him. He grabbed his drink, gave a nervous laugh. "Say it again."

Mickey shook his head, gave a sigh of exasperation. "I said we hit them early Sunday morning. Let them have a few days to think they've got away with it, then go in early while they're all sleeping, leave them in no doubt who did it, make it quite clear that if they fuck with us, we'll wipe them out!"

Martin said nothing for a moment, thinking. When he finally spoke, he was all business. "Brick, you get the lads together. We need five plus ourselves. No amateurs, no cowboys, only the best, understand?"

Brick nodded.

"And don't tell them anything. Get them together for Saturday night, we'll keep them here overnight, so they're all sober, and there's no leaks. Got it?"

Brick nodded. They had all learned that when Martin talked, you listened. Mickey might be the boss, but Martin took care of the details, and woe betide you if you deviated from his plan.

Martin turned to Darren. "I want someone watching that place every minute between now and

Sunday morning. What was that bloke called who did the recce for the job at the chippy last year?"

"Jason?" offered Darren.

"That was him. Get him on it. He was good. I want to know everything about that place, who's there, the entrances and exits, security, how often they take a shit, everything."

Darren nodded. "Got it."

Finally Martin turned to Scrubs. "You get us tooled up. This isn't a time to fuck around. We want the best, untraceable. You know the score."

Scrubs nodded.

Mickey slowly drained his glass, set it down hard on the table. "This isn't just a warning, you all understand that? These cunts killed Del and that kid Charlie. That's two of ours. We're going to put at least two of theirs in the ground, then burn their fucking place to the ground. Anyone who's not up for that, forget them." He looked around the room, met everyone's gaze, his dark eyes burning with fire. "We're not starting a war with this lot. We're fucking ending it!"

Mandy

Mandy sat in her car, stuck in traffic, listening to the radio. They were playing oldies, and every song that came on reminded her of Mickey. Whatever she did, wherever she was, her thoughts always returned to Mickey.

The final straw was when they played Percy Sledge, "When A Man Loves A Woman." That was their wedding song, their first dance together, Mandy and Mickey's song. She leaned forward, snapped off the radio, anything to get him out of her head. But it made no difference, she was totally consumed by him.

She tried to peer ahead, see what was holding the traffic up, but all she could see was a line of cars disappearing into the distance, a snake of red lights that seemed to go on forever. With a deep sigh she slumped back in her seat, let her mind drift back to the good old days, when things were good with Mickey, when sex was good, something to share, not something to be taken on demand.

When she had first kissed Mickey all those years ago, it had felt like nothing she had ever known. She had wanted to relive every magical moment with him, the touch of him, the taste of him, just being in his arms. The sensation of Mickey touching her had made her feel so good, so alive, he was intoxicating.

Even then she had known that he was no good, but Mandy couldn't help herself, she had loved him with all her being. Then, she was a naïve sixteen-year-old girl, now she was a grown woman, but she still felt the same way, nothing or no one could ever change that.

When they started dating, Mickey had done things to her that she had never experienced before, but it was more than that. She felt safe with him; he was frightened of nothing or no one, and that was a feeling she had wanted to last forever …

The first time she saw Mickey was in her sister's pub. There was an instant attraction; she couldn't take her eyes off him. He had a wicked body – hard abs, firm arms, a muscular chest – but it was his dazzling, heart-warming smile and mesmerising eyes that captivated her. From that moment on, she was besotted with Mickey Taylor.

It had been a good day, a charity event for a little boy with leukemia, a friend of Mickey's. Mandy tried not to keep staring at him, but she just couldn't help herself, he was just sex on two legs. She knew from the start that she didn't stand a chance, she was a Plain Jane while Mickey had a bunch of birds flocking round him and fluttering their eyelashes. So she was totally shocked when she suddenly noticed him walking towards her. She blushed, tried to look calm.

"You wanna dance?" said Mickey, staring intently into her eyes.

Mandy felt her heart beating erratically, couldn't speak, could hardly breathe. She nodded, felt a shiver run through her as he took her hand, led her through the crowded pub and out onto the dance floor. When he pulled her close, his body pressed against hers, she knew she was lost, but she didn't care. She wanted him, wanted him for her own, and would do anything to have him.

After that day, she would find any excuse to walk past his house just to catch a glimpse of him – she had never been up the shops so much. People must have thought she had a drink problem the amount of time she spent in her sister's pub, just waiting for him to walk through the bar door.

It all happened so fast, yet she felt powerless to stop. He was so good looking and beguiling; she couldn't stop herself from falling in love with him. Just looking at him sent shivers down her spine, her heart accelerated when she thought about him.

Over the years, Mandy had tried many times to understand why Mickey affected her so strongly. Of course, he was handsome, but it was the dangerous edge that hooked her. It was a lethal combination, and Mandy knew from the first moment that he asked her to dance that she should have said no. Her heart was telling her one thing and her head another, but she couldn't help herself, she simply shut off the warning signs and gave in to him.

After they started seeing each other, she had wanted to stay a virgin till she was married. Mickey was a real gentleman about it, never pressed her, but in the end she was the one who cracked, she just couldn't help herself, she wanted him too much. They were at a friend's party; it was getting late, people were getting out of control, throwing up, fights starting. Mickey, who had been off talking to someone, suddenly appeared beside her, wrapped an arm around her waist. "Come on, let's get you home." He had a way of saying things that you didn't argue with, you just accepted. If Mickey said to do something, it always sounded like exactly what you should be doing.

He led her out of the party, Mandy enjoying the heat of his hand through the fine material of her dress. She was more than happy to leave the party, it meant that she would have Mickey to herself for a while. When they were out and about, he always had someone talking to him, there was always someone wanting a piece of him. Now she would have him to herself for a few minutes.

They walked outside into the cold night air, and Mickey opened the door of his car for her, helped her in just like a proper gentlemen. It was only a few minutes to her house; he parked up a few doors away.

They sat in his car for ages just chatting, getting to know each other, giggling and laughing together, kissing softly, gazing into each other's eyes, dreamy and soft.

Mickey walked her to her front door. "Night, Mandy," he said softly, then moved close and kissed her. But this was not like any kiss she ever felt before, this time he kissed her with real passion. Mandy felt like she was melting inside as their tongues danced and twisted, their bodies pressed close together.

"I've wanted to do that since the first time I saw you," he mumbled pulling her closer to him.

She could feel his hardness against her. She took a deep breath. "Me too."

They kissed again, even better than the first. His lips were insistent but soft, his tongue exploring, and Mandy just lost herself in his kisses, sighing softly as he pushed his hands through her hair. "You're so beautiful," he whispered, kissing her faster and faster, both of them wanting more.

No one had ever told Mandy she was beautiful. Pretty, yes, nice, yeah, everyone said that, but not beautiful. Waves of desire overwhelmed her. She felt like she would do anything for Mickey. She wanted him so much. "Come on, I'll sneak you into my room, you can creep out in the morning," she said suddenly. She giggled like a naughty school girl. "I've got a lock on my door; no one will come in."

Mickey looked deep into her eyes. "Are you sure about this? You haven't got to do it if you don't want to."

Her head was filled with conflicting emotions, her body urging her to say yes, her head kept telling her not to. What if she got pregnant? What if he thought she was a slag, an easy lay? And worst of all, what if she didn't know what to do, didn't do what he liked? Mickey must have had hundreds of girls. How could she compete with that? But as the thoughts swirled round inside her head, she simply stared intently into his dark eyes, whispered "I'm sure …"

"Honestly?"

"Yes, honestly," she said, pulling him close to her, kissing him hard on the lips.

There was no need for further words. She rooted through her handbag and took her key out, opened the front door. Tiptoeing together, they crept upstairs to her bedroom.

Mandy locked the door behind them, walked quickly over to her bed and switched the lamp on. Her eyes quickly scanned her bedroom, suddenly embarrassed by the posters of Donny Osmond and David Cassidy. Thank God her mum had been in today, polished, hoovered and changed the bedclothes.

She turned around, found Mickey standing right behind her. He pulled her into his strong arms, began covering her face with hot kisses, his hands exploring her body through her thin dress. He had a gentle touch, caressing her breasts, her flat stomach, her firm buttocks.

Her heart was beating faster and faster as he slowly undid the buttons on the back of her dress. Mandy would have normally felt self-conscious about her body, but she had no inhibitions with Mickey, she wanted him to rip her clothes off. His hands moved down to her thighs, lifting her dress inch by inch, slowly pulling it over her head.

She stifled a moan as he expertly unclipped her bra, gently cupped her breasts, then brought his mouth down to kiss them, his tongue circling her nipple. She closed her eyes, savouring the moment, the feeling of his hands and tongue, waves of desire washing over her.

She feverishly began unbuttoning his shirt, desperate to feel his skin against hers. Mickey helped, undressed himself quickly, peeling off his shirt and wriggling out of his jeans. Her eyes feasted on him. What a body.

His hands moved down to her waist, then he bent to his knees and slowly slid her knickers down her legs. She stepped out of them as he softly kissed her thighs, driving her crazy. He stood up, his hands moved to her breasts, gently touching, feeling, stroking, and all the time his lips on hers.

He stood back and stared at her naked body. "God, you're gorgeous," he muttered in a husky voice. He pulled her close, warmth sweeping through her body as he took her in his arms, his hard thighs moving against her. She trembled as his fingers travelled down her spine, began tenderly stroking his smooth flesh, feeling his passion and urgent desire pressing against her, their hips moving in rhythm together.

Mickey scooped her up in his strong arms, cradling her like a baby, carried her over to the small bed and gently placed her on the soft covers. He lay down beside her, began kissing her all over, her forehead, her eyes, her cheeks, her jaw line, her nose, neck and shoulders, Mandy feeling his hot breath against her skin. He was touching and holding her so intimately, planting tender kisses all over her, nibbling her neck, running his tongue across her skin.

Mandy found herself gasping and moaning, digging her nails into him, running her fingers over his firm body. And still he kept kissing, down her throat, her shoulders, across her collarbone to suddenly take her breast in his mouth once more, his tongue swirling round her nipple.

She pulled him closer, their hips moving together, feeling him hard against her thighs, little moaning noises escaping her lips. Their eyes met and locked together, and they exchanged an intimate smile. Mandy felt like she was melting inside as his tongue moved slowly from nipple to nipple. She let out a long drawn out sigh. "Oh, Mickey, don't ever stop doing that …"

But to her surprise, he began to move down the bed, his tongue working its way across her stomach until suddenly his head was between her legs, and he was licking her.

She had never imagined anything like this, the waves of pleasure that surged through her as his fingers slid inside her. She felt momentarily embarrassed; she was soaking wet, but his tongue licked eagerly at her, devouring her, and she let go, lost herself in the moment, sighing as his hands and tongue explored the most intimate area of her body. His fingers went deep inside her while his tongue flicked across her clitoris.

It was amazing; mind blowing. She couldn't help herself; her hands went down and grasped his hair, and she began moving her hips in rhythm, arching her back as he buried his tongue deep inside her, pulling his hair as she rocked her hips faster and faster. She'd never experienced anything like it, felt a huge wave of pleasure as she came against his mouth, shivered and pulled him up to hold him, her eyes sparkling, her cheeks flushed.

"I want you inside me!" she gasped, still breathless.

Mickey smiled. "I thought this was your first time?"

Mandy blushed. "It is."

Mickey slowly climbed on top of her, started rubbing himself against her soft skin, felt her legs part as his hardness pressed between them. "You catch on fast," he laughed.

Mandy gasped as he slipped inside her, gentle at first, probing, pushing, then with a sudden thrust she felt him deep inside. There was a second of pain, then a surge of ecstasy.

"You OK?" he whispered softly.

Mandy said nothing, just nodded, biting her lip, lost in his rhythm, his fervent passion. She wrapped her arms and legs around him, wanting to hold him tight, never wanting to let him go, savouring every wonderful moment. He was taking her, overwhelming her, and she wanted him, needed him.

She could never have imagined it being this good. She ground herself against him, pulling him closer, her fingers sliding over his skin, his voice sweet and soothing as he touched her body, whispered his love.

She lay back and gave herself to him completely, panting, her heart beating faster and faster, she felt like she couldn't breathe as she called his name, groaning, his mouth on hers, kissing each other harder and harder, both wanting more. Mandy tried to move in rhythm with him as he slowly eased in and out of her, her body moving and jerking in response to his touch, her skin burning, her legs stiffening.

She ran her fingers through his hair, falling further and further under his spell. "Oh Mickey, it feels so good!" she gasped. The feeling was so amazing she didn't want it to end, she wanted more – wanted to laugh and cry with happiness.

The excitement built, rising and falling as one until they finally climaxed together with a series of grunts and moans. As she fell back on the bed, Mickey cradled her in his arms, her head resting on his chest. She could hear his heart beating, feel his warm skin against her. Mandy wanted this moment to last forever.

They lay quietly on the bed, their bodies entwined. Finally, she gazed up at his handsome face. "I will always love you, Mickey," she whispered. "Nothing can ever change that."

For a moment, she thought he wasn't going to say anything, then he put his big hands to her cheeks, pulled her soft lips to his, stroked her face. "I love you too," he whispered.

If her life had ended right there, Mandy would have died happy. She would never have had to experience his affairs, his lies, the police at the door, the trial, the fourteen years he was inside, and then the final rejection, leaving her for Miranda. Where had it all gone wrong? What had changed from that magical night?

The beeping of a car horn brought Mandy back to reality. The traffic had started moving again, at last. She put the car in gear, inched forwards, still smiling at the recollection of that magical night. She had fallen asleep with a smile on her face, feeling tranquil and serene, and all night they had cuddled close, their bodies fitting together perfectly.

When they woke up early in the morning, they made love again, and this time she was able to relax, enjoyed it even more than the first time if that was possible. Mandy knew that day that this was the man she wanted more than anything else in the world. She had found her soulmate.

She lay quietly while Mickey dressed, watching him, thinking. Mandy Taylor. She liked the sound of that.

He glanced over, that wicked smile on his face. "Penny for them!"

Mandy blushed. "Nothing. Just thinking about, you know, what we did."

He strode over to the bed, buttoning his shirt. "Me too!" he grinned. "Amazing, wasn't it?"

He kissed her on her forehead as he left her house, and she watched him stroll casually out of her gate. As he reached his car, he turned and looked back at her, smiled his dazzling smile, then climbed into his motor.

Mandy crept back into the house, climbed back into bed. It was still warm, and she could smell

Mickey

The street was quiet. Though it was early on a Sunday morning, the summer sun was already creeping over the horizon. There was a familiar rattle as a milk float trundled down the road towards the restaurant, the crates clanking as it bumped over the uneven tarmac. The driver peered out from underneath his cap, eyes scanning the premises as he passed, reached the corner of the street and turned onto a side street.

Mickey sat in the front passenger seat of an old dark green Land Rover, Darren beside him, Martin in the back with two other lads. Mickey's eyes met those of the driver as the milk float passed. A quick nod. All clear.

Mickey took a deep breath, checked his gun one more time, then nodded in turn to Darren. "Let's fucking do this."

The engine was already running. Darren floored the throttle, and the Land Rover leapt forward and round the corner, spewing smoke from the exhaust, a large black transit van right behind them.

The Land Rover's tyres screeched as they cornered, still picking up speed. As they reached the restaurant Darren yanked on the wheel, turned sharply towards the restaurant, ploughed straight through the front window. Glass showered the car as they smashed into the counter, sending menus and mints flying, the Land Rover coming to rest almost in the kitchen. They had barely stopped before Mickey was out, Martin jumping out of the back, hard on his heels. With Darren and two others behind him, he stormed inside.

The black van hit the wooden doors of the warehouse at about thirty miles per hour, splintering them and smashing the front windscreen of the van. Brick didn't care, he knew what was inside – Jason's recce had been thorough, Brick knew the layout of the loading area, knew they weren't going to hit anything unexpected.

The doors split and crashed inwards, and the van skidded to a halt. Brick was out straight away, Scrubs and three others with him.

It was dark in the warehouse, it took a second before their eyes adjusted to the light. The warehouse had two levels, shelves all along the right-hand wall stacked with cooking supplies, offices on the left side.

In the back corner were metal stairs leading to the second floor.

As Brick jumped out of the van, the office door to his left opened, and two young Vietnamese guys came tumbling out, guns in their hands, bleary eyed, hair still mussed from sleep.

Brick didn't give himself time to think, just did what Mickey had ordered. The gun kicked hard in his hand as he fired, two, three, four shots blasting out into the confines of the warehouse. Scrubs behind him did the same, unloading his pistol into the Vietnamese guys. The sound was almost deafening in the confined space, an assault upon their senses, ripping the air apart.

The young guys didn't stand a chance. The bullets hammered into them, stopping them cold as they scampered out, throwing them around like marionettes under the control of a drunken puppeteer. Their bodies flopped and flailed, then slumped to the ground, blood quickly pooling beneath them on the hard concrete.

Brick hurried forward through the haze of smoke, kicked both the bodies to make sure they were dead. One of them rolled over onto his back, blank eyes staring upwards, half his lower jaw gone where a bullet had ripped through it. "Scrubs, with me, offices," Brick ordered, then turned to the others. "You lot check upstairs. We'll meet back here in two minutes."

The guys nodded, trotted towards the stairs. Two of them had compact submachine guns under their arms, the third carried a Glock. Brick watched them as they took the stairs two at a time. He'd known all of them for several years, they were among the hardest bastards in London. He trusted them to do their job, no fuss, no fuck-ups.

"Ready?" Scrubs stood beside him, still slightly breathless from the excitement. He was a good bloke, still only in his early twenties, one of Mickey's former boxing protégés, never panicked, always did what he was told. Brick felt comfortable with him at his back.

Scrubs, grinned, nodded.

"Let's do it!" Brick took two deep breaths, then kicked the office door open …

Mickey stormed through the kitchen, Martin at his side. It was deserted, everything cleaned and put up from the night before, the smell of spices and cooking oil heavy in the air. Mickey glanced to his side as he strode between the work benches, saw his reflection staring back at him from a gleaming silver pan. The eyes that met his were cold, hard, fierce. From the direction of the warehouse came the crackle of gunfire. Mickey grinned. The revenge had begun.

It was at times like this that Mickey lived up to his name, Dangerous. When the shit hit the fan – when other people panicked, or froze, or shit themselves – that was when Mickey was at his best.

For Mickey, it almost felt as though time slowed down. He saw the danger first, reacted without thinking while others were still wondering what to do, made his move and was gone before anyone even knew what was happening.

Mickey was the first to reach the door at the far end of the kitchen, kicked it open with brutal certainty.

It led into a hallway, a stained red carpet on the floor, two faded photos on the wall. There was a set of stairs straight ahead on the left, a corridor to the back door on the right.

As the door from the kitchen flew open and Mickey looked around, two teenage boys were hurrying down the stairs, had just reached the hallway. They looked scared, startled, unsure what was happening. Mickey didn't hesitate. A vicious left hook floored the first one. Mickey didn't even look at his body as he crumpled in front of him, just stepped over him, slammed his right fist into the gut of the second bloke, a thunderous punch that almost lifted him off his feet.

Behind him, Mickey could hear Martin and the boys kicking the shit out of the first geezer as Mickey crunched his forehead into the second teenager's nose, splintering it. The kid screamed in pain, a scream that was cut off by a strangled gargle of pure agony as Mickey rammed his knee into the lad's balls, tossed him to the ground behind him as he took the stairs two at a time, not even breaking stride. "Cap 'em!" Mickey threw back over his shoulder, and two gunshots immediately ripped through the small house.

Mickey paused at the top of the stairs. There were four doors. Martin and the other lads were right behind him, all carrying guns. Mickey signalled to them, one door each, then moved smoothly towards the first door.

The others spread out, each moving to take up position by one of the doors. At a signal from Mickey, they each threw their respective door open, strode inside.

Mickey gazed into a bedroom. There was a double bed, a mess of clothes on the floor, a Vietnamese woman in her thirties huddled in the corner, clutching a small child, maybe three or four years old, who stood in front of her. The woman had a bright blue silk dressing gown wrapped around her, her feet crammed into fluffy pink slippers.

The rest of the room seemed to be clear, but Mickey checked just in case – took a quick look under the bed, threw open the wardrobe doors. Clear.

He turned back to the woman. She was whimpering, clutching the child. The kid, however, wasn't crying, just looking up at Mickey with blank eyes.

"You're a creepy little fucker!" growled Mickey.

The child continued to stare at him.

"All right, on your feet!" Mickey ordered the woman.

Neither of them moved.

Mickey sighed in exasperation. "Come on, chop, chop, we haven't got all fucking day!"

Still they didn't move, just stared at him with their dark eyes.

"Fuck me, let's go!" Mickey reached down, grabbed the woman by her shoulder, hauled her to her feet.

As he did so, the woman pulled a knife out from inside her dressing gown, jabbed it towards Mickey's stomach. He saw it just in time, half turned away from her, so the blade missed his stomach, nicked his arm as he half blocked it.

"Fuck!" Mickey half stumbled backwards, and the woman came for him again, still clutching the kid with her other hand, dragging him forward as she lunged for Mickey.

This time Mickey dodged better, cuffed the woman round the head as she dived towards him, sent her and the child sprawling. As they started to fall, the woman tried to grab the kid, the knife still in her hand, and the two of them wound up in a huddled heap at Mickey's feet.

He stepped back, looked down at his arm. Blood was flowing from the cut, down his arm to drip from his fingertips. He pulled a handkerchief from his pocket, wrapped it around the wound. Not only was he bleeding, but she'd ruined a good Armani suit. "Stupid fucking cunt, look what you did to my suit!" he complained. "Now fucking move it!"

But the woman didn't move. She just sat back on her heels and began wailing, a high keening sound that cut through the air and shredded Mickey's nerves.

"Shut the fuck up and let's go!" he demanded.

Still the woman rocked and wailed, the child clutched tight in her arms. It was only when Mickey reached for her that he realised what had happened – there was a rapidly deepening pool of blood staining the kid's Mickey Mouse pajamas where the knife had impaled his guts as the woman had tumbled to the floor with him. His cold eyes clouded over as Mickey watched, still never leaving Mickey's face.

Mickey looked away, reached up a hand, ran it through his hair. "Fuck! Fuck, fuck, fuck!"

The woman still had the knife in her hand, seemed unable to do anything, but rock and wail, her other hand clutching the child tight to her chest, his blood soaking her lap, running down onto the pale carpet.

As Mickey watched, the child's eyes closed, his head rolling against the woman's chest. She gave an even deeper wail of pure animal anguish, buried her face in the child's neck.

Mickey reached down, gently took the knife from her. "Sorry love," he muttered.

Brick and Scrubs moved cautiously towards the back of the warehouse. They had found – and killed – two more guards in the office while the others had cleared the upstairs. But there was something bothering Brick. The back of the warehouse was in darkness, but he could hear something, a faint sound he couldn't quite put his finger on.

It was the sound of someone breathing softly, of bodies moving around, reminded him of when he was a kid, his old man used to take him out to a friend who had a plot of land near Basildon. While the men drank and played cards, Brick would wander out back to the sheds, where his dad's mate kept a couple of scrawny ponies.

Brick would crawl in through the broken planking to hide with the ponies, the rain beating down on the roof, comforted by the animals' soft breathing, the noise of them moving slightly in the dark …

"Can you see anything?" he whispered to Scrubs.

"Nah. But there's something back there that's for fucking sure!"

Their eyes had adjusted to the dim light of the warehouse, but the back corner was a pool of inky darkness. The only hint that there was anything there was that soft sound, and the odor of warm bodies …

Scrubs paused as the other guys came clumping down the stairs.

"Thirty seconds, guv!" shouted one of them.

Brick glanced back over his shoulder. "Any of you got a torch?"

"Yeah, I got one here." One of the lads was ex-army, always came prepared for anything. He flicked the light on, strode forward towards them. "You got something back here?"

"Yeah," Scrubs told him, "shine it into that back corner."

The torch beam cut past Scrubs and Brick, lit up the deepest back corner of the warehouse.

Brick peered in disbelief at what they saw. "Fuck me!" he finally muttered. "Mickey will want to see this!"

Mickey stepped back into the dimly lit hallway, blood still dripping from his fingertips, the knife in his hand. Martin appeared seconds later, immediately noticed the cut in Mickey's arm.

"You all right?"

Mickey nodded, still stunned.

The other lads led a Vietnamese man towards them. He was in his early sixties, with a shock of white hair, a calm, dignified expression. Mickey recognized him immediately from the dossier Jason had produced. Nguyen Phong was his name, the boss of the Vietnamese gang. According to everything they had learned, if anyone had ordered the hit on Mickey's boys, it would be Phong.

Mickey stepped forward slowly, carefully examined Phong's face. In that circumstance, most men would have showed some sign of fear, even an involuntary twitch, a quickening of their breathing, something. Not Phong. He met Mickey's cold-eyed stare eye to eye, never breaking contact, looked supremely indifferent as Mickey stopped right in front of him, brought the knife up to eye level, turned it over in his hand.

"Mickey Taylor," said Phong suddenly.

"I knew you knew who I was," grinned Mickey.

He turned to Martin. "See, told you it wasn't random!"

Mickey looked thoughtfully at Phong. "Here's what I don't get, Phong. If you're smart enough to do your research, smart enough to jack one of our shipments, here's the question that's bugging me …"

Mickey paused, eyeballed Phong again.

"How come you're so fucking stupid that you didn't know that no one, no one, ever fucks with me and gets away with it!" As he spoke, Mickey's voice got louder and louder, his face closer and closer to Phong's. By the end, their noses were almost touching.

Phong's calm demeanor never changed in the face of Mickey's rant. "I had hoped you weren't as stupid as your reputation," he said softly.

Mickey had half turned away from Phong. As he heard Phong's reply, he turned back, his face like thunder. "Tell me," he hissed, his voice a violent whisper. "Please tell me you didn't just say what I think you said?"

"We sent you a clear message," replied Phong calmly. "Anyone with any intelligence would have realised what that message meant."

Mickey was seething, his fists clenching and unclenching, but he fought himself back under control, forced his reply out between gritted teeth. "Go on then, why don't you tell me, since you are so fucking smart, and I am so fucking stupid, exactly what that message meant!"

Phong started to reply, but before he could say anything, Mickey cut him off. "And just for the record, since you are the smart one, and I'm the stupid fucking one, how come we're in your house right now, and I have your balls in my hand!" As he said it, Mickey reached out, grabbed Phong's balls, squeezed and twisted them.

The older man grimaced, gasped in agony.

Mickey got right into Phong's face again. "Speak up sunshine, we can't hear you. Can you hear him boys?"

The others laughed, shook their heads.

Mickey gave another twist. "Come on, speak up, what's the message?"

Phong had to force the words out past his pain. "It is a simple one," he gasped, "one that someone of your limited intelligence should be able to understand …"

Mickey exploded. He threw down the knife and with his free hand grasped the front of Phong's shirt, smashed his head into Phong's face, crushing his nose.

The old man hung from Mickey's grasp, blood pouring from his nose and mouth, swallowed hard, spat out two teeth, then gasped out the words. "You are finished …"

Mickey just looked at him for a moment, turned back to Martin and the other two. "He's a brave little fucker, I'll give him that!" One hand was still clutching the old man's balls, the other held his shirt front as Phong hung, bleeding and gasping from Mickey's huge hands.

Mickey pulled him in close, whispered in his ear. "Well, here's my message for you, Phong …"

With sudden violence, Mickey lifted Phong off his feet, turned and hurled him down the stairs. He bounced, twisted, landed in a heap at Brick's feet, his neck at a freakish angle.

Brick had just come into the hallway from the warehouse as Phong's body came tumbling down the stairs. He looked up at Mickey, grinned. "I guess you're all done here?"

Mickey nodded. "I think we've shut this lot down for good." He started down the stairs, Martin and the others at his heels.

"We've made a lot of noise," said Martin, "it's time we were gone. Did you find our stuff in their warehouse?"

Brick stood waiting for them at the bottom of the stairs. "All of it, plus a major shipment of heroin. The boys are loading the van right now."

Mickey reached the bottom of the stairs, stepped over Phong's body, the corpses of the two teens they had met on the way in. "Let's go."

"There's one thing you need to see in the warehouse before we go," said Brick.

Martin checked his watch again. "We need to be gone. Right now."

But something in the way Brick spoke had caught Mickey's attention. "What is it?"

Brick pointed towards the back door. "You need to see it. This way."

"Fuck me!"

Mickey, Brick and Martin stared at the strange scene as the torch beam played across it.

Behind them, their guys were busy loading their recovered drugs, plus the Vietnamese shipment of heroin, into the back of the van. Meanwhile, Scrubs backed the Land Rover out of the lobby of the restaurant, pulled up outside.

Bricks moved the torch beam left and right. In its harsh glare they saw a dozen or so dirty, frightened faces, cowering from the glare. All of them were young women.

"What the fuck is this?" demanded Mickey.

"Trafficking," said Martin in a flat voice. "They bring them over, clean them up, stick 'em in a brothel."

Mickey stepped forward, peered at the young girls more closely. "They can't be more than twelve or thirteen years old!" he protested.

"They don't care, that's old enough to suck and fuck."

Mickey looked back at Brick and Martin. "What are we dealing with here? These little Vietnamese fuckers are fucking animals!" He was outraged. "This lot should be at home with their mums and dads, eating rice or whatever the fuck it is they do over there!"

Scrubs called to them from the entrance to the warehouse. "Got static on the police band. Old Bill's received reports of gunfire from down here."

Martin nodded. "We're coming." He turned to go, but Mickey grabbed his sleeve. "Wait! Wait! We can't leave this lot here!"

"What do you want to do Mickey?" demanded Martin. "Take them with us? Send them home?"

Mickey scowled. "No. I mean, we should …" He looked around at Martin. "I don't know, but we've got to do something."

"We can't take home every stray puppy you find, Mickey. And we've got to go. Now!"

For a second, Mickey looked torn, indecisive, then he suddenly pulled his gun from the pocket of his jacket, stepped up to the cage in which the girls were huddled, shot the lock. Once, twice he fired, and the padlock fell away.

Mickey ripped the door to the cage open, called to the girls. "Come on, let's go!"

No one moved. They simply stared at him with their terrified brown eyes, huddled deeper into the far corner of the cage.

"Come on, we haven't got all fucking day!" And suddenly Mickey was in amongst them, dragging them to their feet, shoving them out the cage, towards the exit, towards freedom.

One by one, they tottered out into the bright sun of an early July day, blinking, weak, dirty, confused.

Mickey marched towards the shattered doors of the warehouse, climbed into the front of the Land Rover, a look of satisfaction on his face. "Torch the place!"

As the Land Rover pulled away, half a dozen cans of petrol were thrown into the shop and the warehouse, another was poured over them. Scrubs jogged back towards the van, packed and ready to go, clicked his lighter and threw it over his shoulder. Before the van had even reached the end of the street, both buildings were engulfed in flames.

PC Davis raced the tired Vauxhall Astra through the deserted Sunday morning streets, dodging and weaving past the parked cars. "What do you reckon?" he asked his partner, Marsden.

"Gunshots my ass!" grumbled the older man, trying to balance his coffee in his lap while the youngster revved and raced the small car. "Probably Chinese New Year or something."

Davis grinned, screeched the car round a corner. "You're probably right. Still, it's not every day we get reports of gunfire!"

"Yeah, well slow down, Dirty Harry. If you spill my coffee, you're going to have a really bad day!"

Davis slowed as they reached another junction.

"Left," said Marsden, cautiously taking a sip of his coffee.

Davis made the turn, immediately slammed on the brakes.

"Fuck! Fuck!" Marsden looked down at the hot coffee staining the front of his blue jacket. "I told you, if you make me spill my …" His words trailed off as he looked up.

The street ahead looked like the set of a movie. A dozen frail, dirty, half naked Asian girls wandered down the middle of the road towards them, like the survivors of an apocalypse, while behind them, two buildings – the Vietnamese restaurant and an adjacent warehouse – were consumed by roaring flames, the orange fingers already wrapping themselves round the upper floors, a plume of black smoke rising high into the crisp morning sky.

Both men stared, unable to fully grasp what they were seeing.

"Fuck me!" said Marsden finally.

Georgie

Georgie slowly stirred the sauce, looked thoughtful. "I've been thinking, you know? About you. About your husband." He glanced back over his shoulder at Terri, who sat at the small table, a cup of coffee in one hand and a joint in the other. "About killing your husband!"

Terri laughed. "I think about that all the time."

Georgie's eyes rested on her for a moment. He could see that beneath her make-up there was a bruise beneath her eye, but he chose to say nothing about it. "The way I see it, there are two ways you can go about it," he continued. "Option one is to be subtle. Kill him in some way that leaves no trace, or looks like an accident."

He reached into the cupboard, found some Oregano, sprinkled it lightly on the sauce. "That used to be quite easy, but it's getting harder and harder, what with all the scientific tests, DNA, all that nonsense. It's getting quite tricky to get away with a simple murder!" He sounded almost outraged.

Terri laughed despite herself, sipped her coffee and took a long drag of her joint. She was glad she smoked cannabis, it kept her calm, sane. She could forgot what was going on around her, it took her into another world, a calm and peaceful, dreamy place of her own.

. "So if I can't slip him something in his dinner, what can I do?"

Georgie gave her a sweet smile. "Let me come over and kill him for you!"

Terri shook her head. "No, if anyone is going to kill the bastard, it's going to be me."

Georgie glanced at her as he lifted a saucepan of pasta off the hob, reached for the colander. "Really? You're going to murder your husband?" He served out some pasta for each of them, spooned the sauce on top. A sprig of parsley and it was done. "You haven't got it in you, Terri. If you did, you would have done something a long time before now!" He set their plates down, settled himself into the chair across from her. "You've never been the one to fight back, that's why your men always trample all over you."

"Tell that to my ex!"

Georgie shook his head. "That was different. You were drunk, he attacked you, you defended yourself. You just happened to have a vodka bottle in your hand at the time …"

Terri said nothing. Was he right? Was she just a doormat that men could wipe their feet on, lying there and taking it like some pathetic, inanimate object? Lying there and taking it was what she'd been doing with Jimmy for a long time. Taking the abuse, the insults, the beatings, taking it when he came home drunk and wanted a shag. It certainly wasn't love making what they did, it was barely even sex. He would climb into bed, even if she were asleep he would jam his fingers between her legs to open her up, shove his cock in, pump away for a minute or two, then come. Not a word spoken, not the tiniest hint of affection, and Terri would just pretend to be asleep during the whole thing, lying lifeless, waiting for it to finish. Then as soon as he was done – and it never took long – he would pull out and roll over. Within seconds, he would be asleep, snoring as usual. Then Terri would slip out of the bed, tiptoe to the bathroom and climb in the shower, run it till it was cold trying to get his filth off of her.

"What you thinking about Terri?" Georgie paused, spaghetti rolled neatly on his fork, looking at her quizzically.

"He's a fucking pig!" she said vehemently.

"I don't think you'll find anyone to argue with that!" Georgie slipped the fork between his teeth, chewed thoughtfully. "Even I wouldn't suck his cock and believe me, I've sampled some dodgy ones in my time!"

Terri shook her head, tried not to smile. Georgie loved to shock her, loved to see how she reacted to his more outrageous statements. She resisted the bait.

They ate in silence for a while, both lost in their own thoughts. Georgie kept glancing up at Terri, but she seemed lost, far away. Finally, he spoke. "What about Mickey? Just ask him, tell him exactly what that pig does, then leave it to him. Jimmy would just disappear, no fuss, no mess, you wouldn't have to do anything. He'd simply vanish from your life forever …"

Still Terri said nothing.

"Imagine what it would be like Terri, with him gone? You could do whatever you wanted. Go out. Go on dates, find someone who really loves, treats you like a princess, treats you like a million dollars not a pound note. You deserve to be happy, be loved, you could come over here and visit me whenever you wanted. I can do your hair and nails every week, every day if you wanted me to!" He grinned at her, but she still wasn't responding.

"Come on Terri, think about it! Never having to explain yourself or justify where you've been. No one slagging you off, no one hitting you …" He paused, refilled his wine glass. "Why don't you just call Mickey? Then it will all be sorted, job done"

Finally Terri looked up and met his eyes. "No! I won't do it!"

Georgie reached out a hand to placate her, but she glared back at him so fiercely that he paused, his hand in mid-air.

"It's not that I don't want the bastard gone, don't want him dead, I do!" She lit another joint, inhaling deeply. "I want nothing more than to know that he's in the ground – but I won't have someone else do it for me, Georgie. That's what's got me into this mess in the first place. Giving myself up to a bloke, letting him do everything for me, and before I know it, I'm doing nothing, nothing except what he tells me to do, except what he allows me to do." She reached out and took Georgie's hand. "See what I'm getting at, Georgie? If I just hand the whole thing over to Mickey, I'm just getting another bloke to do something for me, just having him bail me out of the mess I've made for myself." She shook her head. "I know Mickey would do it, in a heartbeat. But I've got meself into this mess, I need to get meself out of it."

"But what if you can't? What if you never find a way to do it, never pluck up the courage to actually do it?"

Terri looked at him sadly. "Karma, they always say you get what you deserve, right?"

Georgie sighed. "It doesn't seem fair, Tel. He should be the one getting what he deserves, not you!"

"And that's the other reason I won't just let Mickey do it for me."

Georgie looked puzzled. "Because?"

"Because I want to see him when it happens. I want him to know that it's me, know why I'm doing it, want him to feel all the hopelessness and pain and despair that I've felt over the past ten years."

Georgie looked down at his empty bowl, then up at Terri. "That's a tall order, Tel. What if you can't ever find a way to do it?"

"Like I said, I'll be getting what I deserve, won't I?"

Georgie didn't know what to say. He picked his bowl up, pointed at hers, still half full. "Are you going to eat that, or what? After all the effort I put into making it!"

Terri laughed. "I saw you – the sauce came out of a jar!"

Georgie grinned. "But it was an expensive jar, and I was still the one who opened it and stirred it in the pan!"

Terri dipped her fork into her food, began to eat as Georgie started cleaning up. "What about you? You found anyone yet?"

Georgie sighed. "I keep finding people, love, but then five minutes later I lose them."

Terri scowled. "What does that mean?"

"It means that there aren't a whole lot of options for a cross-dressing sixty year old gay man with a long history of mental illness!"

"Well, have you been trying, at least?"

Georgie shrugged. "Depends what you mean by trying."

"Well, aren't there places you can go? I mean clubs and so on?"

Georgie smiled at her. "You mean where other gay guys hang out?"

Terri nodded. "I guess so."

He shook his head. "You have no idea, love, what those places are like."

She frowned. "Do I want to know?"

"Trust me, no."

"So what do you do? Don't you get lonely?"

Georgie stiffened. Terri had hit a nerve. "I get by."

"Well, do you go out?"

"Sometimes."

"Where do you go?"

Georgie kept his back to her. This was something he didn't want to talk about. "Out."

"Out? Where?"

He turned suddenly, his usually gentle face enraged. "Christ, Tel, can't you just drop it!"

Terri sat back, held her hands out towards him, palms out, placatory. "All right, all right. I was just asking, Georgie. You know how I worry."

He turned back to his dishes, plunged his hands into the soapy water. "I'm fine. You don't need to worry about me."

Bobby

Martin relaxed in the soft leather chair, looked around. Miranda knew how to make a place look good that was for sure. Mickey had good taste in clothes and cars, but when it came to decorating, to a house, even he would admit that he didn't have a clue. But this place, Mickey's house, it was class. Not over the top ostentatious like a lot of people Martin knew who had moved up. No, Miranda had ensured that Mickey's money was well spent.

There were acres of soft, pale carpets, high-end leather furniture, a glass dining table that could seat a dozen people, expensive modern art on the walls. Martin couldn't help but grin, wondering what their mum, Lizzie would have made of it if she'd still been alive. Christ, even in her last few years, Lizzie was still chuffed that their little house in Dagenham had an inside toilet! What would she have thought of this place with its seven bedrooms, each with their own en suite bathroom?

"There you go, mate." Mickey padded barefooted across the carpet, he handed Martin an expensive cut glass generously full of Scotch and ice.

Mickey had a glass of his own in his other hand, took a sip as he settled into a matching chair the other side of the fireplace from Martin.

Martin took a sip of his drink, leaned forward. "So you got them?"

Mickey grinned, pulled a sheath of papers from his back pocket. "There you go."

Martin took the papers, set his glass on the stone hearth, pulled a small pair of reading glasses from his shirt pocket and peered at the papers. For a moment, the room was silent while Martin studied the documents, Mickey sipping his drink, watching his brother, a half smile on his face.

Finally, Martin sat up, took off his glasses, looked across at Mickey. "Has Sol looked at them?" Sol was their lawyer. He was expensive, but he was also sharp, knew every little loophole and twist going. Good value if you could afford him.

Mickey nodded. "Said they're cast iron. The land is ours."

Martin picked up his drink, took a sip. "So how the hell did we wind up owning this?"

Mickey grinned. "Well, before I tell you the story, you have to bear in mind that in addition to being the biggest cunt that ever lived, your old man, Bobby, was also prone to embellishing a tale when it suited him."

Martin nodded, smiled. "Don't we all?"

Mickey laughed out loud. He'd been in a good mood ever since they'd shut down the Vietnamese, and with the Stratford land looking like it was for real, he felt that nothing could dampen his spirits. "All right, so here's the story as Bobby told it …"

Bobby Taylor was a good looking bloke, there was no denying it, and the fashion renaissance of the 1960s had come along at the perfect time for him. The thin ties, narrow collars, slim-cut suits all emphasised his powerful build, made him stand out in any crowd – especially somewhere as rough as the Church Elm in Dagenham.

Even in his mid-30s, he was that bloke that all the women wanted, and all the men wanted to be. Tough, cunning, always with money in his pocket, a bird on his arm, a flash car parked up outside. The fact that he had a wife and four children at home was no more than an occasional annoyance to him.

But right now, he wasn't looking at his best. Right now, he was sweating hard, eyes locked on the man across the small pub card table. Bobby looked at his cards, stroked his chin thoughtfully.

"Come on Taylor, we ain't got all fucking day!" The man across from him was Charlie Willis, known locally as Willie, a down and dirty crook who made his money the old-fashioned way – he stole it. Willie was everything that Bobby wasn't. In his 40s, he had thinning, greasy dark hair, an ill-fitting shirt with stains under the armpits, and a face that only a mother could love. It didn't seem to quite fit together. His nose was too big, his lips fleshy, his eyes small and slightly uneven.

Willie looked around. A dozen or so people had gathered round to watch their card game, and now the game was reaching its end point, now that the chips were down, now that he was certain that he was winning, Willie was loving it, soaking up the attention. "Fuck me," he added. "My wife takes less time to have a shit than you do to make up your fucking mind, and she's permanently fucking constipated!" He grinned. "So are you in or are you out, Taylor?"

Bobby held his cards close to his chest, literally, peered at them again.

"They ain't fucking changed since you last looked at them!" laughed Willie, his beady eyes on Bobby. "They were shite then, they're shite now!"

Laughter rolled around the table.

Bobby put his cards on the table, leaned back over his chair, called out to the barman. "Harry? Bring me another, would you mate?" He held up his empty glass – Bacardi and coke, the fashionable drink of the day – then finally turned back to Willie. "Now, where were we?" Bobby gave his million dollar smile, the one that made women drop their knickers, men drop their guard.

Willie wasn't being taken in by it. "I just raised you a hundred quid, and you were about to fold if I remember right!" Willie's eyes strayed to the pot, a big stack of cash, lying in the center of the table. There was enough to buy a flash car lying there, maybe even an E-Type Jag, and Willie could almost taste it already.

Harry, the barman, rumbled over, shoved the glass into Bobby's hand. Bobby took a long sip, finally turned his attention back to Willie. "A hundred quid, you say?" He grinned. "Piece of piss." He pulled a thick roll of twenties out of his pocket, began to pull them off the roll, throw them on the table. "There's your hundred," he kept peeling and throwing, peeling and throwing, "and I raise you another three."

The pub fell silent. Three hundred quid? That was a small fucking fortune by itself. When you added it to what was already there …

Bobby looked through the haze of smoke at Willie, a charming smile on his face. The smile of an alligator, a predator.

Willie just gaped. He had been certain that he had won, sure that Bobby wouldn't meet his bet of a hundred pounds, let alone triple it!

"You've gone quiet, Willie," observed Bobby. "A minute ago you were running your gob like there was no fucking tomorrow. Now you've gone all silent on me …"

Willie was still staring at the table, his jaw working while he fumbled for something to say. Finally, he blurted it out. "I don't have three hundred quid!"

Bobby leaned back in his chair, shrugged. "Oh dear. What a fucking pity." He looked around at the crowd, grinned. "Looks like you'll have to fold …"

Willie glared at him with pure loathing in his eyes but knew Bobby was right. Bobby leaned forward, reached for the money, stopped suddenly as Willie grabbed his hand. "Just a minute!"

Bobby raised an eyebrow. "Please don't ask me if you can give me a fucking IOU, coz you know what the answer will be …"

"No, no, I've got something else …" Willie licked his fleshy lips. He hated to do this, but he was certain that Bobby was bluffing, certain that if he could just come up with something to get Bobby to lay his cards on the table …

Willie glanced at his cards one more time. Full house, Queens over Tens. A winning hand, he just knew it.

"Looking at your cards won't change anything, Willie," laughed Bobby. "It's time to shit or get off the pot."

Slowly, reluctantly, Willie reached inside the pocket of his creased jacket hanging over the back of his chair, pulled out a sheath of papers. He looked at them for a moment, then laid them on the table.

"What the fuck is that?" Bobby peered at the papers suspiciously.

"Deeds," Willie told him. "Deeds to some land, in Stratford."

Bobby sat back, waved a dismissive hand at them. "What the fuck would I want with a shitty piece of land in Stratford?"

"It's worth a bit!" Willie told him. "I paid six hundred for it, but I reckon it's worth a lot more! It's got nothing built on it right now; you could put anything you wanted on it, it would be worth a fortune!" He was desperate, desperate to see Bobby's cards, desperate to beat the cocky bastard.

Slowly, showing no sign of interest, Bobby leaned forward, picked up the papers, glanced at them. He read for a moment, then tossed them back on the table. "All right. Three hundred quid."

Willie glared at him. "That cost me six hundred quid!"

"More fool you. It's worth nothing to me, but I'll take it as your three hundred quid if you want to see me."

Willie glared at him for a moment, then finally smiled. "Fine. Three hundred quid it is!" He picked up his cards, leaned forward, slowly turned them over. "Full house, Queens over Tens," he announced.

Bobby looked at them for a moment, his face expressionless, not moving.

The smile on Willie's face grew broader and broader. "You were bluffing, weren't you? You were fucking bluffing!" He looked around at the crowd, jubilant. "I knew it! Bobby fucking Taylor has been caught with his pants down, ladies and gentlemen!" Still smiling, he reached to scoop up the pot.

As he did so, Bobby tossed his cards out onto the table, landing them on top of the pot. Willie paused, his eyes scanning the cards …

Seven of hearts, seven of diamonds, jack of spades, seven of clubs … the final card had landed face down. Willie scrambled for it, turned it over with shaking fingers. Seven of spades …

"Four of a kind!" whispered Willie.

"Looks like I win," said Bobby quietly. He leaned forward. "So get your filthy, fucking hands off my money, you fucking tosser!"

As the game broke up, Bobby carefully stacked and folded the cash, stowed it away in his trouser pocket. He gave the deeds another cursory glance, then put them in his jacket pocket. He stood up, nodded to his mate, Big Frankie. "Room at The Top?"

Frankie was sitting close to a young blonde girl in a short skirt, had spent most of the last hour snogging and fondling her while everyone else was watching the card game. He reached out, stroked her thigh with his thumb. "What you think, darlin'?"

The girl smiled, clearly drunk. "Shounds wonderful!" she slurred.

Frankie nodded. "Always Room at the Top for you and me, Bobby!"

Bobby laughed. He liked Frankie. He was one of the few blokes who could keep up with Bobby. A gypsy, Frankie went toe to toe with Bobby at just about everything – fighting, fucking, drinking, and, of course, crooked business. They often did jobs together, knowing that the other would have their back whatever happened. He was a big bloke, Frankie, certainly earned his name. He stood about six four, with fists like hocks of ham, a heavy featured face beneath a shock of black hair.

Bobby and his date stood up, the girl a little wobbly on her feet.

"I need a pee!" she giggled.

Frankie put a protective arm around her. "Course you do!"

Bobby grinned. "Take your time! I need a fag. Meet you out back."

As Frankie led the girl towards the toilets, Bobby wondered if Frankie intended to shag her in the loo, or just leave her there. You never could tell with Frankie.

Pulling a cigarette from the packet, Bobby headed for the back door, leaving twenty quid on the counter for Harry on his way out.

The fresh air felt good after the smoke and heat of the pub. It had just rained, leaving the ground wet, puddles dotting the gravel car park, their surface a rainbow of colours from the oily ground.

Bobby was fishing for his keys as he strolled to his car when he noticed several shadows detaching themselves from the darkness, moving towards him. Trouble.

"Allo Bobby!"

Bobby should have known that Willie wouldn't take his loss with good grace. He was a cunt, a low life with no standards. He also had three mates with him.

"Willie. What a lovely surprise." Bobby scanned left and right, sizing up the other three guys. All of them were big, all of them the kind of bloke you didn't want to get into it with. Not that Bobby was scared. He hadn't got to where he was by being afraid of a fight – one on one he could take any of these geezers, probably two on one. But three of them plus Willie ... "As if staring at your ugly fucking mug across the table for three hours wasn't enough, now I've got to see you again?" he told Willie.

Willie moved closer, let Bobby see the knife in his hand. "This doesn't have to end badly for you, Bobby. I just want what's rightfully mine."

"What the fuck's that then?"

"The money and deeds you cheated me out of!" snarled Willie.

Bobby glared back at him. "Now you're accusing me of fucking cheating, you're a very silly man!"

"I'm not fucking with you, Bobby," said Willie in a low voice.

Bobby stepped closer to Willie, the fire in his eyes suddenly alight. He wasn't going down without a fight. "That's exactly what you're doing, Willie. Fucking with me."

He looked round at the other three, made eye contact with each of them, one after the other. "You know who I am? Do you?" None of them replied. "I'm Bobby fucking Taylor, that's who I am, and unless you are prepared to put me in the ground in the next two minutes, you'd better all fuck off right now, because if you don't finish this tonight, I will hunt you down, I will find you, and I will kill you. Then I'll find your family – I'll rape your wives, your girlfriends, your mothers, your daughters, then I'll put them in the fucking ground too! Do I make myself fucking clear?"

Willie's full lips parted in a smile, his small dark eyes gleaming in the dark. "You want us to put you in the ground? Sounds fine to me!" He flashed the blade towards Bobby's face. "Hold him boys!"

Bobby was prepared. He took a quick step back, met the rush of the first bloke. He paid for his over eagerness with an elbow to the face that spread his nose halfway across his face, sent him tumbling backwards to land hard on the ground.

The second one grabbed Bobby's other arm; the third took a swing at his head. Bobby dodged the blow, but took a punch to the kidneys from the bloke who'd grabbed his arm.

Bobby grunted, but yanked hard on his arm, got the bloke off balance, nutted the side of his face as he stumbled past Bobby, sending him down. He would have finished him off as he landed in a puddle, but the third geezer jumped on his back, wrapped his legs around Bobby's, his arm in a choke hold around Bobby's neck.

As Bobby wrestled to throw him off, Willie's knife suddenly appeared in his face, close to his eyeball. Bobby froze, and Willie grabbed his shirt front, slid the blade across his cheek, drawing blood, left it resting there pointing directly at Bobby's eye, daring him to move. "Nice try, Taylor!" He sounded grudgingly impressed.

Behind him, the first bloke was still sitting on the ground holding his broken nose, the blood soaking his shirt. The second climbed back to his feet, glaring at Bobby while the third, the one who had subdued him, dropped down off Bobby's back, held his arms behind him.

Willie nodded to the second man, who was brushing the dirt of his jacket, glaring at Bobby. "Get the deeds – they're in his jacket pocket. And the money is in his trousers."

As the lad stepped forward, a deep voice startled them all. "That doesn't look like fair odds to me!"

Frankie stepped out the back door of the pub, zipping his trousers as he came. There was no sign of the girl he'd been with.

Willie knew Frankie, knew his reputation. He licked his lips, looked past Bobby to where Frankie had paused, weighing up the situation. "You don't need to get involved in this, Frankie. It's a private matter."

Frankie stepped forward, adjusted his collar, his cuffs. "I can see that."

"Just walk on, pretend you didn't see anything, you don't need to get hurt," continued Willie. "Better for all of us that way."

Frankie nodded. "Sounds reasonable." He walked towards them. "My car's over there."

Willie let out a sigh of relief. The last thing he'd wanted was Frankie getting involved. Frankie was the King of the Gypsies, a title he'd earned by winning a series of brutal bare-knuckle fights a few years back. He was one of the few people who were as dangerous as Bobby Taylor, so he was relieved as Frankie walked past them towards his car.

"See you around, Bobby," said Frankie, as he strolled past.

His eyes met Bobby's. "Where you heading?" asked Bobby.

"Room at the Top." Frankie grinned. "Always Room at the Top for you and me, Bobby!"

Bobby was moving even before Frankie landed the first punch, a vicious clubbing blow to the side of the head that took the second geezer out of the game.

Bobby knew he had to avoid Willie's knife, so he simply dropped his legs out from under himself, pulled the lad forward who was holding him. The bloke stumbled, knocking Willie out the way, was off balance as Bobby suddenly straightened up and threw him against a parked car, span and rammed an elbow into his gut.

The guy buckled, his head dropping down as Bobby's knee came up into his face. There was a loud grunt; then he flopped backwards, out cold, landed on the bonnet of a tiny Mini, slid down to the ground.

As Bobby span back around, he found Frankie holding Willie, wrenching his arm back to take the knife from him. He shoved Willie forward towards Bobby, who met him with a straight left to the jaw that dropped him to the ground. Frankie tossed Bobby the knife, turned and kicked the lad with the broken nose flush across the jaw, sending him sprawling, out cold.

Bobby looked around, couldn't help but grin. Four bodies littered the car park, three unconscious, Willie sitting dazed and dizzy.

"I was hoping for a bit more of a rumble," admitted Frankie with a regretful look, flexing his knuckles.

Bobby nodded. "Thanks."

Frankie shrugged. "You'd do the same for me."

"Don't be so sure of it!"

Frankie grinned, grabbed Willie under his arms, lifted him to his feet like he was a child. "What do you want to do with this one?"

Bobby flipped the knife over in his hand, strutted slowly towards them. "He was about to kill me before you came along."

"No, no," gasped Willie. "I was just joking, Bobby. I wouldn't have actually done it!"

Bobby stopped in front of him. "See that's the difference between you and me," he murmured. Without warning he stabbed Willie in the stomach, three, four times, plunging the blade in and out.

Willie gasped, went limp in Frankie's arms. Frankie dropped him to the ground, and the two of them stood over him, watched as he slowly bled out, twitching, shaking.

Bobby pulled his cigarettes back out, gave Frankie one, took one for himself.

Frankie pulled out a silver lighter, lit both cigarettes. "So what was he so pissed off about?"

Bobby shrugged. "Not sure." He reached in his pocket, pulled out the deeds. "I think it was this."

As Bobby handed the papers to Frankie, Willie gave a final twitch, lay still. Frankie glanced at the papers, handed them back to Bobby. "Deeds?"

"It's a bit of land in Stratford." Bobby started to put the deeds in his pocket, suddenly paused. "Didn't you say your settlement in Stratford got moved on last month?"

Frankie nodded. "Been there three years, we had. Nice spot."

"So why don't you check this place out? If it's big enough, if it suits, you can set up there, free of charge."

Frankie looked thoughtful. "You sure?"

"It's the least I can do."

Frankie nodded. "All right. We'll check it out."

Bobby slid the papers back into his jacket, looked round the car park at the collection of unconscious men. Two of them were starting to come to. Bobby glanced at the knife in his hand. "You take care of them, I'll deal with this." Frankie nodded, walked over to the guy with the broken nose, grabbed him by the shirt, hauled him half to his feet, smashed him on the jaw again, knocking him back out.

Bobby wiped the handle of the knife, then slid it in the hand of one of the unconscious guys. By the time he had done, Frankie had clubbed the remaining one back into the land of dreams.

Bobby wiped a few specks of blood from his hands, smiled.

"Room at the Top?"

"Always Room at the Top for us, Bobby," laughed Frankie.

"For all the old man's faults, he was loyal with his mates," concluded Mickey.

Martin looked troubled. "Have you been by there recently?"

"The place in Stratford?" Mickey shook his head. "Nah."

"I went by last week," Martin told him, "had a nose around. Not only have they got that scrap metal business, which pulls in a ton of cash, they've built an office, and a house on back."

Mickey shrugged. "Those are the breaks. We'll give them fair value for it."

"I don't think it's as simple as that," argued Martin. "You know how close our families have been down the years – they looked after Mum after Bobby died, visited you in prison – Christ, you and Frankie Junior were at each other's weddings!"

Mickey was getting aggravated. "A thousand fucking people were at my wedding! Your point is?"

"My point is, they won't be happy, Mickey. They've been like family over the years."

Mickey's eyes narrowed. "Fair's fair, Marty. That's our land, and they've had the benefit of it for forty-odd years rent free. If they can't see that what we're doing is fair, then fuck 'em! It's not like we're throwing them out on their ears!" Mickey drained his Scotch, met Martin's eyes. "Stop worrying about everything, Marty. I'll go by, have a word with Frankie; he'll be fine." He stood up, reached for Martin's glass. "Refill?"

Martin held out his glass, forced a smile to his face. "Sure, why not?"

But as Mickey disappeared to refill their drinks, it was clear from Martin's expression that he didn't share Mickey's optimism. "Blood was spilled when we got the land," he muttered to himself, "and blood will be spilled again before this is all over …"

Tommy

Tommy sighed as he passed the ketchup across the table. It was an involuntary reaction; there was so much on his mind, so many things happening right now, he sometimes felt he couldn't keep them all inside.

"You all right Babe?"

Tommy looked up, found Sarah, his wife, looking at him. She was a sweet thing, her little blonde bobbed haircut surrounding a cute pixie face. Tommy forced himself to smile, but it was a tired, half-hearted smile. "Yeah, course, why wouldn't I be?"

Sarah smiled in return, but her eyes were guarded – they were at the table with their girls, Molly, aged eight, and Lucy, ten, not the time to talk.

"I'm just a bit tired that's all," Tommy added quickly, "lot of stuff going on at work."

That was a fucking understatement.

Sarah was still looking at him, concern in her blue eyes. "As long as you're all right?"

Tommy forced a huge smile onto his face this time. "All right? Cause I'm all right, I've got my three beautiful girls here, right?"

The girls giggled. They loved it when Tommy was playful. "So what film are you watching tonight?"

"Finding Nemo!" they chorused together.

Tommy glanced at the fish fingers on their plates. "Finding Nemo? How can you watch Finding Nemo after eating fish fingers? Nemo will think you are murderers!"

"Daaad!"

"Don't be silly," little Molly told him. "It's a film. They won't know what we had for dinner ..." her voice lost some of its certainty. "Will they?" She looked worried.

Tommy stood up, rubbed her head, mussing up her blonde curls. "Course not, love!" He leaned over, gave her a kiss, then did the same to Lucy. "You girls enjoy the film. When I get back, will you tell me if Nemo's dad finds him this time?"

"Daaad! It's a film!" Lucy reminded him. "It always ends the same."

"Oh, right. Silly me."

He leaned over, gave Sarah a peck on the cheek. She looked up at him, concerned. "You going to be late?"

Tommy looked at his reflection in the kitchen mirror, straightened his tie, smoothed his hair. "Probably. You know what it's like when my dad gets a bee in his bonnet about something." He turned and blew them all a kiss. "See you later my lovelies!"

Tommy slumped into his car, wrapped his hands around the steering wheel, let out a deep breath, trying to calm himself. He'd been feeling the strain more and more lately, felt it building up on him in waves until it sometimes felt like it was going to overwhelm him. There was way too much shit going on, way more than anyone else knew. The Taylors were a family of secrets, everyone had them, it came with the territory, and right now Tommy had a bunch of his own that he was trying to keep a lid on, things that Mickey didn't know, Martin didn't know, and especially Sarah didn't know.

She knew he was a Taylor, had some ideas about what that meant, but because of the way Mickey tried to keep Tommy sheltered, she'd never really been exposed to it.

There was no hiding it at family do's. Mickey insisted they all celebrate Christmas and birthdays together, and half the crooks in Dagenham showed up, but Sarah had never seen it like his grandmother Lizzie, or Mandy, his mum. They had both seen all sorts of shit going down. But Sarah, she knew Mickey had served time, knew what people said about the Taylors, but she thought Tommy was clean, wasn't a part of it. If only …

Mickey thought that Tommy knew nothing, but he really should have known better than that. Tommy was a Taylor – there was no way he was going to sit around while his dad and uncle built a huge criminal empire around him, and just pretend he didn't know what was happening. People talked, and over the years Tommy had spent time, and money, cultivating contacts who had their ear to the ground, who could keep him in touch with what his dad was doing.

Not that Tommy had any reason to complain. Not only had they set him up with the dry cleaning businesses, they also used their muscle to drive off the competition, make sure that Tommy made a really good living. But that wasn't enough for Tommy. He wanted more. More excitement. More intrigue. More money. More trust. Fuck it all, he was a Taylor, and it was about fucking time they started treating him like one, not like some kid who couldn't keep his mouth shut! Tommy wanted to be on the inside, not the outside; he wanted to really feel like a part of the family, not some red-headed step kid.

He cranked the engine of his car, pulled out into traffic, the big engine purring. Sure, he drove a big Merc, but Mickey had a 7 Series BMW, a Porsche 911 and an Aston fucking Martin! And as for Martin, well his collection of vintage cars just made Tommy drool.

That was what he wanted, real power, real money. When Mickey or Martin walked into a room, whether it was a pub, a club, a shop, just about anywhere, heads turned, people stopped their conversations to point them out. He drove on autopilot, turning his thoughts over in his mind. It was his mum that was the problem, he was sure of it. Ever since Mickey had come out of prison and run off with that whore Miranda – that's what his mum called, her, that and much worse! Ever since then, Mickey had been a bit distant with him, had kept him at arm's length.

Sure, he was there at times – he had always supported Tommy's boxing, had brought him into the club – but when it came to the real business, then he was shut out. What did Mickey think, he was going to go back to Mandy and spill the beans about everything, run his mouth off to her about what Mickey was doing? He would never do that! Give him some credit.

He knew what it was like between his mum and dad – bitter barely scratched the surface – but Tommy tried to stay out of it, never took sides, never told the one what the other was doing. Not that his mum didn't ask. Jesus, she was always probing, asking about Miranda, "the whore," or about what else Mickey was up to. Right obsessed with him she was, had never got over him, never forgiven him, never stopped believing that one day soon Mickey would dump Miranda and come crawling back to her.

No fucking chance, thought Tommy. He could see clear as day why Mickey had left his mum, even though she had cleaned herself up the past few years. He loved her, of course he did, she was his mum, but she could be a right fucking whinger and didn't stop moaning. There were times he just wanted to tell her to shut it, stop complaining about Mickey, stop blaming everything on Miranda and just get on with her own fucking life.

And then there was Miranda. Even though she was twenty years older than him, Tommy could barely think about her without getting a hard on. Right top fucking totty she was, sex on two legs. Blokes still turned their heads when she walked into a room, eyes on her, devouring her. Many were the time that Tommy had wanked himself off thinking of Miranda naked, imagining her going down on him …

Tommy shook his head. Christ, he was getting right bloody wound up tonight. What he needed was some relaxation therapy.

He pulled into the car park of the big Sainsbury's, rolled to a stop in the far corner, away from the bright lights. There was just one other car parked there, a red Mini. Tommy pulled up next to it, cut the motor.

Almost immediately, the Mini opened, and in the brief flash of the car's interior lights Tommy saw her climb out of the car, a smile on her face. Jeanette. His Jeanette. Young, slim, with legs that seemed to go on forever, and a mass of dark, tumbling curls around her fine-featured face.

She skipped straight to Tommy's car, climbed into the passenger seat, bringing a waft of perfume and excitement with her. "You're late!" she protested half-heartedly, wrapping her arms around his neck and looking into his eyes.

Tommy gave his tired smile. "Long day. Lots of shit going on."

"You need some relaxation therapy!" She kissed him, hard, passionate, their tongues dancing together as they greedily kissed each other.

Tommy's hands went straight to her legs, stroking her thighs, feeling her soft, warm flesh as Jeanette reached for his crotch, rubbed and squeezed.

"Mmmm, someone's feeling horny!" she grinned as she felt his hardness. "You've obviously been thinking of me!"

"Always." croaked Tommy, his voice husky with lust.

"Let's see what we can do with that!" She kissed him lightly on the lips, unzipped his trousers as he eased back in his seat. Her cool, skillful fingers slid his stiff cock out of his pants as her head dropped to his lap. "Oh, you are so ready!" she gasped, then her mouth engulfed him, sucking, stroking, her tongue dancing.

Tommy gave a deep sigh, his head back, eyes closed, imagining Miranda's full red lips wrapped around his cock …

Mandy

Mandy stared vacantly into space, her mind filled with a pent up rage. Night after night she went to bed thinking of revenge, still angry at Mickey, angry at Miranda, angry at the world. How could he walk out on her? Didn't he understand how much it hurt? Every time she closed her eyes, his was the face she saw. Dancing with her, holding her hand, buying her chocolates and flowers, kissing her, making love with her, all the wonderful things he used to do for her. At times she felt that those moments had never existed, that all that had ever happened was the pain, the torment.

She wanted to believe that she could win him back, but how could she? How could she compete with Miranda? Miranda was sophisticated, worldly, knowledgeable, sexy, everything she wasn't. Her mind turned as always to the thought of the whore in bed with Mickey. Her guts churned just at the thought of it, she felt physically sick.

Not that she hadn't been warned. As her best mate Denise had pointed out countless times, Mickey had always lusted after money and power, always had one eye on trading up.

"Well? Are you going to show them to me or not?"

Mandy blinked and looked at Denise. Short, round, with red cheeks and a cheeky smile, Denise had never changed. She was as down to earth as they came, always there for Mandy, always supporting her, offering advice, holding her hand, making her endless cups of tea as she poured out her troubles.

"Yeah, I 'spose so …" Now that it came to it, Mandy felt self-conscious.

"How much did you say they cost?"

"Ten grand," said Mandy quickly.

Denise grinned her cheeky grin. "Bet he didn't know that's what his money was going to!"

Mandy couldn't help but laugh at Denise. At times it felt as though she was the only one who kept Mandy going. It was her who had pushed Mandy to do it. "There are plenty of good men out there who would love you," she told Mandy. "You just need to get your arse off the couch, get out a bit."

Course, Denise was a one to talk. Married and divorced three times, still, she was just what Mandy needed to get herself moving, quit her pity party and finally do something. "Go out and find yourself someone," she said, "someone who will make you happy, treat you how you should be treated." Denise had got that look in her eye. The one that said you'll bleeding do what I say. "I'm not letting you sit here alone every day wallowing in self pity," she had told Mandy. "I'm going to help find you a decent man."

She had no idea what she was unleashing …

Mandy giggled. "All right, here goes!" And she pulled up her T-shirt.

Denise just stared, open mouthed, said nothing.

Mandy felt silly, embarrassed, still holding her T-shirt up high. "What? What is it? Say something for fuck sake! Denise? Do they look all right?"

And then Denise laughed, her cheeks almost hiding her small, bright eyes. "Christ, girl, those are some great looking tits! I almost want to cop a feel meself!"

Mandy couldn't keep the smile from her face as she dropped her T-shirt, stepped forward and gave Denise a hug. "It's all thanks to you."

"Me? What do you mean me? What are you talking about, girl?"

"Don't you remember? About six months ago, you came round one day, found me lying on the couch crying?"

A look of recognition crossed Denise's face. "Oh, fuck, yes. I was pretty rough on you, wasn't I?"

Mandy had been drunk and asleep on the couch as usual, had tried to ignore Denise when she came barging in, but she was too insistent, too loud. "It's time for some home truths, girlie!" Denise had declared.

Still Mandy tried to ignore her, but Denise pushed herself onto the couch beside her, forcing Mandy to sit up. "What are you getting out of this?" she had said. "Letting him in here whenever he wants to, so he just turns up for a blow job, bungs you a few quid? You need to fucking wake up! Get your head out the sand. You're living a lie if you think he's ever coming back to you. Your whole marriage has been a lie, and he's sucked the energy out of you like a vampire! You girlie, need to grow a pair of bollocks"

Mandy said nothing, just stared sullenly at Denise, hoping she would shut the fuck up and go away. No chance!

"It's time to turn all this sentimental shit off, Mandy, it ain't doing you no favours."

"I'm getting his attention, his love, a bit of sex," she protested.

Denise stared at her, wide-eyed. "How can you give him head when he's been shagging that dirty trollop? How can you share him?"

"I love him," sobbed Mandy.

Denise had laughed in her face. "Love? Christ, Mandy, what the fuck am I going to do with you? All the years you've wasted with him, the way he's treated you? Like shit, that's how! You deserve better, you do. You deserve to be happy, to be treated like a princess, not a fucking spare part, a bit on the side!"

Looking back on that conversation, it had really opened Mandy's eyes. Although she hadn't said anything at the time, deep down, Mandy knew that Denise was right. Mandy hadn't been happy for years, she had made her own prison. She was heading towards a nervous breakdown, with Mickey like a heavy hand pushing down and down, bringing bad energy every time he came around. She was in a prison of her own making, that's what Denise had said, yet when Mickey came out of prison he looked like a man who had been on a spa holiday. He was tanned and healthy, his body fit from using the prison gym.

And who brought the kids up alone, sorted out all the shit? Went to visit him every week, never missing a visit, not once? Getting into debt to pay for his clothes and the other things she kept sending him while he had no bills to worry about, never had to worry where the next meal was coming from, never had to worry about whether he had enough money to go in the electric meter.

But once Denise had said those things, they couldn't be taken back. Deep down, Mandy knew she was right. And that's when she began to change. She still lay awake most nights thinking of Mickey and Miranda together, couldn't completely shake those gut-wrenching feelings, but they no longer overwhelmed her. Instead, they made her stronger.

When Denise had finally left her alone that day, she had got up off the couch, joined a gym, got her hair done nice, had her nails manicured for the first time in years, even started going to a tanning place. Within a few months Denise could barely recognize her. The breast implants were the final piece in the jigsaw. In six months, Mandy had gone from fat, fucked up and well past forty to lean, tanned and sexy. "Fuck," said Denise in admiration. "Seriously fit, Mand! If I was a man I'd wanna shag ya."

But where Denise had thought Mandy was doing it to find herself a nice man, someone to look after her, Mandy had a different plan in mind, a plan driven by hatred. Hatred of Mickey. Hatred of what he had put her through. But above and beyond everything else, hatred of Miranda.

The bitch had it coming to her. Miranda had led him on, tempted him, seduced him. It was her fault that Mandy spent her nights alone, alone in the house, alone in her bed. Miranda had Mickey, and what did Mandy have? Painful memories, an empty house, and a bottle of Scotch.

She looked at her list and smiled. Today was the beginning of the end of Miranda and Mickey. Mandy's war was just started, and after years of taking shit from the two of them, this was a war she was going to win.

This wasn't going to be some half-assed revenge. Mandy was taking her time, doing it properly. Her list already contained several pages of ways she could kill Miranda. But that wasn't the first step. The first step was to get Mickey to see Mandy with new eyes, see the stunning new Mandy.

Then once the bitch was dead, where else could Mickey turn? He would come back to Mandy, she would have him in her arms again, in their bed together, skin on skin, no cold empty space next to her. She dreamed again and again of the day when he would be back and fill the void in her life. He was her love, her life. Without Mickey she had nothing, but now she had a plan, she was determined to see it through, and the first step was to get Mickey to realize just what he was missing.

She looked at herself in the mirror. Not bad. She wore a silky black night gown, barely long enough to cover herself, her firm nipples pushing through the thin material. She nodded in approval. That would certainly get his attention.

Then she reached down, lifted the hem of the nightgown and peeled it off, let it fall to the ground.

Even to her own critical eyes she looked good. She had knocked the boozing and smoking on the head, worked with a personal trainer three times a week, only ate healthy food, had done everything she could. And the results? Her body was firm and toned, lightly tanned, her breasts full, pert. She was shaved down below, just the way Mickey liked it, and her hair and make-up made her look at least fifteen years younger than she really was.

"I know it's been a while," she whispered, gazing into the mirror, imagining Mickey standing there, "but I was hoping you might want to maybe, you know …" She gave a coquettish smile. "Oh, Mickey!" She gasped. "Right here?"

Mandy closed her eyes, reached her hand between her legs and started stroking herself. "Oh yes, Mickey, yes, yes, yes …"

She was ready.

Sharon

Sharon stood in the rain, only partly sheltered by the lee of the building, feverishly drawing on a cigarette as the wind swirled the damp air around her. She could do this. Millions of people all over the world did it every day, and no one could tell her that they were tougher than her. It was all down to motivation. Some people said you needed willpower, but Sharon had never really believed that, and anyway, she had less willpower than a kid in a sweetshop. No, if she was going to do it, it was going to be because she had a really good reason – and right now she did.

It was Miranda's fault, as usual. She and Miranda had spent a lifetime leading each other in and out of trouble. Miranda it was who had got her into cocaine in the first place. When she'd first gone to a party with Miranda her idea of a wild night was ditching the Babycham for a Bacardi and coke. Right sophisticated she thought that was.

Then she'd gone to a party with Miranda's mates – Christ, her eyes had been well and truly opened! Everyone drank champagne, and there were lines of coke on the counter in the bathroom for anyone who wanted a snort. Sharon was nervous at first, but after a couple of glasses of champagne, she was up for anything, and with Miranda egging her on, she had tried her first snort of coke.

She could still remember the buzz, the euphoric feeling. It was unlike anything she had ever experienced. She felt she was flying, wanted to dance all night, fuck every bloke in the room. When she finally woke up the following morning, her head thumping with a hundred jack hammers and some good looking bloke lying buck naked beside her, Miranda told her she'd had a pretty good go at both!

Sharon didn't care, she'd found a new way of living, something that took away all the hurt and guilt and pain that festered inside her, and she couldn't get enough of it. Soon her whole life revolved around the next party, the next high, the next snort, and then that glorious moment as the cocaine kicked in and her feet left the ground.

As the first rush of discovery wore off, she quickly came to realize that it was no good for her, but she'd come to depend on it. She needed it to relax and unwind with her mates, needed it to get her through a day shagging punters for money, needed it at the end of the night to finally allow her to clear her mind of all the shit that haunted her, the only thing that allowed her to finally sink into a deep, untroubled sleep.

She'd tried to give it up several times – on her own, with help from friends, and even in the Priory with Mickey footing the bill – but every time she had come back to it. The booze and the cocaine had been her constant companions for over forty years. They had been there for her in the good times, had helped her through the bad times, and ultimately had sucked her dry of every last penny she had.

She was still making good money turning tricks, but all her savings, her share of the diamond money, all of it had gone, most of it up her nose. Now she was living week to week, whipping and fucking guys every day to support her habit.

Like every addict, she'd thought she had it under control, could stop if she wanted to, but it was a lie.

Miranda, on the other hand, seemed able to turn it on and off like a tap. Christ, she'd been with Mickey almost fifteen years, and he'd never suspected her coke habit, she could easily go for weeks without it. Sharon couldn't do that. Even a couple of days without a snort drove her crazy, the need just built and built, then she'd wind up going on a bender and wake up, yet again, beside some bloke she'd never even seen before, wondering exactly what she had done the night before to pay for her fix.

Funny thing, Miranda had been trying to get Sharon to go with her to the fortune-teller for years. Sharon had always resisted, had never been that interested before, although her mum, Lizzie, had done it all the time. But for some reason, this time, when Miranda suggested it, Sharon had said yes. Why not, she thought, she'd done everything else in life at least once!

Sharon had insisted that Miranda go in first, had sat nervously in the little waiting room, unable to stop from tapping her feet, tapping her fingers, getting up, pacing back and forth, sitting down again. How could it take so long?

Calling the room a waiting room was something of a stretch. It was the old lady's sitting room, the décor like something out of the 1950s, everything covered in heavy floral patterns – the carpet, the furniture, the curtains, the wallpaper, even the lampshades hadn't escaped! And then there were the nick-nacks, covering every surface, hundreds upon hundreds of glass or ceramic cats of all shapes, sizes and colours. Everywhere Sharon looked she found a dozen or more beady yellow eyes gleaming back at her. Right creepy it was.

When Miranda finally emerged, she had a dead serious look on her face, like she'd heard some seriously bad news. Sharon peered at her face. "You all right?" She was nervous enough already, the last thing she needed was a freaked out Miranda right before she went in.

Miranda glanced up at her, distracted, gave a fleeting smile that did nothing to dispel the worried look on her face. "Yeah, yeah, I'm fine."

Sharon stopped in front of her. "Miranda? What is it?"

This time Miranda looked up properly, made a real effort to smile properly. "Nothing, nothing. I'm fine." She squeezed Sharon's arm. "It just takes me a little while to process everything she says." She nodded towards the hallway. "Go on, she's waiting for you."

Sharon gave Miranda a last glance, then slowly walked down the hallway to the kitchen, peered at the woman sitting at the kitchen table beckoning her to sit down. "Hello, my dearie. Cross my palm with silver, as they say and I'll tell you your dreams and fate."

Christ, thought Sharon, could you get any more corny than this? She pulled a twenty pound note from her purse, held it out to the woman. She took the note and in a flash it vanished somewhere in her voluminous dress.

As Sharon sat down, she could see that the woman was old. Not just old, but really old, ancient, probably one of the oldest people she'd ever seen in her life. Wisps of white hair peeped out from under her headscarf, and the hand she held out to Sharon was gnarled and covered in liver spots, shaking slightly as she reached for Sharon's hand. She sat hunched in a bundle, pulling her shawl tight around her.

Sharon sat on the cheap kitchen chair, peered around the kitchen. It was as dated as the living room, with old, stained Formica cupboards, the kind they'd had back in the old house in Dagenham when she was a kid.

"Tell me your birthday, dearie," said the old woman. "Nothing else, just your birthday, and let me take a look at your palm. Then I can tell you what you want to know."

"It's the twentieth of December," Sharon said softly, holding her palm out.

The old woman shrieked as she grabbed Sharon's hand, startling her, and began speaking in a singsong musical voice. "Dearie, I can tell you things about yourself, what has happened and what's to come, who you'll love and who will love you. Everything that's happened, everything that's happening and everything that's to be is written in the stars and here on your palm."

The old woman beamed as she leaned forward to speak in a confidential tone. "I can see your life path, Sharon."

"How did you know my name?"

The woman ignored her and continued. "The numbers twenty and twelve are coming to me."

Sharon sighed. "Yes, that's right, that's my birthday, the twentieth of December. I already told you that."

The woman pulled a face as if Sharon had said something particularly ridiculous.

Sharon shrugged and decided to go along with her and listen to what she had to say. Miranda had probably said her name, but even though Sharon didn't believe there was anything in it, what was the harm in listening?

Sharon smiled encouragingly as the woman peered more closely at her palm.

"I can see that you are a very special person."

Ain't we all? thought Sharon.

"You have been chosen to lead. The angels are directing me, and I can guide you through your journey."

Come on, get on with it. I'm getting bored.

"You are a good person, but you have let yourself place materialism above everything else in your life."

Anyone could tell that from my designer clothes, my Jimmy Choos, thought Sharon.

"Deep down you are dependable and trustworthy, but you have never taken that path. But it will soon be time for you to sacrifice what you have for the greater good of all."

It sounded good, but not exactly specific, thought Sharon. I mean, really, she could say that to anyone. But Sharon found herself getting impatient, hoping that this was the build up to something more interesting and exciting.

"You will never marry, but you will nonetheless become a mother to many."

A mother to many? Sharon's mouth dropped open. She was far too old to have kids, what was the silly old bat going on about?

The woman suddenly looked up at her quizzically.

Sharon nodded at her. "Go on."

"You have lived a hard life, it has taken its toll, and it would be easy for you to be bitter. It is one of your life challenges to learn to be more tolerant of other people. You are blessed with a brilliant creative mind that is never at a loss for a solution to a problem, but you haven't ever really put it to good use. You don't know it yet, but the reason you are here in life is to serve others."

Sharon was getting bored. Most of that stuff could have been said to anyone, it was probably a con. Her attention began to drift as the woman continued.

Noticing that Sharon was barely paying attention, the woman suddenly raised her voice. "Oh my!"

"What is it?" Sharon leaned forward. Maybe this was where it got interesting?

The woman dropped Sharon's hand and stared into her eyes as if she was trying to see into her soul.

"What is it?" Sharon repeated, but with a little more urgency this time. She shuffled uncomfortably.

The woman made a dismissive gesture and sat back. "I don't need to look at your palm anymore. I know what's coming up for you."

Sharon shivered and waited. Suddenly it seemed more real, as though the woman had just been going through the motions before, but was now suddenly serious. This felt personal.

"You have the sight. You know what to do. You don't need me."

Sharon frowned. "I don't know what you mean."

The woman sighed. "You will. You can see things just as well as I can – maybe even better. You just don't realise it yet."

"But what's going to happen?"

"Everything's going to change. You won't believe how much it's going to change. It will feel like your world is spiraling towards its own collapse. Death and destruction, violence and hatred. And you will have to rise to the challenge. Oh, there will be so many challenges ahead."

Sharon felt a chill. "For everyone?"

"For you and your family. There's something about your family, something that happens, and they are going to need you, going to need you like never before." The woman briefly closed her eyes and went silent, then suddenly opened her eyes and grabbed Sharon's hand, making her jump. This time though, she wasn't reading Sharon's palm, she was simply holding her hand as if to give her comfort. She leaned forward until her face was almost touching Sharon's and spoke in a low voice. "You must prepare yourself for what happens, for the future. They will need you!"

"What sort of thing? What's going to happen?" Sharon's mind was a whirl. Sharon couldn't think of any situation where her family would need her. She started to panic and tried to remind herself that she didn't really believe in all this stuff, it was all nonsense.

The woman let go of Sharon's hand and sat back. "It will be tough, Sharon." She looked deep into Sharon's eyes as she spoke. "Sometimes things have to fall apart before you get the chance to experience something new and something better, to learn about yourself, what you are capable of." She grabbed Sharon's right hand and pointed to one of the lines running across it.

"See how long that line is? That says that you'll have a long life, but all those little lines crossing it ..." The old woman shook her head. "These are all the troubles in your life, troubles to come. But your lifeline is strong, and you will be able to overcome those challenges."

She sat back in thought. "This is not something far, far away, this is something that is rushing towards you, and you must be ready." Her old eyes met Sharon's, held her gaze for a moment, then finally she smiled. "That's it, my dear, that's all I have for you." Despite her smile, she looked exhausted, as though she had just done something incredibly difficult.

Sharon climbed slowly to her feet, still uncertain what to think. "Yeah, right. Well, thanks."

As she stood and turned to leave, the woman called to her. "Prepare yourself, Sharon. You can't stop what's coming. You can only be ready for it …"

Sharon walked out of the kitchen, took a deep breath as she stepped into the living room, found Miranda standing gazing out the window. "All set?"

Miranda turned and looked at her, a searching expression on her face. "So? What did she say? Anything interesting?"

Sharon sighed. "Exactly what I expected. A load of old bollocks, waste of money if you ask me. Come on, let's go, I'm dying for a fag."

Miranda gave a short nod. "Yeah. You're probably right." She took Sharon's arm as they stepped outside the house towards Miranda's convertible Mercedes. "How about lunch and an early cocktail? My treat?"

Sharon grinned. "That sounds more like it!"

They were both smiling as they got in the car, but both of them knew that something had happened in the old lady's house, something that was giving them both pause for thought.

Sharon gazed up at the dark, rainy sky, stubbed out her cigarette, puffed out her cheeks. The old woman had said to be ready, to be ready for whatever happened, to be ready to accept the challenge. If she was going to do that, there was one essential first step. "Here goes nothing," she muttered to herself, and pushed the heavy wooden door open.

Stepping inside, the church hall was everything she had feared. Plastic chairs, bad coffee, earnest looking people in crap clothes and bad hairstyles, but she had come this far, and she was determined to see it through. She sat down on one of the uncomfortable, orange chairs, looked around at the sea of expectant faces. She took a deep breath, forced the first words out. "Hi. My name's Sharon and I'm an alcoholic and a drug addict ..."

Mickey

Mickey parked on the narrow street, turned off the motor. He needed to just sit for a moment. All around him were the fag ends of Stratford, run down two-up two-down houses, little back street businesses, yards, garages, warehouses, all with a washed up, grimy look to them as though the tide of progress had washed over them and moved on, its fleeting presence marked only by the line of scum and detritus it had left behind. How many of them had figured out that they were sitting on a small fortune? wondered Mickey. His eyes strayed to the end of the street. A pair of high metal gates topped with razor wire, a single, rusting sign:

Frankie's Scrap Metal

Cash Paid

The gates were open, and as Mickey watched, a battered flat bed rumbled past him, its metal sides bulging with old appliances, rusty bikes, the flotsam and jetsam of a consumer society.

Mickey was not looking forward to this meeting. Big Frankie was now in his late seventies, but he was still a formidable presence, a huge man who had never backed down to anyone. Mickey had a feeling he wasn't about to start now.

Martin had wanted to come with Mickey, of course, but Mickey had met Frankie enough times to know that he'd be better off alone. Frankie didn't know Martin, would immediately be more on his guard if Mickey brought his brother along.

Not that Frankie would be by himself. Family was central to the travellers' way of life, and any time Mickey had dropped by to visit in the past, there had always been a stream of family in and out of their meetings. It was only when they got down to brass tacks, hardcore details that Frankie ever cleared the room.

They had done some jobs together over the years, both helping the other to make money. Mickey helped the travellers when they were getting grief from someone and needed some outside muscle, and in turn, Mickey knew they could always rustle up someone with calm nerves and hard fists when he needed some extra help on a job. Not that you could totally rely on them – Mickey had tried having some of their boys on his crew, but they weren't consistent, would just not show up if something else took their fancy that day, but when push came to shove, they each had the other's back. Until now. Would this change everything for them both?

Mickey leaned forward, cranked the car, slid it into gear and rolled forward. No point putting it off. The land was his, and he was going to sell it. All that was left was figuring out how that was going to happen – the easy way, or the hard way…

"Mickey!" Big Frankie's voice was a deep baritone rumble, coarsened by a life time of cigarettes. He had one hanging from his lips as he enveloped Mickey in a huge bear hug, slapped him on the back. "You don't come down here enough!" he complained as he finally released Mickey. He pointed Mickey towards a battered armchair, held together by dirt and grease, dropped into another such chair himself.

Mickey would normally shit himself before he sat in something that filthy, but he had been there often enough to know what to expect, had put on an old suit that morning, a dark shirt that wouldn't show the dirt.

"Liam! Get us a drink!"

They were sat in the small office that overlooked the entrance to the yard, the spot from where Frankie had overseen the business for the past forty-five years. The walls hadn't been painted in decades, were stained a dirty yellow brown from thousands upon thousands of cigarettes, the windows grimy.

There was another office on the side, where the boys who worked in the yard hung out, drank their coffee, smoked their cigarettes, told their tall stories.

A young kid in his late teens popped his head round the door. He had a close shaved head, bright eyes. "What will you be having?"

"Scotch!" Frankie looked at Mickey, who nodded.

"Straight up for me."

"How's business, Mickey?"

Mickey shrugged. "Can't complain."

Frankie looked good for his age. His hair was still full, just greying above the temples, his face alive, alert, the lines around his eyes and mouth just serving to add character to a face that had seen its share of good and bad times. There was a long scar that ran from his left eyebrow down to the corner of his jaw, and his nose had been flattened countless times in fights, but he still moved like a much younger man, waved his huge, scarred hands around when he talked. "I heard there was an incident down in Mile End the other day, some Chinks or something got put in their place?"

Mickey grinned. "Yeah, I heard that too!"

Liam trotted in with their drinks, handed one to Frankie, one to Mickey.

Mickey took a sip, continued. "Vietnamese. You know the way it is, they fucking show up, think they can start sticking their noses in without paying their dues, without so much as a by your leave!"

Mickey swirled the Scotch in his glass, admiring the amber liquid. "Shut the fuckers down. They won't be bothering us again."

Big Frankie leaned forward, held up his glass. "Here's to business as usual!"

Mickey looked uncertain, but couldn't refuse the toast. He clinked his glass against Frankie's. "Business as usual."

They sat back in their chairs, each eyeing the other, two heavyweights waiting for the other to show his hand. "So what brings you down here?" wondered Frankie, looking over the top of his glass at Mickey.

Mickey could feel the sweat forming on his brow, trickling down his back. Ten in the morning and it was already turning into a scorcher. "Got some news," he said, in a hard flat voice, "something we need to discuss."

"Discussion is good," replied Frankie carefully. "As long as it benefits both of us."

Fuck! thought Mickey. Does he know already? Has he heard about the site for the Olympics, put two and two together? No point dancing around the thing, that wasn't Mickey's way. Straight to the point, that was the only way he knew, get it out there, then deal with it. "It's about this place," Mickey replied, looking for Frankie's reaction, "and if we are both smart we could both benefit from it."

"Our place." Frankie's voice was flat, cautious.

"My land," asserted Mickey.

There it was. Cards on the table.

The two men looked at each other, both thinking, waiting for the other to say something. Mickey hated fucking waiting. "This is right where they want to build the stadium. You know that."

Frankie nodded, his hard eyes on Mickey.

"This land is worth a fucking fortune."

Still Frankie stared at Mickey. As Mickey had expected, he wasn't making this any easier for him.

"We have to sell, Frankie."

Big Frankie settled even deeper in his seat, tipped his glass back and emptied it. "Liam!"

The youngster appeared again in the doorway. "Refills!"

Mickey drained his glass, held it out as the lad trotted in.

"I own this land, Frankie, have a right to sell if I want. You know that."

Still Frankie said nothing, still his dark eyes bored into Mickey. The only sign that gave away the turmoil beneath the surface was his hands. They were in his lap, clenching and unclenching into giant fists, over and over again.

They sat in silence until Liam delivered their drinks, then left.

Mickey leaned forward. "You know I'll take care of you, Frankie. Always have, always will."

Frankie gripped his glass tight, stared at Mickey.

"But in the long run, there's no choice. They are going to build here, going to turf you out, whether you like it or not."

Mickey sat back. He had expected outrage, arguments, threats, not this stone cold silence. He sipped his drink, waited for Frankie.

Finally the old man sighed. "My father liked gold, Mickey. Never had a lot of money, but over the years, whenever he had a bit of cash, he'd buy himself a little more. By the time he passed, he had several ounces, carried it round in a wee leather pouch. What do you do? Didn't seem right just to sell it. It meant the world to the old man, he hoped he was giving us something valuable, a legacy. He would have been heartbroken if he'd realised how little it was really worth. So we kept it. Kept it to remember him." As Frankie finished speaking, he smiled at Mickey, and the sun that had forced its way through the grimy windows gleamed off his gold teeth. "Frankie Junior, Liam, Roy, all the boys have one, have a part of their grandfather that's always with them …"

He leaned forward. "We stick together, we keep our family close, and here, right here, this is the heart of it. This is our home, Mickey. The only one my family has, the only one they've known. We've built a business here, lived, loved, fought, cried, had babies …" He sat up straight again. "This is our home. We won't leave!"

Mickey shook his head. "Jesus, Frankie! Wake up and smell the fucking coffee! You don't have a choice! In five years' time there's going to be a big, fucking stadium sat right here, millions of people traipsing in and out to watch the poxy Olympics, and there ain't nothing you or me or anyone can do about it! The only thing left is for us to figure out the details between us!"

"It's our home," replied Frankie, his voice soft, compelling. "They can't move us out of our home."

Mickey could see the fear, the emotion, the resolution in the old man's face, tried to lighten the tone. "Come on Frankie, you've had a good run! Forty-five years, rent free! Not bad by anyone's standards, right?"

Big Frankie looked up, met Mickey's eyes. "I saved your father's life."

"And we have honoured that debt many times over. But that was a long time ago, Frankie. Times change, people move on, Bobby's been dead for years –"

"He gave this land to us!"

"No! He let you stay here for a while, but he didn't give you the land. That's why I have the fucking deeds!" Mickey was getting pissed off. The old man was being obdurate, unreasonable. "It's time to move on, Frankie. If it's not me, it will be the government, they'll just put a compulsory purchase order on the place. Send the bailiffs in, the Old Bill, the whole fucking kit and kebang to get you out of here. You realize that, don't you?"

Frankie looked at him, uncomprehendingly.

"See, these compulsory purchase orders – that's what the government does, Frankie. They fucking turf you off your land if they want it, no choice, and pay you what they want." Mickey sipped his drink, waited for a reaction. Nothing.

"I told you I'll give you a fair shake of the stick. The money I give you, you'll be able to set up wherever you want, out of town somewhere if you like, room for some ponies, all that guff you like!" He peered at Big Frankie, who still sat, unblinking, immobile. "Sounds good to me."

Finally Frankie looked up at him. "This is our home," he said firmly. "We're travelling people, I can't deny that, but this place, this place has given my family somewhere to come back to for forty-five years." He was getting animated, waving his huge hands around. "You can't imagine what it's like moving from town to town, every few days being turfed off and moved on by some sour faced fucker. That's the way I grew up Mickey. Then your dad gave me this place. It was dirty, shitty, the worst fucking piece of crap you've ever seen – but it was mine! Mine to do as I pleased! No one could turf me off, no one could tell me what to do, no one could move me on." He gazed out the window, a claw crane framed against the clear blue sky as it lifted a crushed car. "Until you. Until you walked in my door today and told me you wanted me to leave." He shook his head. "I won't do it, Mickey. I won't leave."

Mickey scowled. What had he expected? He knew Frankie was stubborn, knew he'd laid down deep roots here. But Mickey could be stubborn too, and he wasn't giving up. "You got no fucking choice!" He waved his hand around at the office, the scrapyard, the small house that stood behind it. "You got no planning permission, no building regs, nothing for this place. The council would shut you down, kick you out and clear the whole fucking lot away the second they got a sniff at it."

Frankie looked puzzled. "But they've never –"

"Because I've kept them off your back! That's why they've never bothered you! The only reason you're still here is because I grease a few palms, get them to turn a blind eye to what's down here!"

"But you wouldn't –"

"Frankie! It's time! Discussion's over. As soon as we get the right offer, we're selling."

Frankie nodded slowly. "So you're kicking us out?"

"No! I'm not kicking you out. I'm just telling you that it's time to move on. Like I said, Frankie, we'll make it well worth your while."

"You're kicking us out."

"Oh come on, Frankie! You know it's not like . . ."

"Liam!"

Again the youngster stuck his head into the room.

"Guess what? Mickey here says he's going to throw us out of our home."

Liam looked puzzled.

"Give it a rest, Frankie, it's not like that!"

Frankie ignored him. "Get the boys."

Liam's bright face turned suddenly hard as he glared at Mickey, then disappeared.

Mickey sat very still, glad for the hard comfort of the .38 tucked in the back of his trousers. He'd hoped not to need it – still hoped he didn't – but you didn't walk into the lion's den, no matter how long you'd known the lion, without at least some degree of protection. "Don't do this, Frankie," he said softly.

Frankie's hard eyes stared back at him, unblinking. "Last time I looked, you were the one doing it, Mickey."

"Our families have gone back over fifty years!"

"And you're throwing all that away."

Mickey could hear the rumble of voices approaching, even before the men crowded into the small office. There were seven of them, tough looking bastards with thick, muscular bodies, powerful, tattoo covered forearms, big, grease stained fists. Their cold eyes went from Frankie to Mickey and back again. One of them pushed his way to the front.

Frankie Junior. The big man's son, the travellers' bare knuckle boxing champion for the past six years. He had his old man's dark hair, steady gaze. "What the fuck is this about, fa? Liam said some nonsense about Mickey throwing us out of our home?"

Frankie looked at Mickey. "Go ahead, tell them."

The sweat prickled Mickey's forehead, ran down his cheek. He had to take the initiative. He climbed to his feet, moved to the center of the room, between the old man and the gang who clustered in the doorway. He had already scanned the room for possible weapons, an escape route. There were some tools on the floor by the window that he could use if he had too – a tyre iron, a club hammer – but his only route out other than the door was out the window. He had no plans to dive out the window and try to leg it, he'd never make it out of there. It was down to his voice, his authority, and if necessary, his gun.

"Here's the way it is," he began. "The Olympics are coming. In five year's time, everything in this area will be gone. Not just your place, but the whole fucking street, the whole fucking neighbourhood. Nothing we can do about it." He met Frankie Junior's eyes. Maybe he would see sense, understand the way the world worked better than his old man. Mickey didn't know him well, but they'd shared a few drinks, a few fights.

"And so Mickey wants to turf us out of our home so he can make a few bob," Big Frankie told them.

Cold eyes bored into Mickey. "Three words!" snarled Mickey. "Compulsory purchase order!" He looked from one face to another. "Know what that means? It means the government comes in, pays you what they want, throws you out. That's going to happen if you don't listen to me, work with me!"

Frankie Junior met his gaze. "And what's your alternative?"

"Simple. I sell the land – which I own – and give you a cut. We're talking millions here. You can go wherever you want, set yourselves up nicely."

Frankie seemed to be listening, taking in what Mickey said, considering it. He turned to the old man. "Fa?"

Big Frankie glared up at Mickey. "We're not selling! We'll never sell! This is our home! You hear me, our home!"

His son nodded. "And what about him?"

"Throw the bastard out. If he ever shows his face here again, kill him!"

The gang moved towards Mickey, menacing. It wasn't going to be pretty, and tough as Mickey was, he knew he could be about to take a serious beating. As Frankie Junior reached for him, Mickey whipped the gun out the back of his trousers, shoved it into Frankie's face. "Back the fuck up!" he snarled.

Frankie stopped cold, held his hands up in surprise.

Mickey jammed the gun against his forehead, right between his eyes. "The rest of you! Outside!"

There was a moment's uncertainty, and then the others all scrambled out of the office.

They stood frozen for a moment, Mickey just glaring at them both, father and son. "I didn't want it to be this way," he said finally.

"Too fucking late for that!" said the old man.

It was the final straw for Mickey. "I've given you every fucking chance! You want it this way, fine! I'll fire up the lawyers, and they'll throw you off, without a fucking penny!"

He stabbed the gun into Frankie Junior's forehead. "Let's go!"

He didn't move. "What if I say no?"

Mickey sighed. "Then I'll shoot you in the leg and leave you bleeding on the floor! Move!"

Frankie looked over at his old man, who nodded. Slowly, he turned and walked out of the office, Mickey's gun pressed to his back.

The sun was dazzling as Mickey stepped outside, it took him a second to realize what was happening. When he did, he cursed. The rest of the gang had surrounded his car, his brand new Beemer, and were scratching and knocking the shit out of it with whatever came to hand. It already looked like a pack of lions had used it for a scratching post.

"Oi! That's my fucking car!" Enraged, Mickey fired a shot into the air. Startled, they all stopped.

"Next fucker who touches my car, I'll shoot! Now fuck off!"

Slowly, reluctantly, they moved away from the car. Mickey eased the remote out his pocket, unlocked the car.

With Frankie Junior still in front of him he walked to the car, a dozen cold eyes on him. As they reached the car, Mickey shoved Frankie hard, sending him to the ground, then quickly climbed in the car.

Even as he was cranking the key the gang moved in again, started pounding on the car, a sea of angry faces and flailing tools smashing against the windows, the bodywork.

Mickey jammed the car into reverse and slalomed out of the yard, the angry mob chasing after him. As he hit the street he wrenched on the steering wheel, executed a perfect J-turn that wiped out one of his chasers, then accelerated hard and raced up the narrow street.

He glanced in his rearview mirror at the mob behind him, falling into the distance, waving their weapons and screaming at him. "You want a fucking war!" he screamed, his voice full of pent up fear and anger, "Well, you fucking got one!"

Mandy

It was getting on for five, time to start getting herself ready. That would let the rush hour traffic die down enough, but still give Mandy time to get there just before Miranda left the house for the evening. Mandy knew where Miranda was going, who she was meeting, everything about her. She smiled as she looked in the mirror, touched up her make-up. Amazing what money could buy you. The divorce money Mickey gave her came in very handy.

Everything had to be perfect. Before getting ready to go out, she'd done an hour of yoga with her personal trainer, flexing her muscles, stretching her limbs, followed by a nice soak in the bath. Then it was off to the hairdressers, a manicure and pedicure, all with Mickey's money. She had a lovely glow to her skin from a recent holiday in Turkey. She couldn't help but feel smug at how successful she had been at transforming herself, and with Mickey staying away these days, he would have no idea, would still be imagining her flabby and pale, a fag smoking wreck. It was over six months since he had last seen her, six months in which she had dedicated her life to this. Was he ever in for a surprise!

Mandy turned her car into the road where Mickey lived with his rich bitch, drove down the neatly kept street, past a series of enormous gated houses. Millionaires Row, that was what she called it, the gardens alive with flowers of all different colours, shapes and sizes, all in immaculately tended beds nestled against close- cropped emerald-green grass. Mandy felt like she was at the Chelsea bleeding flower show. As she neared Mickey's house, she passed Miranda on her way out. Mandy smiled behind her sunglasses – stupid whore, her head stuck too far up her own arse to even notice that Mandy had just driven past her!

Mandy slowed down, enjoying the moment, savouring it, the fruit of her labours, everything she had planned about to come to fruition. Miranda turned at the end of the road and was gone, and seconds later Mandy pulled up onto the driveway outside their house.

As she parked the car she took a deep breath, forced herself to relax. This was it, this was her big night, her big performance, and it was crucial that she got it right. Truth be told, she was dying for a fag and a stiff drink, but she had knocked both of them on the head. Instead, she practised her yoga breathing for a moment, tried to calm the butterflies dancing round her stomach. Slowly, breath by breath, she felt herself start to relax.

She was ready, she could do this. She checked her hair and make-up in the mirror one last time, then climbed from the car, wrapping her mink coat around her. A quick glance around, making sure Miranda wasn't coming back, then she walked up the long path to the front door, pressed the bell.

Mickey would answer the door thinking it was a cab to take him out, but she had already cancelled his cab. Mickey wasn't going anywhere. He was going to do exactly what Mandy wanted. Nothing more, nothing less.

She heard his footsteps approaching, echoing on the polished wooden floor, then stop as he picked up his keys, pulled on his jacket. The final few footsteps, then he pulled the door open, dressed immaculately in a silver grey double-breasted suit, a crisp white silk shirt, silk tie, handmade Italian shoes on his feet, he looked so horny!

It took Mickey a second to register what he was seeing, to recognize her. "Mandy? What the fuck are you doing here? I thought it was a cab, I'm on me way out."

"I cancelled your cab," she said matter-of-factly.

Mickey scowled. "What do ya mean? I'm going out."

She tingled inside. This was the crucial part. "No, you're not."

"Mandy, I ain't got time for this, I've got an important meeting to get to."

She raised an eyebrow. "I just want to talk. Are you going to keep me standing out here?"

Mickey sighed, leaned out the door and glanced around quickly, then pulled her in. "Five minutes, then I've got to go." He kissed her on the cheek as she stepped inside, caught a whiff of her Chanel No 5, it had always been his favourite.

Mandy glanced around, trying to look shy, demure, uncertain, as though she had never been in his house before. Christ, he would shit himself if he had known that she had been here twice before, checked out every room, looked through his drawers, his wardrobe, everything.

"Living room's this way." He gestured, led her into the vast room, the gleaming chandeliers throwing soft light on the pale walls.

Mandy followed, her stiletto heels clicking on the wooden floor of the hallway before she stepped onto the thick carpet.

Mandy had spent years reading Mickey's moods, trying to avoid his anger, keep him sweet, she could tell exactly what he was thinking. He was intrigued, curious, had clearly noticed the difference in her face, her hair, thick and wavy as it cascaded down her shoulders. "So what's this all about?" Mickey walked straight to the bar in the corner, poured them both a drink, the ice clinking in the glasses.

Mandy gazed around the room, pretended to be impressed, even a little overawed. "Your house is lovely."

Mickey handed over her drink, and for a brief moment their eyes met. He held her stare for a moment, then walked over to an oversized cream leather settee, sat down and patted the seat beside him. "Have a seat, then tell me what's on your mind."

Mandy walked over, stood in front of him, her drink in one hand, the other still holding her coat wrapped tight around her. "I had something I wanted to share with you," she said softly, and as she did she set her drink down on a side table, let her coat fall open, turned back to face him, then shrugged the coat off her shoulders.

Mickey just stared. Mandy was naked beneath the coat, her toned body almost glowing with health, her breasts perfect, her shaved sex almost at Mickey's eye level.

Mickey licked his lips, took a sip of his drink, his eyes feasting on her body. "Fucking hell Mand!" he finally croaked.

Mandy moved closer, her body now just inches from his face. She knew Mickey, knew he couldn't resist, not when she looked like this. He couldn't, could he? For a second Mickey did nothing, then suddenly he put his hands around her waist and pulled her close, his mouth on her firm stomach.

His hands explored her bottom, feeling the firm, taut muscles as his tongue slid down her body licking and kissing her softly then traced a line back up towards her breasts.

He climbed to his feet, pulled her in close as he sucked on first one breast then the other. She could feel him getting hard as his body pressed against her. Mandy quickly unbuttoned his shirt, pulled it off him and threw it to the floor, touched his chest, fingering his nipple.

Mickey kissed her neck, her mouth, her face, his breath hot, rapid. "You've got my full attention," he laughed softly, "so what did you want?"

"I'm gonna show you." Mandy whispered, unzipping his trousers. She bent to her knees, opened his trousers, pulled out his cock, began tantalizingly licking up and down the shaft.

Mandy smiled to herself as she engulfed his hard penis in her mouth, felt him moan and push against her, his fingers locked in her thick, dark hair as she gave him long hard kisses, her full lips stroking and sucking with each stroke.

Their sex was hot, frenzied, carnal. Mickey soon came in her mouth, but she wasn't done with him. She wanted to own him, she wanted all of him, wanted to intoxicate him, do everything she knew he did with Miranda.

She pulled him down on the carpet beside her, straddled his chest, then slid her body up to his face, sat on his mouth, taking her pleasure from his tongue, writhing, bucking, all her frustrations and hatred pouring out as she climaxed.

Before he could even catch his breath, she lay on her back on the soft carpet, pulled him on top of her. He was already hard again as he slipped easily inside her, began thrusting. This was what she had missed, her Mickey, his firm, strong body claiming her, his hands all over her, his thick cock inside her. Fuck you, Miranda, she thought as Mickey rode her hard, building towards another climax. Fuck you, you stuck up whore. Who's the silly bitch now!

As Mickey came inside her, Mandy clung tight to him, her mouth clamped to his shoulder.

"Easy, girl," he gasped. "Don't leave any marks!"

But Mandy didn't care. Mickey was hers again, she would do what she damn well pleased. Mickey was hers!

She fell back on the carpet, happy, sated. That was part one of her plan completed. Time to start planning part two …

Mickey

Sol settled back in his chair, half hidden in a haze of cigar smoke. Mickey watched him carefully, looking for clues in Sol's face as he scanned the deeds to the land in Stratford.

Sol had handled all the Taylor's legal matters for decades, was the ultimate fixer, the man they turned to in almost any tricky situation. Whatever problem you had, whatever you needed, Sol would know a bloke who knew a bloke who could get it sorted for you.

Mickey studied Sol's face. He had no idea how old he was. He was one of those men who had probably started looking old when he was in his twenties, with receding hair badly combed over, flabby jowls, a paunch. He could be anywhere from forty to seventy, badly dressed, always grumpy, but with one of the sharpest minds Mickey had ever encountered.

He puffed on his cigar, tapped the ash into a cut glass ashtray, then set the papers down on his cluttered desk. "You've got them by the balls," he began. "The deeds are unimpeachable, and I've done some research on the zoning. Everything they've built there is illegal."

"I could have told you that for free," said Mickey. "I'm the one who has paid off the council to turn a blind eye."

"So how do you want to handle it?"

"Can't we just get an eviction order or something, get the council in to condemn all the buildings and throw them out?"

Sol shrugged. "Sure. Legally you're solid. But there are downsides to going that route."

Mickey frowned. "Such as?"

"Firstly, once the council are involved, they'll be in your hair for the long haul. And if your friends are smart, they'll do what travellers do best, which is disappear like morning mist on a sunny day."

Mickey couldn't help but grin at the metaphor. Sol was so pale he looked like he'd never even seen a sunny day. "And if they do that," Sol continued, "you're fucked."

"How's that? It sounds perfect?"

"Oh, they'll be gone all right. But the council will be looking for someone to pay the bill – for the eviction, for the demolition, and for whatever horrendous environmental clean-up is needed. The only person they can go to will be the landowner – you."

"How much are we talking?"

Sol puffed out his cheeks, shrugged. "Who can say? Depending on what kind of mess they've created there – and I'm guessing that after forty years of dealing scrap it will be huge – it will run into hundreds of thousands, maybe more."

"And I'd have to pay it?" Mickey looked outraged.

"It's your land. You are ultimately responsible."

"That ain't fucking right!"

"Plus – and you probably know this better than me – word will get around, and you'll have the whole traveller community looking to cause trouble for you."

"I can deal with them!" bristled Mickey.

Sol looked dubious. "Really? You really want that lot on your back for years to come?" He shook his head, pointed his cigar at Mickey. "Think carefully Mickey. I've met some vindictive bastards in my time, but that lot, Christ, it's like a fucking religion for them. They can carry a grudge for generations, long after everyone has even forgotten what it was even about. If there's an alternative to having them on your back from now till kingdom come, I would look at it very hard!"

Mickey rubbed his brow. "So what is the alternative?"

"A bit of legal, a bit of cash, a bit of muscle."

"Meaning?"

"First, I send them an eviction order, a bit of legal bluster to intimidate them. Then we make them an offer, something that will make them feel like they aren't getting shafted. Then you add some muscle to provide them with the motivation to move on. You can still do that, I assume?"

Mickey snorted. "You fucking assume! Don't ever assume, mistake me or confuse me for anyone else. I'm Mickey Taylor, scared of no fucking man, don't ever forget that!"

"I have to ask," said Sol suddenly. "You have already offered to pay them off, haven't you? I mean, that is most people's first weak spot."

Mickey nodded. "I told Big Frankie we'd take care of them. But money don't mean much to him. For Frankie it's all about family, having a place of their own. Even if it's fucking mine!"

"Still, I would pursue that option further before we become confrontational with them."

"Become confrontational!" Mickey looked outraged. "They threatened to kill me, and smashed the shit out of me brand new beemer! If I hadn't have had a shooter on me they would have kicked the crap out of me too!"

"My suggestion still holds."

Mickey took a deep breath, tried to calm himself down. He knew that getting worked up, emotional about it, would just wind up in bloodshed. "I'm listening," he said finally.

"Offering a vague amount of money doesn't have the power of a clear, specified amount." Sol leaned forward. "Based on the research I've done, that land could be worth anything from ten to twenty million."

Mickey looked surprised.

Sol grinned at his response. "Right. So we set up a meet, neutral ground, legal counsel present, and make them a concrete offer."

Mickey's eyes narrowed. "How much."

"I would think that two million would provide a high enough level of motivation to resolve this."

"Two million?" Mickey spluttered. "You want me to give those cunts two million to get off my fucking land! After what they did to me and my car? You are fucking shitting me, right?"

Sol puffed his cigar, said nothing, waited for Mickey to calm down.

Mickey stood up, paced to the window, gazed out. Sol's office overlooked the back of a chippy. Very low key was Sol, no one would guess who his clients were, how much money he made. Mickey turned it over in his mind. Much as he hated giving two million of his money to those thieving bastards, it would be better to resolve it quickly, with no fuss.

"And you would still net at least eight million," Sol reminded him.

Mickey turned, looked at Sol. It was almost as though he was reading Mickey's thoughts.

"We can make it contingent upon the final sale price," continued Sol. "Say twenty percent of anything up to ten million."

Mickey shook his head. "Nah. Greedy cunts will immediately say twenty percent of everything. You were right first time. A fixed amount, something concrete they can get their minds set on."

Mickey nodded as if in confirmation of his own statement, turned to the door. "You'll set it up?"

Sol nodded. "I have a colleague who has worked with the travellers before. I'll have him set it up."

What a surprise. Sol knew a bloke who knew a bloke … Mickey straightened his cuffs, buttoned his jacket. "Tell me when it's set."

Georgie

Dave couldn't believe his luck. When he'd asked the woman if he could buy her a drink, he'd expected her to say no. Ninety percent of women did, but you had to keep trying, didn't you? And with a looker like this one, well he'd figured his odds were even lower than usual.

"Sure, vodka and cranberry," she'd replied in a husky voice.

Dave got over his surprise quickly, ordered the lady a drink, slid up onto the bar stool beside her, started reeling out his best chat-up lines.

Up close, he could see she was a bit older than she probably liked to let on, but he'd watched her as she had sashayed to the bar, and no matter how old she was, she had the kind of figure he liked – slim through the hips, firm ass, nice tits. And that voice, the way she talked, it sent tingles through Dave.

Dave wasn't a bad looking bloke, mid-30s, divorced, but he tried to keep himself in shape, went to the gym a couple of times a week, and his job as a brickie helped, on the go all day long. But still, you get into your thirties, the hair starts receding, it becomes harder and harder to compete with the young blokes. And now that he was divorced, suddenly thrown back out into the deep water, there were times when he felt like he was drowning.

It had all seemed so much easier when he was younger. In those days he'd felt invincible. Full head of hair, lean and muscular, with some cash in his back pocket on a Friday night, well, he'd pretty much always pulled. And even after he and Stacey had got married, he'd still scored a few times, still had the touch when he fancied a bit on the side.

But over time he'd done it less and less, had settled into married life, looked on in envy when one of his mates who was still single had picked up some girl, headed out for a bit of fun, leaving Dave and his married mates to bury their frustrations in another pint.

Then fuck me, if he didn't find out that Stacey had been screwing his friend Mark for the past two years! He knew he'd not been paying her much attention for a while, but it was hard with the kids always screaming, Stacey never seemed to make an effort to look nice anymore, and anyway, after the third kid she'd really let herself go. Her tits had sagged, her arse had expanded, she'd even cut off her lovely long hair, said it was too much hassle to look after it.

So the past few years the most they'd managed was the occasional Saturday night shag when Dave came home from the pub boozed up and randy.

So what the fuck did Mark see in her? A lot, apparently! Dave had found out through a mate who had heard Mark boasting to someone that she gave the best fucking blowjob he'd ever had.

Stacey? His Stacey? Giving Mark blow jobs! Fuck me! Dave had never managed to get her mouth anywhere near his dick, Stacey had always said the thought of it disgusted her, and yet here she was, apparently sucking Mark off like there was no tomorrow.

Right fucking to do it was. He and Mark had had a huge fight in the Three Bells one night, tearing lumps off each other until their mates pulled them apart, and after that it was all downhill. Stacey still lived in their house with the kids, while Dave had rented a tiny flat just around the corner …

"So do you want to go somewhere more exciting?" said the woman suddenly.

Fuck me, Dave couldn't believe what he was hearing. Her hand was on his thigh, stroking softly, dangerously close to his junk, her seductive voice in his ear, her perfume in his nostrils. Jesus Christ, he'd pulled! In the two years since the divorce, Dave had had sex once with a woman, a one-night stand with a fifty-year- old slapper when he was drunk, the rest of the time it was him alone in his apartment with his laptop, wanking himself to internet porn.

"Yeah, yeah, I'd love to!" he gasped. Their eyes met, and Dave could see the lust in them. There was no doubt about it, he was going to score!

Dave threw some money on the bar, trying to play the big man, took her arm and led her towards the door.

Christ, where could they go? His flat was a right bloody tip, dishes all over the place, bed unmade – he hadn't changed the sheets in months – dirty clothes all over the floor. He doubted a classy woman like this would appreciate a tip like that. Maybe she had a place?

"My place isn't really ideal for entertaining," he mumbled as they walked to the door, hand in hand.

The woman smiled that wicked, seductive smile of hers. "That's OK. Do you have a car?"

Another embarrassment. "I've got me work van," he admitted.

"I'm sure that will be fine."

It was one of those beautiful warm, summer evenings where you just wanted to be outside as long as you could, a blanket of stars visible despite the lights of the city.

Dave led her to his van, parked a block away on a narrow side street, remembered to help her into the van first. He was rewarded with a flash of thigh, the top of a lacy stocking as her skirt slid open.

His heart beating, Dave raced around to his side of the van. "You're going to get some tonight!" he told himself, unable to keep a grin from his face.

He slid into the seat, slammed his door, turned around to find the woman already moving towards him. One hand slid behind his neck, the other into his lap, and their lips met.

Christ, she was hot! Their tongues darted back and forth while her hand found his dick, squeezed it through his jeans. He gasped in surprise, his hand all over her arse.

She suddenly broke off the kiss, pushed him back in his seat, began to unbutton his trousers. "Let's see what we've got here, shall we?"

Dave felt powerless, held in thrall by her assertiveness, not believing what was happening, barely even daring to think what she might do next.

He didn't have to wait long to find out.

Her strong hands slid his cock out of his jeans, gently stroked up and down, then without another word she dropped her head into his lap, took the full length of his cock in her mouth.

Dave gasped. It was all he could do not to shoot his wad straight away, but he managed, settled back in his seat, eyes closed, enjoying every last second as her mouth slid up and down, up and down, her tongue dancing around the tip, sending surges of pleasure racing through his body.

God, it felt good! Dave reached down, pushed on her head, his hand in her thick, dark hair as she sucked faster and faster.

He could feel himself coming, closer and closer, her mouth moving faster and faster, and then he came, a hot torrent, holding her head in place as he thrust up against her mouth, gasping, shaking, finally sagging against his seat with a deep sigh.

She sucked and licked him for a moment more, then slowly sat up, smiling. "I think you needed that."

Dave looked at her in amazement. He'd always fantasized about something like that, but never actually believed it would happen to him. "Christ, yes," he mumbled.

To his surprise, she immediately reached for the door handle.

"Wait, where are you going?"

She paused, gave him an enigmatic smile. "You got what you wanted, didn't you?"

"You'd better fucking believe it!"

"So we're both happy." She opened the door, climbed out.

Dave leaned across, unable to follow her, his trousers still open, his limp dick still out. "But I don't even know your name!"

She closed the door, and without looking back disappeared down the dark street. "Believe me, honey," said Georgie, in his normal voice, "you don't want to know my name …"

Mickey

Mickey sat and glared at Martin. "What do you mean disappeared?"

"Exactly what I said!" snapped Martin. "Brick said he went to the dead drop as usual, nothing there. He called Si, Si swears he put the money there, was careful, nothing different, saw no one …"

"Nothing different!" stormed Mickey. "Nothing fucking different! That's the third drop this week that's gone missing, and you say nothing fucking different!"

The sounds of the gym pounded through the window, like a staccato soundtrack to their conversation. The pounding of fists against heavy bags, the clank of weights, the grunt of the boxers training, the thump of the music blasting out of the boom box. Mickey had had double glass installed to keep the sound of their conversations from carrying out to the gym, but no glass could keep the noise of the gym out of his office. Usually Mickey loved it, but right now it was giving him a fucking headache.

"Are we going soft, Marty? Is that what it is? Are our boys starting to take the piss, knowing we won't do anything about it?" Mickey glared out at the gym, the boxers working, Kenny Jackson attacking the speed bag, his fists a blur. "Maybe we should bring them all in, bust a few of them up, let the others see what happens?"

Martin shook his head. "Bad idea."

Mickey bristled. He wasn't used to being told no.

"The whole point of the dealer network is that we never meet them," added Martin quickly, seeing Mickey starting to react. "They don't know who we are, nothing can be traced back to us." He looked up, met Mickey's fierce gaze. "And anyway, that's not the problem."

"Oh, and how come you suddenly know so much?"

"Listen to me a minute, Mickey. It's part of a bigger pattern."

"What the fuck are you talking about?"

"Last week, when the cops busted the club, you said it was just one of those things," explained Martin. "Every so often the cops have to do something to make it look like they are doing their job, and it just happened to be us."

"Right," agreed Mickey. "Christ, it's been over three years since they last stuck their nose in there."

"And then when those kids jacked Tommy's dry cleaning shop last week, emptied the till, you said it was bad luck."

"You can't connect that to the club!" protested Mickey. "Tommy's not even a part of what we do. Everyone knows that!"

Martin shook his head. "That cuts both ways, Mickey. He's still a Taylor. Everyone knows that."

Mickey looked seriously at Martin for the first time. Did he have a valid point?

"And now, three drops vanished in one week," concluded Martin. "So. Do you still think this is all bad timing, bad luck, dodgy couriers?"

"Fuck me! Someone's got it in for us big time!"

Martin nodded.

"It's the fucking pikies!" snarled Mickey. "I should have known they wouldn't take this lying down!"

"It makes sense," agreed Martin. "Who else would have the manpower, the connections to squeeze us like that?"

"Sol warned me," Mickey admitted. "He said no one holds a grudge like the travellers."

"When's the meet set for? Tuesday?"

Mickey nodded. He'd been pretty cocky about the meeting, confident that with the eviction looming over them, even Big Frankie would jump at the chance to take two million quid and walk away. But now he wasn't so sure. If it had become a matter of pride, a true vendetta against the Taylors, they might not back down. It could drag on into a war of attrition that lasted for years. That was the last thing that Mickey wanted. Something like that could drag the whole family into it, would cost them millions over time – and not just that, there was the effect something like this could have on his family.

They'd had troubles before, rival gangs they'd had to put in their place, but it had always been over pretty fast, had never involved family, friends. But if they had the balls to hit one of Tommy's dry cleaning places when he wasn't even part of the business, then there was no limit to what they might do.

Mickey got a sudden chill as he thought of Miranda. He had always kept her right out of what he did. She stayed in Upminster, met her friends there or in London, had never even visited the gym or any of his clubs, even though she begged him to let her come see where he worked, the places he owned.

But now she seemed suddenly vulnerable. She was a creature of habit, had a set schedule – the beautician, the hair salon, her yoga classes, coffee with Madge every Thursday … and that baby blue convertible Bentley of hers was hardly the most inconspicuous car around.

He looked up to find Martin looking at him. "Call Sid. I want him in here within the hour."

"You thinking of Miranda?"

"I'm thinking of fucking everybody! Miranda, Georgie, Terri, Sharon, my kids, my gran kids, the shops, fucking everything! Until this is resolved, we are on a full fucking war alert. We have to assume that we are going to be hit, again and again until this is resolved."

Martin nodded. "I'll call him." He reached for his phone, then paused.

"What?"

"And that's it? We go on the defensive, wait for them to pick us off, hope we can be ready?"

Mickey glared back at him, the mad, cold-eyed look on his face that had done so much to earn him his nickname. "Fuck no. We send them a little reminder of who they are dealing with!"

Darren crouched on top of the wall, carefully cut the razor wire, holding the strands as he cut them so that they didn't fly off when the tension was released. Three strands, then he was clear.

He gazed around the scrapyard. Mickey had said there were two big dogs – he could see them, German Shepherd crosses, both asleep outside the main office. As long as he was quick and quiet, they shouldn't bother him, but he had a big can of pepper spray in his pocket just in case.

The air was crisp, daylight already starting to creep up from the east even this early. Just after 4:00 a.m. it was, but in July, morning came early. It was a perfect time – almost everyone was sleeping, it was too early for milkmen and paper boys to be out, but there was just enough light for Darren to see his way around without a torch.

He lowered himself down onto the roof of a rusting transit van. The van creaked as Darren's weight landed on it. He paused to see if the dogs had heard anything, but they slept on.

Relieved, Darren jumped down, landing softly on the oil-soaked ground. To his right was the office, a small brick and timber building with several haphazard extensions tacked onto it. Behind it was the house, one level to not attract the attention of the council or any other busybodies. No lights were on.

Darren turned to his left, slipped between several huge mountains of scrap, looking for just the right place to plant the bomb …

Mickey sipped his coffee, gazed up the street, waiting for Darren's return. He could have sent any of his boys to do this, but he was pissed off, the attacks by the travellers felt personal. They were bringing it to him, and now he was going to bring it to them. And besides, he liked being a part of it, going out and causing trouble, rather than always sitting in his office. He had missed this – the raid on the Vietnamese had been the first time in years he'd done something like that, and the buzz he got had lasted for several days. Miranda said he was like a man reborn, a randy stallion she called him. Not that she was complaining …

Martin had been against it, of course, said they should send someone else, but that was his job, wasn't it? To be the sensible one, the voice of reason, the businessman. And Mickey's job was to do the dirty work, stir up shit, put people in their place when they stepped out of line, which the pikeys were definitely doing now.

Mickey grinned. Darren should be inside by now. The pikeys were going to get a right bloody shock when the bomb went off. It wasn't anything big, just enough to make a loud bang, create a bit of a fire, lots of smoke. Not a bomb so much as a really loud message, delivered Taylor style. Mickey style. Dangerous style.

He fucking loved it, loved being a part of this, loved paying them back for the shit they had caused Mickey. Yep, Miranda was going to get a really good seeing to later today!

Darren looked around. Piles of crushed cars towered over him. Perfect. Mickey had wanted something that looked a lot worse than it really was, and scrap cars were the perfect things. The residual oil and petrol would burn quickly, the tyres would send up a big plume of smoke, but as they were mostly metal, they wouldn't burn that much.

He slipped the small bomb from the backpack he wore. It didn't look much, all contained in a tiny wooden box, a little light and a switch on the top for him to turn on once he'd set it. But the geezer who had made it for them was ex-army, had spent three years blowing things up in Iraq and Afghanistan, said it would do its job. Apparently the geezer was the dog's bollocks, and dirt cheap too, according to Mickey. Said the bloke work almost for free just for the fun of making bombs. Christ, thought Darren, there were some right fucking nutters out there.

He stopped and looked up – the biggest pile of cars in the scrapyard. That would do nicely! The sort of thing Mickey would choose himself. Darren couldn't believe that the guvnor, Dangerous himself, was his driver on this job. It really made you want to get it right, knowing that Mickey was on the job, was waiting for you in a car outside.

He looked at the pile of cars, gently shoved the nearest one. Rock solid. The bomb in one hand, Darren used the other to haul himself up onto the car, look inside the massive pile. That looked like a good spot, the back end of a crushed Mondeo, near the petrol tank.

He peered at the bomb. Turn the switch, the nutter had said, and the little light will come on. That means the bomb is primed. Then click the detonator switch, which Mickey had, and as long as you are within a hundred yards or so – boom!

Here goes nothing, thought Darren. He turned the switch, and sure enough, the little red light came to life, started blinking. He squeezed himself in through the open window of the red Mondeo, dropped the bomb on the back seat, turned to jump down, stopped cold.

Fuck! Standing below, looking up at him, were the two dogs, ears back, lips curled in a low snarl. Christ, he hadn't realised quite how fucking big they were. They looked like German Shepherds, but what were they mixed with? Fucking horses!

"Nice doggies!"

The low snarl turned into a low growl.

Darren glanced back towards the office, the house. No movement there yet, thank Christ. Just two enormous fucking dogs thinking that he would make a good breakfast. He reached in his pocket, pulled out the pepper spray. Everyone said it worked, but had they ever had to actually use it? And how close did you have to get? He didn't fancy jumping down there with them to use it.

He flipped the cap open, put his thumb on the trigger, started to climb down. As he did so, the dogs leaped up towards him, barking. It was just what he needed – the monsters coming to him!

Darren reached out as far as he could, his hand just a couple of feet from the dogs' snapping, snarling jaws, pressed the button. There was a loud hiss as the spray was released, and suddenly the dogs dropped down, howling, whining, rolling on the ground and pawing at their eyes.

Darren didn't wait around to see what happened next. He jumped down from the pile of cars, landing between the two dogs, then legged it back the way he'd come. Up onto the transit van, haul himself onto the wall where he'd cut the wire, then drop the ten feet to the ground below. He landed awkwardly, half twisting his ankle, hobbled off up the street as fast as he could.

Mickey was in the middle of a hot daydream that involved taking Miranda across the kitchen table when he saw Darren come limping round the corner towards him.

Mickey immediately cranked the engine of the car. It wasn't one of his own cars, he wouldn't be so stupid as to risk his car being spotted when he was out on a job. Instead, it was one of several nondescript cars they kept around for jobs like this, a battered Vauxhall Astra that no one would look at twice.

Mickey threw open the door as Darren limped up to him, grinned as the lad dropped into the passenger seat.

"What the fuck happened to you?"

"Twisted me ankle when I jumped down from the wall."

As Darren slammed the door shut, Mickey pulled forward. "Muppet! Everything else go all right?"

"Bomb's planted and primed … fucking dogs woke up though!"

Mickey's eyes sparkled with humour as they turned the corner towards the scrapyard. "No shit! Did they get you?"

Now it was Darren's turn to grin. "Nah! That fucking pepper spray worked a treat. One minute they were jumping up, snapping and snarling at me, ready to tear me balls off, next minute they're lying on the fucking ground whimpering like a pair of bitches!"

The car pulled alongside the wall of the scrapyard, Mickey cruising slowly. The detonator was already in his lap. "I think it's time to send a message, don't you?"

Darren grinned. "Wakey, wakey pikeys!"

Mickey pushed the button. There was a second's pause, then a satisfying "crump" broke the early morning quiet.

"Message delivered!" laughed Mickey as he accelerated away down the narrow street.

Mandy

Mandy knew she was dead, she had watched her die, had blown her life away, her new life with Mickey, her man.. It serves her right, she thought, she shouldn't have done what she did to her. But if she couldn't have Mickey, then nobody else was going to, not while Mandy was alive and breathing. Miranda had chosen the death card when she chose Mickey, and now her karma had come to repay her in the form of Mandy.

She stared at the gun in her bloodstained hand, trying to recall what had brought her here, but she couldn't clear her mind. She knew she had to do something, but she didn't know what it was, her thoughts were spinning out of control, the room was spinning around her, she was confused, disorientated. Nothing was familiar, everything looked strange. Was that the way it was now Miranda was dead? Everything different, everything changed? She could hear some music playing in the background, but she couldn't place the song, there was something wrong with it.

The gun slipped from her bloody fingers, fell softly on the thick carpet. Mandy looked at it, trying to focus, but she couldn't grasp anything. What should she do with the gun? Hide it? Throw it away? Leave it where it lay?

Her eyes went to her legs – her jeans were soaked in blood, it was on her hands, her arms, her chest, blood everywhere. Was any of it her own? Then she looked at Miranda. She must have shot her several times, there was blood everywhere, soaking her white T-shirt and forming a deep burgundy pool on the cream carpet.

Mandy knelt down next to her body, a beautiful blood-soaked body. All she could see was blood – blood oozing through her silky white skin, blood running from her neck, over her shoulders, across her stomach. Her fingers reached out, touched the t-shirt – it was wet, warm, sticky. Mandy's stomach wrenched, she felt sick and queasy, had to fight back a gagging reflex at the sight and touch and smell of the blood.

The music had stopped. Silence. Just the sound of Mandy's own breathing, fast, laboured as she hovered on the verge of panic.

She could feel the sweat oozing from her pores, prickling her forehead, running down her back. She felt hot and giddy. Oh my God! What had she done? Murder, kids, prison, the images flashed through her mind. She had to save herself, had to save Miranda! She felt her wrist for her pulse, flinched at the feel of her warm skin. So alive she felt, but she knew she was dead even before her lifeless wrist confirmed it. She had watched her die, heard her take her last breath, heard the last word she gasped as the air caught in her throat:

"Mickey …"

The music had returned, louder now, filling her head and leaving no room for thought. If only she could step back in time, turn back the clock to the way things used to be, when she and Mickey were together, to when he loved her, to when she was the only woman in his life.

She looked around, squinted. She couldn't make sense of where she was, had her death changed everything that much that nothing was familiar to her anymore? It felt like a jigsaw puzzle in her head, the parts were there, but she couldn't piece it together, there were some bits missing.

A sweet smell hung in the air, the smell of blood, hot and sweet and nauseating at the same time, like a sweet food when you eat too much of it, suddenly it starts to turn your stomach. She climbed to her feet, certain she was about to gag, throw up.

She felt herself growing hysterical. She felt a giggle trying to escape her lips, clamped her mouth shut, slapped her hand across her own face to keep the bitter bile from escaping, then almost gagged again as she smeared warm, sticky blood across her skin.

Mandy looked around, frantic. She needed to go to the bathroom, wash away the blood, wash away the traces of what she had done, but she didn't know where anything was. She was in a strange house covered in blood, looking down at Mirandas' dead body. She stepped back, the carpet wet with blood, hurried from the room, leaving deep, bloody footprints behind her.

The next room added to her disorientation, the lights were dim, the furniture seemed all wrong, shapes and angles that didn't make sense. Mandy felt overwhelmingly tired, her hands hung by her side, her legs felt like jelly. She collapsed exhausted in an armchair, saw a phone on the table beside her. She should call someone!

She picked the phone up, dialled 999. The phone felt hot and slippery in her hand, the blood from her hand coating it, making it hard to hold on to.

"Emergency Services. Which service do you require?"

Mandy stared at the phone stupidly. What was she doing! She had murdered Miranda, there was blood, and her fingerprints everywhere, why was she calling the emergency services?

The room seemed to be closing in on her, she felt like she couldn't breathe.

There was a loud pounding in her head, the phone in her hand, accusatory, covered in her incriminating bloody prints. Randomness, wantonness, savagery, ferocity. What had she done?

Someone grabbed her, and she sat up with a gasp.

"Mandy? Mandy? Wake up! I've been knocking on the door for ages, I was worried about you so I let meself in with me spare key." Denise hovered over her, her face full of concern.

Mandy gazed around, could feel her clammy nightdress sticking to her from her sweat. She looked at her hands – no blood.

"You all right, girl?" Denise peered at her, her brow furrowed.

"I feel like shit!"

Denise grinned. "You look like it too"

Mandy didn't know if she was relieved or disappointed that it was a dream. She took a deep breath. "Do me a favour," she gasped through parched lips. "Put the kettle on."

Denise gave her a funny look then trotted off, muttering to herself.

Mandy lay back and closed her eyes. Murder still lay heavy in her heart. There was no turning back now, she had been lonely for too long. It was time for someone to pay.

Mickey

Terri shook her head slowly, met Mickey's eyes. "I don't know, Mickey," she said. "What he gets up to is anyone's guess."

Mickey nodded as the barman set their drinks on the bar. Scotch on the rocks for Mickey, orange juice for Terri. Mickey was so proud of her, she hadn't had a drink for a few years now. "And he's not sharing anything with you?"

"He was, for a while, but lately he just smirks when I ask him how he is, what he's doing." She sipped her drink. "I'm worried about him, Mickey."

Mickey was always worried about Georgie. He'd worried about him when he was locked inside Rampton for twenty years, he worried about him now that he was out.

It had taken a lot to get Georgie out, and there were times when Mickey wondered if they all would have been better off just leaving him there. Did

Georgie really care where he was? Georgie seemed so out to lunch sometimes that Mickey wasn't sure. But Terri had been insistent. She was the one who visited him every week when he was in Rampton, the one he would actually open up to, and she had insisted that Georgie was just dying in "that fucking place" as she called it, insisted that Mickey get him out. Get him out, like it was the easiest thing in the world …

The doctor – Philips or something, Mickey never could remember his name – stared at the large envelope, licked his lips. Twenty thousand in cash was a lot, even for someone on a cozy doctor's salary. "The thing is, it's not just up to me," he whispered. Although they were alone in his office, the man was nervous, peering through his round glasses, licking his thin lips, looking at Mickey with his pale, watery eyes. "For your brother to be released requires two signatures." He held the envelope tight to his chest as though afraid it might slip through his fingers. "Obviously you have my support. But Doctor M'Banga is a hardliner. He never wants anyone to be released. Sees it almost as a matter of pride, feels it is his job to protect people from those who might do them harm."

Mickey had had enough of this bloke's simpering. He stood up suddenly, reached across the desk, grabbed the envelope and ripped it from Philips' hands. "You told me that you could get

Georgie released. You didn't say nothing about no fucking doctor whatever his fucking name is blocking the process!"

Mickey shoved the envelope back in his jacket pocket, glared at Philips.

The doctor licked his lips again, ran his hand through his thin red hair. "Yes, well, when we talked before, the other doctor on the panel was Willis. He is a pushover, would always follow my direction. But he had a heart attack last week, and M'Banga replaced him. As I said, M'Banga is a totally different kettle of fish." As he spoke, his eyes strayed to the envelope, still slightly visible in Mickey's jacket pocket.

Mickey turned back, leaned over the desk again, got right in Philips' face. "There are two ways this goes, Doctor. We can either convince people the nice way –" he tapped his jacket pocket, "– or the nasty way. You've opted for the nice way. Smart man. But apparently this Banger bloke will require a different form of persuasion."

Philips blinked his watery eyes. "Oh dear!"

"Oh dear in-fucking-deed!" snarled Mickey. "So here's the way it works. You get me Banger's personnel file. I'll apply the pressure."

Philips gulped. "By pressure you mean –"

"Don't you worry about what I fucking mean – the less you know, the better, right?"

Philips nodded, gulped, his eyes never leaving Mickey's. "Right …"

Some jobs, Mickey preferred to handle himself. This was one. It was all about family, all about Georgie, so he was going to be the one to do it. The file on M'Banga had arrived on Mickey's desk a couple of days later, contained everything he needed to know about the bloke. Where he lived, who he lived with. There were just three days until Georgie was up for review, so he had to move fast, but Mickey knew how to apply the maximum leverage. Hit the bastard the night before, that was the plan, don't give him time to think, to consider, doing anything stupid. Let him still be shitting himself when he went into the review panel so he was fully motivated to cooperate.

M'Banga lived on a quiet suburban street, new built semi-detached three bedroom houses, each with their own little garden, a garage. Probably all come with a cat included, thought Mickey as he and Darren sat at the end of the street, waiting for the lights to go out in the doctor's house. The doctor was obviously a lightweight – by midnight the lights had already been out for more than an hour, but still Mickey and Darren waited, sitting and smoking, chatting or dozing until the moment was just right. Three o'clock in the morning – that was the perfect time – that was when you could catch people cold, deep in sleep, scare the living shit out of them.

Darren followed Mickey round the back of the house, keeping close to the wall, in the shadows. As soon as they were round the back, Darren went to work. Breaking and entering was his game, and this place was a piece of cake – no alarm, no dog, and a simple lock on the back door. Within seconds, they were inside.

Mickey could feel the adrenaline rising as they tiptoed across the kitchen floor. The light from the moon cast pale shadows across the floor, highlighting a neat kitchen, everything clean and tidy, cereal boxes, bowls and spoons already set out for the next day. According to the file Philips had sent Mickey, M'Banga had a wife, and two girls, aged five and six. Lots of pressure points …

They crept up the stairs, grateful for the thick carpet to muffle their footsteps. At the top of the stairs were four doors, all open – three bedrooms and a bathroom – but they knew exactly which one to go to. Darren had done his research, visited a house for sale on the same estate, so he knew the layout, knew which one was the master bedroom, where the doctor and his wife would be.

Mickey stepped softly into the doctor's bedroom. M'Banga was on the side of the bed closest to Mickey. Perfect. Darren took up station in the doorway, to listen in case the kids woke up, and provide an added level of threat.

M'Banga lay on his side, facing towards Mickey. Slipping a knife from his pocket, Mickey crept to the bed, clamped one big hand over M'Banga's mouth, held the knife up where the doctor could see it.

M'Banga's eyes popped open, he started to struggle, but then he saw the knife, and though he still looked panicked, he stopped struggling, lay still.

"We need to have a little chat," hissed Mickey. "Understand?"

Wide-eyed, his gaze flicking back and forth from the knife to Mickey's face, M'Banga nodded.

"See my friend over there?" Darren waved from the doorway, making sure his knife was also visible. "The first squeak from you, the first hint of trouble, he goes straight to your daughters' room? Understand?"

M'Banga was breathing hard, sweat beading on his forehead, but again he nodded.

Slowly, Mickey removed his hand from M'Banga's mouth.

"Please!" he gasped in a frantic whisper, "I'll do anything you want, just don't hurt my babies!"

"That's what I like to hear," whispered Mickey. "So here's the deal. You have a review panel tomorrow. There's someone there we want to be sure you release."

For a second it looked as though M'Banga was going to argue, but just as quickly, the fight went out of his face. "Who?"

"No need to know now. Philips will tell you tomorrow. When he says this person should be released, you will agree, understood?"

M'Banga nodded.

Mickey gave a big smile. "There, that wasn't so hard, was it?" He suddenly moved the knife close to M'Banga's face, the tip almost touching his eye. "As long as you do as you're told, don't ever mention this to anyone, we are fine, right?" He slid the tip of the blade across M'Banga's cheek. "But if you do something stupid – call someone, shout out, tell the police – then we will come back. Maybe not tomorrow, or next week, or even this year. But sooner or later we will return, and this house will run with blood. Do we understand each other?"

The whites of M'Banga's eyes shone in the darkness as he nodded.

Mickey slowly stood up, patted M'Banga on the cheek. "I really hope, for your sake, that we never see each other again …"

Less than a week later, Georgie was released from Rampton.

Mickey led Terri to a quiet table in the corner of the pub. "So you've got no clue what he's up to?"

She shook her head. "Maybe it's nothing. But he's changed. I know his moods, Mickey, and there's something different."

Mickey sighed. It was the last thing he needed right now. "So what do you want me to do about it?"

Terri shrugged, spun the ice around her glass with her fingertip. Christ, thought Mickey, she's looking old. She's had it tougher than all of us, what with her lousy choice of partners … "I don't know. I just worry about him." She looked up at Mickey with her tired eyes. "Maybe you could go talk to him?"

"Christ, Tel, you really think that will achieve anything? He barely talks to me, and if he does, it's always in fucking riddles. You're the one he trusts, the one he talks to. If anyone's going to get any bleeding sense out him, it has to be you!"

Terri said nothing, buried her face in her drink.

Mickey rubbed his head. Christ, why couldn't things be easier? Why couldn't Georgie have stayed the way he used to be? It was growing increasingly hard to remember what Mickey thought of as "the real Georgie" – his brother when he was growing up. That Georgie was a lovely bloke. Everybody said so. He was bright – easily the smartest member of the Taylor family – funny, loyal, caring. Many were the time Georgie had looked after Mickey when he came home bruised and bleeding from yet another fight. And for all his caring side, there was also a toughness hidden within him. On several occasions when they were kids, when someone was giving Mickey a hard time, Georgie had sorted them out, given them a right good hiding.

What had changed him? There was no doubt about it in Mickey's mind. It was their dad, that cunt Bobby Taylor. Whereas Bobby's abuse had just made Mickey tougher and tougher, made him the cold-eyed bastard he was today, it had somehow broken Georgie. Already the most sensitive of the kids, he had somehow gradually been battered and crushed, his normal cheerful demeanour worn away, one abusive day after another.

What had been the tipping point? Probably the affair with the priest. Christ, in those days no one had any idea that Georgie was gay, it was something you didn't talk about. Poofs were like another breed of people, they had something wrong with them, weren't normal, so there was no way that their Georgie could be one of them. He was a man that all girls wanted as a husband. But he was, and he had fallen in love with Father Jim. Of course, that nasty cunt of a dad, Bobby Taylor had found out about Georgies' love affair with the priest, and before you knew it, Father Jim was back in Ireland. And when a few months after that he was found in a ditch with his throat cut, well, they all knew who was behind that.

After that it seemed like a light had gone out in Georgie's eyes. He became more and more withdrawn, kept to himself, rarely laughed. Even Terri, who was the one he was closest to, couldn't get through to him.

From there it was a steep, slippery slope – killing Bobby, then abducting his childhood tormenter and winding up in Rampton.

And that's when Samantha had emerged, his tough, female alter ego. She still came and went. You never knew which of them you might find when you went round to Georgie's place, but Mickey had fooled himself into thinking everything would be all right with Georgie now that he was out, surrounded by his own family …

"So?"

Mickey looked up. Terri was staring at him. "Sorry, girl. What did you say?"

"I can try to talk to Georgie, but I think it might help if you went to see him. Would you do that?" Terri's sad, tired eyes implored him. "I've got all kind of shit going on with Jimmy right now. I don't have the energy to deal with Georgie."

Mickey nodded. "Course I will love." He fixed her with a serious look. "Is that prick fucking you around again?"

Terri looked away. "You know the way he is …"

"Terri?" He got her attention, her sad eyes on him. "If you need me to sort Jimmy out – whatever you need – you tell me, right? You know I'll take care of him if you just ask me?"

Terri forced a smile onto her face. "Don't you worry about me." Her smile deepened as though she was remembering something secret, something that brought her comfort. "I can take care of him …"

Tommy

Tommy sat in his car outside the gym for a long time, composing himself, trying to find the right words to say. He had put this day off his whole life, avoided the confrontation, the conflict, avoided doing anything to rock the boat. Why? Was he scared? Scared of Mickey? Scared of what his dad might say or do if he confronted him? Probably. But if that was the case, the time for fear was over. There was something going on – something big – and Tommy was no longer prepared to sit on the sidelines and watch while Mickey and his uncle Martin dealt with everything.

What did Mickey think, that he wasn't up to it? That he couldn't handle the heat? That he'd crack up or cry like a baby at the first sign of trouble? He was a fucking Taylor for Christ's sake, he'd grown up tough, no matter what Mickey thought. Shit, who did Mickey think had helped Mandy keep things together when he was inside? How many times had

Tommy had to answer with his fists when some lairy cunt had made a comment about his dad being inside?

How did he think they had survived financially when Mickey was inside? Tommy had done his fair share of dodgy deals to make sure there was money on the table, and what was his reward when Mickey came out? To be treated like a little kid, sidelined, shunted off into a fucking dry cleaning business! Was that really any sort of job for a Taylor? For Mickey Taylor's son? Running a fucking dry cleaning shop? "We have a two for one special on men's shirts this week, ma'am. Of course we can get that wine stain out of your suit, sir!" Fuck all that!

Tommy glared up at the gym. Taylors. That was the name of the gym. That was his name. And that was Tommy, a Taylor. He should be a part of all of this. The gym, the night clubs, the wheeling and dealing and drugs and dodgy deals. It was his birthright, and, God forbid anything should happen to Mickey, his inheritance.

What did the old man think would happen if Tommy had to take over without being eased into it? He had to be a part of it now, had to learn the ropes, get to know all the ins and outs, the connections, the rivals, everything that went into running a business as diverse and dangerous as the Taylors.

Tommy took a deep breath, clenched and unclenched his hands on the steering wheel. He had to be calm but decisive, couldn't show any weakness, his dad would pounce on that. Try to appeal to his business instincts – that was the way to go, he had to argue that the business needed Tommy – that it was a good time, they needed someone else to share the burden, needed to be training him, teaching him the ins and outs. It was a win-win for all of them. That was the right approach. Keep it factual, keep the emotion out of it.

Tommy slid the keys out of the ignition, opened the door, climbed out of the car. He quickly checked his reflection in the driver's window, straightened his tie, smoothed his hair, buttoned his jacket. You had to look good for Mickey, he valued appearances, style.

"Fuck me, look at you? Going on a date or something?"

Tommy looked up, startled. His dad was standing in the doorway of the gym, giving him an amused look. "No, no, I –"

"We're just off out." Mickey held the door open, and Martin strode out, cool and immaculate as always.

This was not what Tommy had planned. He thought he had timed it to perfection, after his dad's morning workout, before they went for lunch. He was almost always in his office at this time.

Mickey and Martin turned and headed towards Martin's Porsche, the car beeping as Martin unlocked the doors with the remote.

Tommy hurried towards them. "I wanna have a word with ya dad!" he blurted out.

Mickey paused, one hand on the roof of the low car. "Better make it quick – we've got a meeting."

All the words Tommy had prepared were suddenly gone, he felt like a tongue-tied schoolboy about to ask a girl for a date. "I wanted to – I mean we need to –"

Mickey gave an impatient sigh. "If it's about the shop getting jacked, don't sweat it, son. We're on it. Martin and I will take care of it." He pulled the door open, started to climb in.

"Wait!"

Mickey paused.

"It's more than that. It's about … everything!"

Mickey stared at him, impatience written clearly across his face. "Everything? What the fuck does that mean?"

Tommy stepped closer, tried to find the words. "The business, all of it. I need to be a part of it. It's good for all of us, a win-win!"

Mickey stared at him as though he were talking gibberish. "Win-win? What the fuck are you talking about, son?"

Tommy cringed when he heard the tone of voice. It was the way Mickey always talked to him, treating him like a kid, like he was still ten years old.

The car roared into life as Martin cranked the engine, almost drowning out Tommy as he replied.

"You can't keep shutting me out, dad. I need to be a part of what you are doing. I can help!" Tommy knew he sounded desperate, but he could see his chance slipping away.

Mickey shook his head, lowered himself into the firm leather seat of the Porsche. "This really isn't the time, son!" He slammed the door and with a sharp rasping roar the Porsche pulled out into traffic. Mickey was gone. His chance was gone.

Tommy stared after them until they were out of sight.

Fuck! He'd blown it!

He turned back to his car, but the adrenaline still coursed through his body, he was too wound up to simply get back into the car and drive meekly back to the shop, spend another day pretending he gave a flying fuck about people's poxy dry cleaning.

Tommy stood by his car, leaned on the roof, tried desperately to marshal his thoughts. He couldn't give up. Wouldn't give up. He had waited too long, was too far down the road – at least in his own mind – to go back.

And anyway, he was a Taylor. What would a Taylor do? What would Mickey do? He wouldn't quit, that was for fucking certain. He would do something. He would fucking do something!

That was it! Tommy straightened up, a new resolve coursing through him. He had been going about it the wrong way from the start. Simply talking to his dad was the wrong approach, made him sound like a whiny kid trying to get his dad's attention. No wonder Mickey had given him that look – Tommy would have got the same response even if everything had gone perfectly, even if he'd caught Mickey in a good mood, he'd delivered his full speech. It was simply the wrong way to go about it.

What he had to do instead was prove himself. Do something, something that benefited the business, showed that Tommy could handle himself, that Tommy was a Taylor through and through. Then even Mickey wouldn't deny him, couldn't deny him.

Tommy pulled his keys out as he climbed into the car. Fuck the dry cleaning shops. He had a job to do – a real job, a job that would make Mickey welcome him into the family business.

Terri

Terri stood in the doorway of her bedroom, ready and waiting. The lights were dimmed, scented candles were burning, low music played in the background, the champagne was chilling in the ice bucket. It all looked very alluring, the perfect romantic evening.

Terri was ready too, kitted out in her PVC figure-hugging outfit, looking like Miss Whiplash. A black basque with a zipped front opening, fishnet stockings and thigh-high boots. Studded leather cuffs on her slender wrists completed the outfit, while she had a latex whip in her hand.

She glanced in the mirror. She was buxom, with a good figure for her age, nothing wrong with her legs. And to top it all off she'd been on the sunbed all week so she looked bronzed and healthy. Jimmy would think he'd won the lottery when he saw her all dressed up like this.

She sat on the dressing table chair and reapplied her makeup. She needed a little more colour on her cheeks, a bit of blusher – or 'rouge' as her mum used to call it – plus another coat of lipstick. She didn't need any mascara, she'd put false eyelashes on earlier, looked like spider's legs they did, but Terri liked them. She thought they gave her eyes a killer look.

Terri heard the key turn in the lock, the door open and then slam closed. She quickly ran her fingers through her hair, turned and twisted, adjusting herself until she was finally satisfied. A quick spray of her favourite perfume and she was done.

She took a deep breath. Right about now he would be reading the note she had left him on the kitchen table. "I'm in the bedroom. Got a special treat for you! XXX." There was no way he would be able to resist that. He was a randy little fucker. She had to be calm and relaxed, no room to be sentimental tonight. She had to be strong, pull herself together, get on with it.

His heavy footsteps laboured up the stairs, then the bedroom door opened. Terri took a deep breath, put one foot up on the chair in her sexiest pose. The huge grin on his face said it all as he took his jacket off, threw it on the floor, walked towards her. "Sexy little fucker, ain't ya," he said smiling as his eyes feasted on her. "Scrub up pretty well when you put a bit of effort in, don't ya girl?" He kicked his shoes off. "Nice bit of tackle you've got there."

Terri sauntered towards him, playing up the sex in her voice. "Come here you horny fuck. I've got some wicked surprises for you." She smiled as she spoke. "I'm gonna do to you some things you've only dreamt of. All your deepest fantasies will come true tonight."

Smirking at her, he said, "It's about time you livened up in the bedroom, Terri, gave me a good seeing to." He peered towards her crotch. "Fucking hell, you've even had a shave, got rid of the forest down there! It's my lucky night."

He walked slowly towards her, a huge grin on his face, too stupid and lustful to even think about what might have contributed to the change in Terri. She knew him well, knew he wouldn't question it, just try and grab it with both hands. She just had to slow him down a bit, keep control. "Fancy a bit of bondage do ya girl?" he laughed.

Terri smiled seductively. "Hey, big boy come here," she said giving a filthy laugh.

Her soft, warm hands pulled him gently towards her and she slowly, one at a time, undid his buttons, pulled his shirt off and dropped it on the floor. She kissed him passionately as her arms wrapped around him, her dark eyes gazing deep into his. "I love you so much, you know?"

Her voice was sweet and soothing as she touched his body, whispering her love. Jimmy put his big hands to her cheeks and pulled her face towards his. "And so you should," he said smiling. "You're lucky to have someone like me." He gave her a cocky wink. "You know that, don't ya?"

Terri stood still in front of him, slowly nodded her head as she unzipped his trousers. "Yes. Yes, Jimmy. I know," she murmured, looking deep into his eyes.

"You'd still be on the ninth floor over the Gascoigne estate if it weren't for me," he reminded her, his green eyes shining with satisfaction. "Wouldn't ya?"

Terri looked at him, at his short, blond hair, stroked his stiff cock in her hand. "I know. What would I do without you?" she replied, her voice sexy and seductive.

He placed one hand roughly on her chin and pulled her closer to his firm, hard body. "Don't ever forget how lucky you are to have someone like me."

Terri started singing, "I was working as a waitress at a cocktail bar when I met you."

He kissed her hard, said in a thick voice, "Bend over, I wanna fuck ya now."

"No," she replied quickly, stepping back from his grasping arms. "I've got all dressed up. Let's take this nice and slow, have a bit of fun first, all right?" She saw his hesitation, quickly added, "Don't worry,

I'm gonna look after you tonight, fuck you over and over again."

"Go on then, watcha got in mind?"

"Hold on a minute." Terri skipped over to the window. She was feeling hot all over, her head felt dizzy, she needed to cool down a little. She opened the window, the cold breeze sweeping across her, giving her goosebumps.

Jimmy had sat down on the bed. "Hurry up and get over here then, you dirty fuck, and open them legs."

She quickly drew the curtains, plunging the room into darkness. "I'm coming." She sauntered slowly towards him. "I'm gonna do things to you you'd die for, you'll be begging me for more and more."

"That sounds more like it!" He peeled off his trousers and pants, lay back on the bed. Terri ran her finger along his body, her hands stroking his chest, leaned forward and began kissing his stomach.

He lay on his back watching her beautiful face move downwards, her soft cheeks against his thighs, her tongue searching, seeking. His hips moved in rhythm, wanting her, and he greedily grabbed her hair, forced her mouth down onto his stiff cock. He closed his eyes, felt the shiver of his skin exploding in a savage impulse, spasms running through his body as her hands ran down his legs to his ankles. Click, click. She stopped.

"Don't stop, it's lovely," he moaned.

She slowly straddled him, leaned over so that he could suck her breasts. She pushed his hands up above his head as she moved across his body, and he thrust up and into her, giving a deep sigh as her warmth enveloped him. Click, click again.

He moaned and groaned below her as she thrust deeper, harder and faster. "Is it nice, does it feel good?" Terri asked.

"Yeah, lovely, lovely!"

"Tell me when you're about to come. Tell me."

"Yes, yes!" She watched his face screw up with pleasure, listening to his moaning, grunting and groaning. "Not long now baby, ooh, yeah, here it comes."

Terri suddenly climbed off him, stood at the side of the bed, hands on her slender hips.

Jimmy looked up, surprised, annoyed. "What you doing, you can't stop now," he complained, agony in his voice.

"I can do anything I want to."

Jimmy tried moving, but he couldn't. He was handcuffed to the bed by his wrists and his ankles.

"Terri!?" He laughed, half annoyed, half uncertain.

She stood and looked at him, said nothing.

Anger started to take over. "What the fuck you playing at?"

She turned and walked away from him, picked her handbag up from the dresser.

"You fucking prick tease, get the fuck over here and undo these things right now!" he demanded.

"I'm not teasing," Terri told him, rummaging through her bag. She found what she was looking for.

"Get the fuck over here now and finish what you started!" he ordered.

"Never been very patient, have ya Jimmy?" She took a joint out of her bag, slowly lit it.

He glared at her, his erection gradually diminishing. "Come on, stop playing games."

"I'm not playing games. This is serious." She took a puff of her joint, felt herself relax.

"You fucking cunt!" he screamed at her.

"Yeah, you've told me that before."

He nodded towards her joint. "You're off your head. You can't leave that fucking weed alone for five minutes can ya? Every time I come near ya I can smell that shit."

She looked at him, feeling sick. Could she go through with this? She inhaled deeply on her joint, making it look exotic, like someone in an old film, Marlene Dietrich maybe, then turned the chair around and sat down suggestively, legs wide apart. "Want me to come finish you off, do you?"

"Fucking right I do!"

"Don't worry. I'm gonna finish you off, baby," she purred. "I'm gonna finish you off good and proper." She reached in her leather Dior bag, took out a gun. For a moment she was lost, staring at the revolver, caressing it in her hands, its dark metal gleaming dully under the candlelight. She looked over at him. "You wouldn't believe how easy it was to get hold of this," she said, pointing the gun towards him.

"Tell me you're joking," he said in abject disbelief. "You're having a fucking laugh ain't ya?"

Terri gave him a sardonic smile, raised her eyebrows. "Joking? I've never been more serious in my life."

He looked at her in disgust. "You dirty fucking whore, get these fucking handcuffs off me."

She smiled at him. "You're right. I am a dirty fucking whore. And know what? This gun is getting me excited. It's turning me on, I'm getting nice and wet."

Jimmy looked around the room, trying to figure out an escape, but there was none. He yanked hard on the handcuffs, but they were locked tight to the wooden bed frame. All he succeeded in doing was hurting his wrists and ankles as the metal bit into them. "You're off your head Terri. Get these fucking things off me!" he demanded angrily. "It's all that fucking weed you smoke; you can't go a day without it. It's making you paranoid, you're a fucking nutter."

Terri said nothing, just took another drag, blew the smoke towards him.

"You're one lazy cunt, all you do is sit on your fat arse all day, drinking and smoking. I should call you the four fucking c's, I should, all you fucking live for is cannabis, cigarettes and chocolate, and you're a fat cunt!"

Terri felt profoundly calm, happy, certain. "I know. You've been telling me that for years." She stood up.

"Get these off me!"

She looked down at him, smiled. How sad and pathetic he looked lying there. "Ain't got a hard on now 'ave ya? Don't worry, you will be nice and stiff very soon." She leaned right over him, blew a deep puff of smoke right into his face.

He started coughing and spluttering. "You cunt!"

"You crack me up,"' she said, taking another puff. "You're quite happy to sell this shit, but you slag me off for smoking it. How many times have you come home, waving a bag in front of me, saying, "You know what this is worth, don't ya darlin'? What is it again? Twenty blow jobs, shag on demand? I see that look in your eyes every time, the pure pleasure knowing that I'm not gonna say no. You know I want it. Your cacks are down before I've got the puff in my hand. You love every single minute of it, holding the carrot out to the donkey. Control, power and manipulation. That's all it's ever been with you. You're one nasty bully, Jimmy, and it's time to pay!"

He stared at her, wide-eyed, real fear gripping his heart.

She ground out her joint, dragging the pinched butt across the ashtray long after it was out, then pointed the gun at him. "You wanna think yourself lucky, 'cause if I didn't have this to smoke, I think I would have put a knife through your heart long before now." She watched his expression shift from outrage to horror. "Look at your fat ugly face. I've waited so long for this day." She looked at him with unexpected menace in her eyes. "I want to make you feel the fear that I've felt for so long, just a taste of what you've put me through."

Terri put one leg upon the bed, began rubbing the gun over her erect nipples, then slid it down between her legs, began rubbing it back and forth. "Mmmm, this is nice, feels good." His horrified eyes were fixed on her, unable to look away. "Soaking wet I am, wanna taste me?" She suddenly shoved the barrel of the gun as far as she could into his mouth. He tried to resist, but she jammed it hard, busting his lip, cracking a tooth. His eyes bulged wide as the gun filled his mouth. "Taste nice do I?" she asked. "Shall I pull the trigger now?"

He shook his head from side to side, choking and gagging, blood trickling down the side of his mouth as he gagged and moaned.

She pulled the gun out of his mouth. "Turning you on, am I Jimmy?"

"Fuck off, cunt!" he roared, his voice cracked and vicious, spitting blood and saliva.

"Don't be like that, I thought you'd like it. You're happy enough when it's you jamming your cock into my mouth."

"Get these off me!" he yelled, flailing about like a fish out of the water.

"No, don't think so," she said slowly, shaking her head. "I told you, I'm gonna hurt you like you hurt me. I've hated you for a long, long time. Every day I look at you, and I hate you a little bit more. But you know what? I hate myself more than I hate you. You've stripped me of everything."

His dark eyes glowered up at her. "You're enjoying this ain't ya, you slag? Getting yourself all turned on, you dirty piece of scum!"

"You should think yourself lucky you've lived this long," she told him. "The number of times I've had to beg Mickey not to kill you when you've fucked up or pissed someone off. He hates you more than I do, would have snuffed you out just like that." She clicked her fingers. "But no, stupid fucking me couldn't do it, didn't have the bottle to say yes. He always told me what a wrong 'un you were."

He glared at her. "Mickey, Mickey, Mickey. Your cunt of a brother always comes into it. You think he's the fucking Godfather and I'm scared of him? You make me laugh, Terri. He's like you – a nothing!"

She whacked him suddenly with the butt of the gun. Blood sprayed from his lip and his face contorted in pain. "Don't you ever slag my brother or any of my family off! I'm sick of listening to you put me and my family down! Our own kids hate me because of you. Mickey's more of a man than you could ever be!"

"Get me out of these!" he yelled, struggling to try and free himself.

Terri whacked him around the face again with the gun as hard as she could. His lip split, and blood poured into his mouth. "Free you? I ain't going to free you, you bastard. I'm going to fucking kill you, blow your fucking brains out."

And suddenly he started to sob, big tears rolling down his cheeks, mixed with blood from his lip. "No, Terri, please. Don't be silly. You'll go to prison. Who'll look after our boys?"

She threw back her head and laughed. "Our boys, oh my God, how funny; it's our boys now, is it? No, they're your boys, I had them for you. Not for me, but for you. I had my children years ago, my family. I never wanted any more and you knew that, but no, you pushed and pushed, and as always you get what you want. You've even made them hate me. Your precious boys treat me just like you do, no love or respect. They treat me like a piece of shit, just like you do. It's just like listening to you when they talk, the three of you, sitting there on the sofa scoffing and munching away, watching your dodgy videos, clicking your fingers or whistling at me when you want something."

"Please, Terri," Jimmy begged, "it's not like that, you've got it all wrong. It's not what you think. I love you, you love me, right? What do you want? Money? It's in my pocket. Take it."

She stood there gaping, her eyebrows raised in astonishment. "You really ain't got a fucking clue have ya? You think you can buy your way out of everything, or buy your way in. And love!" She gave a harsh bark of laughter. "You don't know the meaning of the word."

"But we've had some good times, ain't we babe?"

"Good times? What, you mean when you're lying on top of me fucking away, grunting and sweating like a fat horrible pig, and I'm screaming and shouting, come on, do it, harder, faster. You think I'm enjoying myself?" She shook her head, laughed. "No. All I'm doing is wishing you have a fucking massive heart attack and die, you obese cunt. You know what? I dread you coming home, dread having to have sex with you, I've done everything I can think of so I ain't got to fuck you. I've made out I was on my period, I would stick my fingers down my throat to make myself sick and pretend to be really ill, I would make out I had a migraine, anything, just so you wouldn't come near me. I have to be stoned to shag you. It's like an endurance test, fucking you. There is no kissing, no cuddling, no love, no passion, no foreplay, no seduction. You're just straight in there, hand down me knickers, a quick flick and a rub and you think that's it. Fucking idiot!"

Terri was warming to her theme, getting all her hatred out in one huge rush. "I'm happy when you don't come home, when you're out with your dirty little slags. It's amazing what they will do for a Louis Vuitton bag, a Gucci necklace, a night out at some fancy restaurant. It's great though because it means you're not near me, not got your horrible hands creeping all over me. When I get in bed next to you I cringe, praying that you are asleep, when you're not I feel those arms around me, I feel physically sick, your dick poking me in the back. I just lie there and think to myself, oh my God, no, not again, please make this quick – get it over and done with. It's not normal to feel like that with your husband is it?"

Jimmy lay still, quiet, hoping she would talk her rage away, come to her senses, release him. Then he would show the fucking bitch who was boss. He would fuck her so hard she wouldn't know what day it was. After tonight, she would wish she had never met him!

"Even watching you eat makes me feel sick, hearing you munching, crunching, slurping on your food, like a fucking pig scoffing. It's like feeding time at the fucking zoo!"

Jimmy eyed her warily. Calm her down. Soothe her. "Please, babe, just uncuff me and let's talk about this. I'll give you anything, anything, just say what you want. I'm begging you, Terri," he whined, "take these handcuffs off me and let's be like we used to. You remember, don't you?"

She looked at him carefully. "Say you're sorry, and I might change my mind."

"Sorry!" he whined.

"Do you mean it?" She looked at him with hope in her eyes.

"Course I do, I'm so sorry, Terri, I didn't mean anything, didn't know I wasn't making you happy."

"Really?"

"Yes really, I fucked up big time, I can see that now, but you're the one for me, Terri, no one else. I'll make it all up to you, do anything you want me to do to make it up to you. I've made the biggest mistake of my life. I promise things will be different, Terri I'm so sorry." He gave his most pitiful, pleading look. "Take these off me now, please?"

"I want you to promise me you will never hurt me again, that you will always love me."

"Of course!"

"Say it then."

"I will never hurt you again, and will always love you."

Terri gave a small smile of satisfaction. "That's good."

Jimmy smiled, trying hard to hide a look of animal cunning. She was going to release him. Then we'd see who was in charge.

"OK. One last thing."

"OK, babe, whatever it is, just tell me!"

"Say, 'I'm a fat, dirty perverted cunt and I deserve to die'."

He glared at her, lapsed into a sullen silence.

"Say it!" she screamed.

He lay there quiet, not responding.

"Fucking say it!"

"No, you fucking whore," he finally yelled. "Just get me out of these fucking handcuffs, right now!"

Terri moved so fast it startled him, stepping forward and jamming the muzzle of the gun hard into his forehead. He closed his eyes, half turned away, felt her weight on him as she climbed onto the bed, straddled him.

The only noise was his frantic breathing as Terri looked at him one last time, then grabbed a pillow, covered his face, thrust the gun deep into the pillow and fired.

Once, twice, three times the gun roared. His body shook, gave a convulsive spasm, then lay still.

Slowly, cautiously, Terri lifted the pillow, stared down at the dead face of her husband. One whole side of his head was missing, but his eyes were wide open, unblinking.

Terri smiled. "Rot in hell, you cunt!"

Mickey

Someone's got a sense of humor, thought Mickey, as he climbed out of the car. The Blind Beggar on Whitechapel Road was probably the most notorious pub in London – it was where William Booth, founder of the Salvation Army, gave his first speech, but more pertinently it was also where Ronnie Kray shot George Cornell in cold blood, the heart of east London gang territory. But it also made a certain degree of sense to meet there – it was always packed, lots of tourists, the most public of public houses.

Sol was waiting outside as Mickey and Martin approached. He rubbed his hands together nervously. "Let me do all the talking," he reminded Mickey. "And no silly stuff." He looked around as though expecting to see a bunch of thugs at Mickey's heels. "Just the two of you, that's good."

Mickey gave his most innocent look. "That's what we agreed, Sol." He didn't mention that Darren,

Brick, and three others were inside, all tooled up and ready for any shit that might happen to hit the fan.

"Good, good," murmured Sol, "follow me, they're already inside."

As Sol shuffled into the pub, Mickey's eyes were everywhere. He might have his boys inside, but the travellers had a huge network they could call upon. Who knew who might be there watching them right now?

He followed Sol's crumpled suit inside. As usual, the place was packed, the bar lined two deep, all the tables taken. Sol wormed his way through the crowd, Mickey and Martin at his heels, directed them to the back corner, where half a dozen wooden chairs had been gathered round a small circular table. Big Frankie, Frankie Junior, and their lawyer, an Irish bloke called Casey who Mickey had met once or twice, were already sitting there.

As they approached, Casey stood up, shoved his chair back, offered handshakes all round.

Frankie and his son didn't move, just glared at Mickey with their big, dark eyes.

"Well good, good, this is great," chirped Casey. "Here we all are, ready to talk and settle this like gentlemen." He sat back down, smiling as though they had come together to discuss plans for a kid's birthday party. Sol had warned them about Casey in advance. A real charmer, was how he described him, with a soft Irish burr and friendly eyes, you immediately felt you could trust him. Don't, was what Sol had said. He's a shark under the surface, always probing, searching, looking for your weak spot.

"So," began Casey, "would you boys like a drink?" He cast around, searching for someone to take their order, but Mickey stopped him cold.

"We don't plan on being here that long. Let's cut the crap and get straight to the point."

Casey smiled. "Mickey Taylor, as I live and breathe, you are as direct as your reputation would suggest."

Mickey gave him a nod of acknowledgement.

Sol cut in before Mickey could say anything further. "Let's do as Mickey said, get straight to the point. My client holds the deeds to the piece of land in question. Your client has lived there rent-free for forty five years. That seems reasonable recompense for any favors that the Taylors might owe."

"I saved his dad's life," growled Big Frankie. "Bobby had honor, knew how to repay a debt like that."

"Bobby was a cunt and would have thrown you off of there years ago if he hadn't died!" snarled Mickey. "It's by my grace that you've been there for over forty fucking years!"

Again Sol cut back in.

"However, my clients recognize that this is quite an upheaval for your clients. As a result, they are prepared to offer some compensation to ease the transition into a new location."

"And what if we don't want to move?" said Big Frankie softly.

"I'm afraid you don't have a choice," Sol replied quickly, feeling Mickey stirring beside him. "If we called the council in, they'd turf you off in a heartbeat, knock down everything you've built there –"

"– and tie you up in court for so long that no one would buy the land," interjected Casey. "You would end up having to settle for a compulsory purchase order at a knock down price –"

"– which is why it is in everyone's interest to reach an agreement today, and settle this amicably," concluded Sol.

"Agreed!" grinned Casey.

They all paused, almost surprised that they seemed to be in agreement over something. Mickey glanced around. This was going too well. There was something wrong, something he wasn't seeing, something he hadn't noticed. As his eyes scanned the crowded pub, he spotted Darren, Brick, and another lad he recognized. But what about the Pikeys? There were a few lads drinking at the bar who he'd lay a penny to a pound were travellers…

Sol looked around the table. "In recognition of the disruption this move will cause, my clients are prepared to offer the sum of two million pounds, to be paid out of the proceeds of the sale of the land, in exchange for relinquishing all claims upon the property."

Casey smiled, leaned back in his chair. "Two million pounds? Really? Is that two million pounds each? To Big Frankie and each of his close family?"

"That is an incredibly generous offer!" said Sol. He looked flustered. "Where else would your clients ever realize a sum like that?"

Casey still had his infuriating grin on his face. "Do you have any idea what that land is worth?" He looked at each of them. "I suspect you do. Up to twenty million pounds according to the estimates I have received. And you offer two million! I don't think so!"

"Twenty million!" scoffed Sol. "Where on earth did you get a pie in the sky number like that? We would be fortunate to get ten. Six to eight is a more realistic range."

"I could get you ten tomorrow!" laughed Casey.

But as the lawyers argued back and forth, Mickey was paying little attention. They sounded like two kids arguing in the playground, and anyway, what they were saying was of little importance. What really mattered was Big Frankie. What was he thinking? And right now Mickey had a pretty good idea what Frankie was thinking. He'd not said a word since they had first arrived, was just sitting glaring at Mickey, his dark eyes never leaving him, his face expressionless.

Finally, he leaned forward, spoke in a whisper. "You set a bomb in my yard!" he snarled.

"You've been fucking with my business!" Mickey spat back. "You think I'm going to take that lying down!"

Big Frankie scowled, his thick eyebrows drawing together and almost hiding his eyes. "We haven't touched your business. You came to my home and set off a bomb!"

"You expect me to believe that?" Mickey shook his head. "I wasn't born yesterday!"

"You have no honor," Big Frankie declared. "You don't come to a man's house, threaten his family!"

"It wasn't a threat to your family," Mickey replied quickly. "It was a message, a warning. Don't fuck with me! Just like you gave to me when I visited you."

"We haven't fucking touched you yet!" snapped Frankie Junior, his face flushed. "But if you want a fucking war, we can give you one!"

"Gentlemen, gentlemen!" Sol flapped his hands at them.

"I agree," added Casey. "This meeting is about negotiation, agreeing a settlement that will resolve this, and I believe we are getting close, right, Sol?"

"Yes, yes!" Sol mopped his brow with a stained handkerchief. It was hot in the pub, hotter still around their small table.

Mickey and Big Frankie were still glaring at each other.

"So, Sol," continued Casey. "Give me something to work with. Come on, you and I know two million isn't a fair –"

"I'm warning you, Frankie. You and your puppy –" Mickey nodded towards Frankie Junior "– had better back off. You come around my business again, I will burn you to the fucking ground!"

"Mickey!" said Sol desperately. "What about three million? Could we go as high as –"

"Forget it!" Mickey glared at Sol, who shrank back in his chair. "Until these cunts apologize for what they've done, I won't give them another penny!"

"Now really, that doesn't help any of us!" pleaded Casey in the most conciliatory tone of voice he could muster. It made no difference.

Mickey stood up. "Evict them. Get the council in. I'll take my chances with the courts."

Casey tried one more time to calm everyone. "Let's not go that route. We all know –"

Big Frankie also stood up, eyeball to eyeball with Mickey. "You have no honor, Mickey Taylor. You will pay for what you are doing to my family." He nodded to Frankie Junior, who climbed to his feet beside him. "If the Taylors want a war, that's what we'll give them!"

And with that they pushed their way through the crowd, marched out.

Mickey watched them until they were out of the door. As he expected, the group at the bar turned and followed them out.

"Well that went well," said Martin. He hadn't spoken since they arrived.

"I didn't notice you coming up with any bright ideas!" Mickey snapped at him.

"With the way you were jumping in with two feet, there didn't seem much room for any intelligent comments!"

The two lawyers looked at each other.

"Do you think you can bring them around?" wondered Sol. "If we went to four million, we –"

"Four fucking million!" shouted Mickey. He was outraged. "To a bunch of thieving pikeys who have just challenged me to a fucking war!" His face was red, but his eyes had the cold, mad look that Martin knew only too well. "I'd rather give the fucking land away than give them a penny!"

Casey started edging out from behind the table. "I'll call you," he told Sol as he passed him. The two men exchanged a brief handshake.

Sol sank back into his chair. "I don't see how that could have gone much worse unless you had actually started fighting each other!" he sighed.

Mickey looked down at him, thoughtful, the mad look gone from his eyes. "It just might come to that before this is over," he said softly.

Mandy

Mandy was sitting at home alone, which was nothing unusual, and like so many times before she had her bottle of whiskey for company, and the stereo playing her favourite songs over and over again. For years, she had cried alone. All she had wanted to do was crawl into her bed and sleep, didn't want to see anyone, didn't want to face anyone. Depression had crept over her, filled in the empty spaces. Where once her life had meaning, held so many promises, now it seemed like a prison, the bars closing in a little closer each year. But that was then, this was now.

Whereas before the bottle had been all she'd had, now she had something else, and the drink was a treat, her first in months, saved for this special occasion. Tonight she was going to wallow in her misery, listen to all the old songs, feel again the bitter gall of rejection clawing at her throat, then take that pain, that anger, and direct it towards her ultimate goal. Miranda's death.

There was nothing else, no other objective or outcome that would make her feel better – that would wipe away the misery of the past ten years. Phase one had been completed – Mickey had been unable to resist her, had got a look and a taste of the new Mandy. Now it was time to complete the job. Kill Miranda, have her revenge, then sit back and wait for Mickey to come crawling back into her bed, into her life.

Plotting and planning her revenge – that was all she thought about, it consumed her daily. It was a dark pathway that Mandy was going down, but she had no choice, she had been left with nothing else, no other choice, nowhere else to turn.

For a moment, a deadly thought crept over her. Sure, when she met Mickey she was a pretty little sixteen year old, but would he have married her if she hadn't got pregnant? She wasn't an outgoing confident young lady, even then she was uncertain, insecure. If she hadn't got pregnant, would she have been just another one of Mickey's conquests? Or was her shyness, her timidity, why he had married her? Someone to stay at home, get pregnant and be the mother of his children, never complain when he came home later smelling of booze, cigarettes and some other slag's perfume?

Mandy could never forget Miranda's words to her: "Mickey never loved you, and he never will!" Was that true? Mandy's mind refused to be still when she thought about Mickey making love to Miranda, picturing them naked in bed together, hands and mouths and bodies all over each other. It was too much for her, it had to end, and she was the only one who could put a stop to it.

But try as she might, she couldn't blame Mickey. Coming out of prison, he had been faced with Mandy, fair, fat and forty from raising the kids, and then that perma-tanned whore throwing herself at him. What chance did he have? Any man would have done the same. No, it wasn't Mickey's fault, it was hers, Miranda, she was the one to blame, and she was going to be the one to pay.

Of course, Mickey had always had a wandering cock, never could resist a pretty face. She had put up it with it then and she would do the same now, he could still have his bit on the side, she just wanted her Mickey back in her arms, in her life.

Mandy put the notepad in her lap, licked the end of her pencil just like she used to do in school. It was time. Time to decide how she wanted to do it.

Mandy could have Miranda killed whatever way she wanted, she had enough connections, enough money, to pay someone to do it, but what would be the fun in that? For Mandy, the real pleasure would be looking Miranda in the eyes, seeing it happen, making sure that Miranda knew that it was Mandy who was responsible, that Mandy had won, and that Mickey would end up back in her arms. Then the bitch could burn in hell.

She wrote a neat "Number 1" at the top of the page, then carefully added the title: The Seduction Dinner.

Set it up so that Miranda thought Mickey was coming home for dinner, then show up herself, and with Miranda tied up to a chair, set out everything for a romantic evening. Tell the bitch what was happening, let her think she was going to live, then slip something in her drink. Her friend worked at a doctor's surgery, could get Morphine, Temazepam, Diazepam, all sorts of stuff that could kill her. Then as the bitch slowly slipped towards unconsciousness, describe in detail how she was going to seduce Mickey and win him back, let him come to her for comfort, having sex with his ex-wife to help him get over the death of the bitch who had stolen him.

She sipped her drink. Not bad for starters. What else?

"Number 2": Hotel Seduction. Book a posh hotel, have someone nab Miranda and bring her there, then strangle her with her bare hands. Just for fun, she would leave some men's clothes lying around so that Miranda would die knowing that Mickey was going to believe that she was shagging someone else.

"Number 3": Dodgy Cocaine. Mandy had done her research, knew the city club Miranda went to, knew the dealers that hung out there, the one

Miranda bought her cocaine from. Pay him enough, and he would slip her something dodgy. Miranda would go to the loo as she always did, take a snort, and as she lay writhing on the floor Mandy would emerge from one of the stalls to watch her die. The bonus? Mickey would finally know that his wife was a drug addict.

"Number 4": Slice and Dice. Simple, but effective this one. She had someone keeping an eye on Mickey, just had to choose an evening when he was away to come over, surprise Miranda. We need to talk, she would say, let's be adults about this, no bad feelings between us. At some point during the evening, Mandy would slip a tranquiliser into Miranda's drink, knock her out. By the time Miranda woke back up, she would be tied up in her bed, Mandy standing over her with a knife. Then Mandy would slowly, little by little, cut the bitch to death, let her blood stain the bed in which she had fucked Mickey so many times. Mickey would then be the one to come home and find the mutilated body of his wife. He would never want to go back there after that, never want to sleep in that bed again with the vision of Miranda's blood-covered body forever in his mind. Where else would he come but back to Mandy?

Mandy nodded. She liked that one. Almost guaranteed to bring him running back to her arms for comfort.

Her drink was running low. She swirled the ice around, tipped the glass up and drained it. Even on a special night like this she wasn't going to go back to her old boozing ways, one was enough. She set the glass down, picked up the pencil. One more to go.

"Number 5": Spiders. A lovely one this, and Mickey had let it slip to her. Miranda was deathly scared of spiders. Couldn't even be in the house if she'd seen one, had a complete panic attack. All Mandy had to do was to wait for a night when Mickey was away and Miranda was in bed, then creep in and put a big, fucking tarantula on her chest. She would wake up, go fucking ballistic, screaming and crying as Mandy put more and more spiders on her, on her face, her stomach, crawling between her legs. The bitch would die of a heart attack, natural causes it would look like, then Mandy could collect up Incy Wincy and his friends and make her escape, leaving no trace.

Mandy sat back, read through everything she had written. She couldn't help but smile, each of them had their appeal, each of them would work if she did it right. But there was one, one that she liked above and beyond the others, one that would achieve everything she wanted. She nodded to herself as she circled it with her pencil. Yeah, that was it, that was the one …

Sharon

Sharon forced a smile to her face as the doorbell rang. She checked herself in the mirror by the front door. Her bleached blonde hair hung straight down her back, her ample breasts spilled out over the top of her black basque, her legs looked good encased in black stockings, perched on her stiletto heels. Just what the punter ordered.

She pulled the door open, gazed at the bloke quivering on her doorstep. He was short, pudgy, with thinning mousy coloured hair, wearing drab clothes and a hangdog expression. She got all sorts, but this was one of the "typicals," as she called them, the easy ones. Pathetic men with empty lives who wanted her to emphasise just how sad they were by beating and debasing them.

That was fine with Sharon, she was in a lousy fucking mood, she would be more than happy to take it out on this poor sod.

"Welcome," she cooed, holding the door wider so that he could cop a look at her body.

His eyes bulged, he was already sweating. He licked his lips, eyes locked on her breasts. Finally he looked up and met her face, a guilty look plastered across his pale mug. "Hi, I …I …"

Christ, thought Sharon, let's not spend the whole fucking day out in the hallway. She kept the smile in place, reached out and grabbed his shirt front, gently pulled him inside. "I know who you are," she said as she closed the door behind him, "and I know exactly what you want."

Dennis, that was the name he had given. Sometimes they used their real names, sometimes they made up a name. Sharon really didn't care, they could call themselves Winston bleeding Churchill for all she cared. As long as they behaved themselves and paid her, she was happy.

"Sit down, Dennis!" she ordered.

Dennis hurried over to the couch, sat down, his hands on his knees, looked up at Sharon.

She came and stood over him, legs apart, hands on hips, her crotch at his eye level. The couch was low, the kind you sink into, chosen to make them feel inferior to her, to allow her to assert her superiority and control right from the get go.

Dennis gazed at her crotch, her long legs, then slowly looked up and met her eyes, licking his lips over and over again.

"You like what you see?"

Dennis nodded quickly.

Sharon gave him a stern look. "That's not the correct response, is it?" She cocked her head to one side. "What is the correct response?"

Dennis swallowed hard, cleared his throat. "Yes, mistress," he croaked.

"Good boy. Say it again."

"Yes, mistress."

"Have you been naughty?"

"Yes, mistress."

"Do you deserve to be punished?"

"Yes, mistress."

Sharon smiled. "Do you want me to punish you?"

Again he swallowed hard. "Yes, mistress."

Sharon suddenly turned, headed towards the hallway. "Follow me."

Dennis climbed quickly to his feet, followed Sharon out into the hallway. She pointed to the chains on the wall. "Go stand over there!"

Dennis hurried over, stood beneath the chains, looked at Sharon expectantly.

"Strip!"

Just for a second he hesitated. Sharon quickly reached for the side table, picked up a riding crop. "I said strip!"

This time he moved, quickly peeling off his clothes to reveal his soft, pink body. Christ, thought

Sharon, why couldn't she ever get anyone who looked worth shagging? Someone with some muscles, a lean, flat stomach, a nice fat cock? Despite years on the game, she still loved getting to grips with a good looking bloke, the feeling of a man inside her – or at least, one that she fancied.

Dennis though, he was the opposite of what she wanted in a man. Everything drooped, from his jowls to his moobs, his belly to his little cock, no more than two inches right now. Christ, wasn't he aroused yet? He was supposed to want this.

Dennis caught her gaze, looked down at his shriveled member. "I'm sorry if I displease you, mistress," he simpered. "I can't ..." He flushed, stammered. "I mean, it won't ..."

Sharon took a deep breath. Sobering up and getting clean was all very well, but for nearly forty years she had been turning tricks, and for all of those forty years she had been half hammered or partly high every time she did it. Sober, it was different. Sober, every emotion that she had kept hidden came racing to the surface. Fear, loathing, sadness, guilt – she was a Catholic girl, so plenty of that – revulsion, pity, they all came crowding forward, all of them fighting for attention now that she was clean, now that she was no longer hiding behind the bottle and the cocaine.

"Mistress?"

Sharon shook her head, looked back at the poor, pitiful figure standing naked before her. Her trick. Her income. The show must go on. She took a deep breath, cracked the crop across the palm of her hand. She could do this. "Turn around," she ordered, "and put your hands above your head!"

Grateful to have her attention again, Dennis turned around, pressed his hands against the wall.

Quickly, without giving herself time to think, Sharon stepped forward, snapped the manacles around his wrists, securing him to the wall. But it was still different, she found herself moving carefully, avoiding any contact with his body, conscious of his smell, the smell of sweat and fear.

"Spread your legs!"

Again he did as told, and Sharon knelt behind him, avoiding looking at his flabby, hairy buttocks, quickly clamping his ankles. That was better; he was under control. She could do this; she could get herself under control.

Sharon stood back, looked at his pathetic form, chained quivering to the wall. Christ, some people are seriously fucked up, she thought.

"You will be gentle to start with, won't you, mistress?"

Sharon looked at his back, his butt. No marks, no scars. Was this his first time? Her answer came automatically, she had said it so many times she didn't need to even think to say it. "You dare to question me? You pathetic little creep! I will give you exactly what I see fit, and you will accept it, gratefully!"

Dennis gave a little shiver. "Yes, mistress," he whispered.

Sharon set the crop on the table, reached for the soft whip. A little gentle lashing to get him started? That was the usual. Then something a little firmer, then gradually moving up to the crop, and finally, if he could stand it, one of the thin canes.

But somehow, for some reason, Sharon's hand didn't pick up the soft whip. Instead, her fingers reached past it, wrapped around the thin cane. It was a seemingly innocent instrument, but one capable of inflicting serious pain, leaving scars. It was not one for the faint-hearted, for a beginner.

She lifted the cane, stepped forward, tapping it gently on her leg. Who did this man think he was? Coming here, asking her to hurt him, to inflict pain.

Without thinking, she flicked the cane across his buttocks. He gave a little yelp of pain.

Did he understand what that was like? What it did to her? Did he think she liked hurting other people?

Again she struck him, harder this time. Again he yelped, sighed, pulling a little against the chains.

All the men through all the years, wanting, wanting, wanting, always wanting her to do something for them. Fuck them. Suck their dicks. Dress up for them. Undress for them. Beat them. Beating her.

The next blow was harder, elicited a real gasp of pain. "Mistress!" squeaked Dennis.

But Sharon didn't hear him. She was lost, lost in forty years of abuse, of greedy grasping fuckers taking from her, taking everything from her, over and over again, do this, do that, give me everything you've got, sucking her dry with their demands.

Faster and faster she struck him, harder and harder, the cane leaving deep welts across his soft skin, Dennis squealing and squirming, calling out over and over again, "Amber! Amber! Amber!"

Tears flowed down Sharon's face, streaking her mascara and leaving deep black tracks on her cheeks, her arm beginning to ache as she struck again and again, venting her fury for a lifetime of abuse on the poor suffering creature in front of her.

"Amber!"

The safe word. Suddenly it penetrated her cocoon. Amber was the safe word. Amber meant stop! You're going too far. Amber means you're really hurting me. Sharon's arm stopped its relentless motion, she dropped the cane at her feet, staggered into the living room and collapsed on the couch, deep sobs wracking her body as years of bitterness welled up and engulfed her. She curled in a ball, wrapped her arms around herself, finally gave in to the emotions she had held back for so long.

Sharon wasn't sure how long she lay there. It was dark when she woke up, the only light the street lights seeping through the curtains.

Sharon sat up, wiped the back of her hand across her cheek, smeared her makeup halfway across her face. Christ, she thought, I must look a right bloody sight.

She looked down at her "working clothes," tried to piece together what had happened. She had been seeing a bloke, had been right in the middle of – oh Christ!

Sharon jumped to her feet, ran to the hallway on her high heels, flicked on the light, gasped when she saw him still there, hanging from the chains, his buttocks red and raw. "Mistress!" he gasped as the light came on.

"Oh my God, I'm so sorry," gasped Sharon, running over to unchain him.

"No, no, it's my fault, mistress," whined Dennis. "I must have displeased you in some way!"

With fumbling hands Sharon unchained his feet, unhooked his hands. He collapsed to his knees, whimpering in pain. Sharon peered at his raw backside, winced. "Let's get some cream on those welts," she said, "then get you home."

Dennis picked up his clothes, followed Sharon back into the living room, bent across the arm of the couch while she applied Savlon to his raw buttocks, wincing and twitching the whole time. Sharon was as gentle as she could be, but she knew it was hurting him. "There you go," she said finally, "get your clothes on."

Dennis quickly dressed, moving gingerly as he slid his pants and trousers on.

Sharon looked at him sadly, all the emotions still lurking at the back of her mind, waiting to surge back up again. "I'm really sorry about that," she said softly. "There's no charge."

Dennis stood in front of her, looking like a schoolboy hauled up before the headmaster. He frowned. "No mistress. I should pay you in full!"

"But I –"

For the first time he showed some assertiveness. "No! It was wonderful! It was exactly what I deserved!"

Sharon goggled at him. "But I really hurt you! You begged me to stop and I just kept going!"

"Exactly! I'm weak and pathetic, I wanted you to stop, but you didn't! You knew what I wanted, what I deserved, and you gave it to me!" His eyes were sparkling, his normally dull face alive. He fumbled in his pocket, pulled out his wallet, began pulling out fifty pound notes.

Sharon shook her head. "Dennis? Listen to me love."

He looked at her imploringly. "Anything!"

"Do you have a wife?"

He nodded glumly.

"Kids?"

"Two."

"You don't need this," she told him.

"But mistress!"

Sharon stood up, moved towards the door, ushering Dennis in front of her, shoving his wallet back in his pocket. "Go home. Hug your wife. Love your kids. Forget this ever happened."

His sad eyes looked up at her as she reached for the door. "I can never forget this. It's the most amazing thing that has ever happened to me!"

Sharon glared at him as she opened the door. "Go home you sad little fuck!" she snapped. And before he could reply, she shoved him out the door, slammed it shut.

Jesus Christ, she thought, there's no helping some people.

She staggered back towards the couch, halfway there stopped and pulled off her high heels, threw them in the corner. What now?

Sharon stood in the middle of the room, looking around. Her job had taken over her whole life. This wasn't a normal living room, it was a tart's boudoir, filled with the bitter memories of her world, of the guys she had entertained here, the suckings and fuckings and beatings and nights spent grunting and sweating under some bloke whose name she didn't know.

She could hardly sit down and relax and watch telly after what had just happened, could she? She still felt raw, nerves on edge, jittery. Against her will she found her feet taking her into the bedroom, found herself sitting down by the beside, pulling out the little bag of white powder, her emergency stash, the one she had kept even though she had been clean for three weeks now.

What would one snort matter? She'd just had a really rough day, needed a little something to take the edge off, change her mood, chase away the sadness that threatened to overwhelm her.

With shaking hands, Sharon opened the bag, pulled the mirror out, tipped two rough lines out. Two little lines. Two deep snorts. That wasn't much, was it? And then it would all be gone, the pain and misery would be chased away for a few sweet moments, just long enough to help her calm down and think what to do.

That was how she rationalised it. It was just taking the edge off, calming herself down, getting her head back together so that she could do the things she needed to do.

No one would blame her for that. It made sense, really, didn't it?

Sharon took a deep breath, exhaled, leaned over the mirror. Just as she was about to inhale, snort the sweet powder up her nose, she saw the reflection of her own eyes in the mirror. Except it wasn't her own eyes she saw – it was the eyes of the old lady, the fortune-teller.

What was it about that woman? She was old – really old – and at first glance her eyes had that rheumy, cloudy look that old people get. But on closer inspection there was a fire in there, an incredible depth to her eyes that seemed to look deep into your soul, see your deepest secrets.

Sharon paused inches above the mirror, her hand already closing off her left nostril. What was it the old woman had said?

Now that she thought about it, Sharon couldn't remember a single word the fortune-teller had actually said. But it wasn't the words themselves that mattered, it was the way they made Sharon feel, the effect they had on her at a deep level, a level beyond words, beyond conscious thought.

Still she hovered above the mirror, the old woman's eyes haunting her.

Could she really see the future? Christ, what was it she had said? That the family was going to need her? Unlikely! They'd got along fine without her for the past forty years. If anything it had been the other way round, her needing them.

But what if she was right? What if her time was coming? What if they needed Sharon, and she wasn't there for them?

One again, Sharon stared into the mirror, but this time it was her own eyes she saw staring back at her.

She stood up suddenly, the mirror in one hand, the white bag in the other, marched into the bathroom, and before she could stop herself or change her mind, she flushed every last drop of cocaine down the toilet.

As the water swirled round the bowl, Sharon looked up at her reflection once again, in the big bathroom mirror this time.

"You've gone and done it now, girl," she told herself. "No turning back!"

She dropped the empty cocaine bag in the rubbish, looked back up. What she saw wasn't a pretty sight. She looked old, her mascara streaked across her face, eyes red rimmed, her hair a mess.

"No more booze, no more charlie, no more tricks," she told herself. It felt important that she actually say it, say it to her reflection. She was her own witness to her promise, her promise to her family.

This time there was no turning back, no change of heart, no weakness. If they needed Sharon, Sharon would be ready. When the family called, she would be there.

Georgie

Another night, another pub. Georgie wasn't sure what compelled him to come out, night after night, picking up guys. Sure, he liked giving blow jobs, but there were lots of gay clubs where he could have spent half the night sucking off all and sundry with a lot less hassle.

As he sat at the bar waiting for the bloke in the corner to make his move – he'd been staring at Georgie's short skirt for the last ten minutes, trying to pluck up the courage to come over – he turned the thought over in his mind.

There was the chase, that was fun. The little moments like right now when the bloke looked over, staring at Georgie's legs, then made shy eye contact when he realised that Georgie was looking at him.

Next came the approach, the chat, the thrill as they left the place together, the bloke wondering just how lucky he would get.

From there it wasn't long to the first kiss, then that moment of grateful wonderment when Georgie dropped his head into their lap and took their cock into his mouth. Most were so surprised and grateful that they came in just a couple of minutes.

But as he gave an encouraging smile to tonight's most likely target, Georgie admitted to himself what the most exciting part was. It wasn't any of the other parts, the chase, the pick-up, the first kiss. It was the thrill of not getting caught, pure and simple. The thrill of getting away with it.

After spending his teen years first of all hiding his sexuality, then feeling guilty about it, he had got used to sneaking around, to sex being something that you did on the sly, secretly, without other people knowing. After starting his sexual journey in that way, he now had a hard time separating sex out from that thrill. For him to enjoy sex, it had to have an element of risk, to be exciting, edgy, to always be wrapped up with the thrill and the fear of discovery. Giving guys blow jobs in their cars in a pub car park had all of that and more. Not just the risk of them being caught in the act, but the possibility that one day, one of his conquests would discover that Georgie wasn't actually a woman. What that would actually mean, what would happen if that occurred, he had no idea. But it gave his encounters a real thrill, and that was what Georgie craved.

He glanced over at tonight's target. Not that handsome, certainly not sophisticated, he looked like a builder or a plumber, with thick tattooed forearms and the beginnings of a beer belly. But he was a big guy, and Georgie was already anticipating what his thick, meaty cock would feel like in his mouth. He liked them a bit rough.

Georgie gave a shy smile then looked away – that was all it took. Suddenly the bloke was beside him, his scent a mix of sweat and cheap aftershave.

"All right love?"

Up close, he was rougher than Georgie had realised. This bloke had been in a few brawls, and now that he had made his move, now that he thought he was in with Georgie, he had a brutish confidence.

"Buy you a drink?"

Georgie gave another shy smile, put on his huskiest voice. "That would be lovely."

It didn't take long before they moved on. Trevor – that was his name – was short on subtlety, direct, to the point. Even as they walked to his van he reached over and squeezed Georgie's butt. "You're built, aren't you?" he leered.

"More than you can imagine," purred Georgie.

As soon as the van door was closed, Trevor was all over Georgie, grabbing at him, taking Georgie's hand and rubbing it against the bulge in his dirty jeans.

"That's what you want, isn't it?" He quickly unzipped his trousers, pulled his cock out, shoved Georgie's head roughly into his lap. "Suck it good you dirty whore!" With his hand holding tight to Georgie's hair, he thrust his cock up into his mouth.

Georgie almost gagged, but took it in, holding on to his little secret as Trevor thrust roughly against him.

"That's a good girl, you suck that thing!" He was thrusting and grunting against Georgie's mouth. "Soon as I've come I'm going to take you in the back of the van and fuck you up the arse!" he snarled.

Georgie tried to focus on what he was doing. This was all happening too fast, it was not what he had planned. Rough was one thing, but this guy was a pig, and Georgie couldn't allow him to get his hands inside his dress – he would discover more than he bargained for.

But in a sudden rush, it was too late. Trevor came, holding Georgie tightly in place, and at the same time he reached his big hand over and grabbed between Georgie's legs.

Georgie was a strong man, but this bloke was far stronger. Georgie was trapped, Trevor's hand burrowing and digging, ripping Georgie's silk underwear off. And then he felt it …

"Jesus fucking Christ!" His hand grabbed Georgie's cock, strapped to his stomach but still very much in evidence if you found it, then quickly let go. "You're a fucking bloke!"

He glared down at Georgie, but for some reason didn't release his head. Georgie's mouth was still filled with his cock. Georgie could say nothing. "A fucking tranny, that's what you are!"

He shoved Georgie's head down even harder, gagging him.

"No wonder you like sucking cock so much!" He grinned. "Well, I hope you enjoyed it, cos it's the last fucking cock you're ever going to suck!"

And with Georgie's mouth still filled with his thick member, he wrapped his big hands around Georgie's neck, began choking him. "Suck on that you fucking pervert!" he rasped, his grip tightening.

Georgie could feel the hands on his throat, feel the waves of blackness coming over him, feel his breath running out. As he started to black out he did the only thing he could – he sank his teeth into Trevor's cock.

The sound that Trevor made was unlike anything Georgie had ever heard, a strangled cry of sheer agony that quickly turned into a full-on roar of shock and horror.

As he screamed, Trevor loosened his grip on Georgie's neck. It was enough for Georgie to break free, sit up, gasping and wheezing. He flopped back against the passenger door of the van, sucking in a deep lung full of air through his bruised throat.

"You fucking cow!" screamed Trevor, gazing down as his bleeding cock. "Look what you fucking did!"

Georgie was slowly coming round, his head clearing as the oxygen coursed through his veins to his brain. He turned, trying to find the door handle, but was stunned by a fierce blow in the back from Trevor. "I'm going to fucking kill you!"

Another punch slammed into the back of Georgie's head, smashing his head against the window. He began to panic as the fists rained down on him, but kept one clear vision in his mind. If he could just get his purse, just find it, get his hand on it …

Blow after blow rained on Georgie's back, his shoulders, but he didn't care, he had found his purse, opened it, felt inside – there it was!

As his fingers wrapped around it, he turned back to Trevor, just in time to catch a hard punch to the cheek that knocked him backwards. But in the confined space of the van it didn't matter, he was close enough, close enough for his right hand, holding the blade, to thrust out, bury it in Trevor's stomach.

Everything froze for a moment.

The blows stopped.

Trevor looked down in confusion at the knife thrust deep into his belly.

Georgie gasped, blinked.

Then suddenly his strength returned, his brain fully cleared, his muscles came to life, and he stabbed the four inch blade into Trevor over and over again. He stabbed him for all the pricks and cunts who had abused and hurt him, stabbed him for every hurt he had suffered from his dad, each miserable day he had spent in Rampton, stabbed him for all the accumulated pain he had felt in a lifetime of misery and confusion.

When Georgie finally stopped stabbing it was from sheer exhaustion. He fell back against the door, his chest heaving, dropped the knife in his lap, his hand falling to his side, completely spent.

In the garish yellow light of the car park, he gazed at Trevor. It was like a scene from a horror film, a nightmare. Trevor was, of course, dead, had long ago stopped writhing and squirming. He looked almost peaceful; his eyes closed, his head rolled to one side, a calm look on his face. But his body looked very different, his T-shirt completely soaked in blood, which had also spilled down across his trousers, staining them black, spilled down across his limp, bleeding cock, covered the seat, formed a thick pool on the floor of the van.

Georgie gasped, like a man awakening from a dream, released from a nightmare vision that has gripped him and controlled him. "Oh fuck!" he whispered. The sharp metallic smell of blood filled his nostrils. He looked down – his hand and arm were also covered in blood, and it had splashed onto his dress. He felt something on his face, reached up with his clean hand and wiped his cheek, smeared more blood across his face.

At that moment three lads came out of the pub, laughing and joking.

Georgie froze, his heart hammering against his chest, didn't move a muscle as the three blokes strolled to their car.

They climbed in, started the car, turned on the headlights. For a moment, the lights shone directly into the front on the van, lighting up the gory tableau, Trevor's blood-soaked body, Georgie wide-eyed and frightened. But none of them were paying attention, and their car soon pulled out of the car park, leaving Georgie alone with Trevor once more.

Georgie let out a huge sigh of relief, slumped in the seat. He could feel a rising tide of panic and sorrow washing over him, wanted to just sit there and cry and scream and never have to deal with the situation, just wait to be discovered, wait for events to overcome him, like a stone lying on the beach and waiting for the tide to come in and wash over it. But then he thought of going back to Rampton, to those sadistic guards, the indifferent doctors, the fruitcakes and psychos he had been incarcerated with for over twenty years. They would send him back there, no doubt about it. And if they did, he would kill himself.

Georgie shook his head. He had to do something, and fast. There was only one thing he could do, one person he could call. With fumbling hands, he pulled his mobile phone out of his purse, punched in a number.

There was a long wait, the phone ringing several times, and for a moment he thought he wouldn't get a reply. Then that familiar voice came on the line. The voice that always brought him comfort. The one voice that could help him in this situation.

"What's up Georgie?"

"Mickey!" gasped Georgie. He gulped, took a deep breath, forced himself to be calm.

"Georgie? You all right, mate?"

Georgie exhaled sharply, blurted the words out before he lapsed back into panic. "I've done something terrible, Mickey! I need your help!"

Mickey

Mickey grabbed his keys, pulled on his jacket as he headed out the door.

Miranda watched him, concern in her eyes. She had seen Mickey in this mood too many times to ask questions. When something urgent came up with the business it was ask no questions, make no fuss, just give him a kiss as he headed out the door and hope he came back alive.

Mickey paused, stroked her cheek as he kissed her softly. "Sorry about dinner, darlin', but it's Georgie, he's got himself in some kind of bother, needs me to go and sort it out for him."

Miranda nodded, understanding. When it was family, Mickey dropped everything and came running. "Hope the silly sod is all right," she laughed.

"Yeah, I bet it's nothing," lied Mickey. Georgie had already told him enough for Mickey to know that this was a big, big, fucking deal. "I'll grab a bite to eat while I'm out. Don't wait up for me."

How many times had Miranda heard that before? It meant another night at home alone with the booze and the TV. But when you married Mickey Taylor, that was part of the package. "Stay safe."

Mickey gave her a smile, the smile that had melted Miranda's heart the first time she saw him. "Ain't I always?"

Miranda watched him strut to his car, didn't close the door until his big BMW had backed out of the driveway and was out of sight round the corner.

But neither Mickey nor Miranda saw Mandy, parked discretely in an anonymous rental car fifty yards down the road, watching, plotting, writing down every detail of Miranda's schedule.

Jesus Christ, thought Mickey, what was it with his fucking family? He'd bailed Sharon out once when one of her clients had died while chained up in her flat, and now Georgie reckoned he'd killed a bloke in the car park of some dodgy pub. It was hard to tell with Georgie what was truth and what was fiction, but he'd sounded pretty shaken up, so maybe the stupid sod had actually killed someone.

Mickey only had himself to blame, mind you. He was the one who had got Georgie out of Rampton, the one who had made it happen. He just hoped he hadn't let a genie out of the lamp. If Georgie was going doolally and killing people, Mickey was going to have to deal with it, he couldn't have his brother out there knocking people off for fun or kicks.

But how do you deal with it if it's your own brother? He certainly wouldn't want to take him to the police, have a trial and all that nonsense. Then they would all have to deal with the whole issue of a mad member of the Taylor family out killing people, the press would have a fucking field day with that. He could always get him recommitted, he had got him out of Rampton; he was damn sure he could get him back in, but Georgie said that Rampton had been a living hell. He couldn't put him through that again.

Fuck it! Thought Mickey, let's see what the situation really is first, then we'll deal with it. He pulled his car into the pub car park, pulled over into a dark corner, then climbed out the car and dialed Georgie. "I'm here. Where are you?"

"White van," gasped Georgie, "back right corner of the car park."

Mickey looked around, peering into the darkness. Then he saw it, Georgie's pale face as he waved at Mickey from the front of the van. Even under a wig and make up, Mickey recognized Georgie. He'd had enough meetings with Georgie's alter ego Samantha to recognize that face anywhere.

Mickey pocketed his phone, strode over towards the van. He could see Georgie's wide eyes following him all the way over.

As he reached the van, Georgie wound down the window. "Mickey, I'm so glad you're here, I didn't know what else to do!"

Mickey said nothing, peered past Georgie into the front of the van. A big bloke was slumped across the seat, blood soaking the front of his shirt. "Christ!" muttered Mickey. "I had half-hoped you were joking!"

"I'm so sorry, Mickey," gasped Georgie, looking up with tear filled eyes. "We were just –"

Mickey cut him off. "I really don't want to know what you were just doing," he snapped. He nodded towards his car. "Let's get you in my car, in the back. Make sure no one sees you."

Georgie nodded. "OK, OK, I can do that." He started to open the car door, but sudden voices made them both freeze.

"Stay where you are!" hissed Mickey. As he said it he melted back into the shadows.

Georgie sat frozen as a couple of blokes came out of the rear of the pub, one of them swaying slightly, made their way to a car. The driver climbed in, waited patiently while his drunken friend pissed against a bush. The driver was looking right towards them, Georgie felt certain that he could see him, see the guilt written across his face, the blood that splattered the front of his dress. He could hear his own breathing, feel his heart beat, didn't dare move. Finally the drunk was done pissing. He staggered back to the car, scrambled in, and they pulled away. The car park fell silent once more.

Mickey emerged from the shadows. "All right, let's go!"

Georgie jumped as Mickey appeared, his nerves shredded and on edge. He threw the door open, scrambled out, taking one last look at Trevor's bloody body, flopped across the seat. "What about him?"

"Once we're clear, I'll call Martin. He'll get some of the boys to come down and clean this mess up."

They hurried towards Mickey's car, the car park thankfully quiet.

Georgie cast one last glance back at the van as he scrambled into the back of Mickey's car, slid down onto the floor behind the front seats. "Clean it up? How will they clean it up?"

The big car started, pulled smoothly out of the car park, quickly picked up speed as Mickey put his foot down. "Don't you worry about that. Right now we need to get you somewhere safe."

But where? thought Mickey. Where the hell could he take Georgie where he would be safe, where someone could clean him up, calm him down, look after him? There was only one place ...

Martin

Martin moved smoothly round the pristine kitchen of what Mickey called his "shagging pad." Perched high in a Canary Wharf high rise, it was close enough to work when he needed to get somewhere quickly, but seemed a thousand miles away at the end of the day when he wanted to relax and unwind.

The flat was spacious, with acres of polished wooden floors, huge windows looking out towards the city, marble counter tops and oak cabinets in the kitchen. Elegant minimalism the designer had called it, and it suited Martin to a "T."

In truth, the place was far bigger than Martin needed, but his time in Australia had got him used to big houses with lots of light and space, and he just couldn't go back to living in a pokey English place with dark rooms and low ceilings. He needed room to move around, liked his high-end designer furniture to have space to be seen, loved the wall space to display the large pieces of modern art that he collected.

Martin chopped the spring onions, set them aside. Cooking was a great way for him to relax at the end of the day, a chance to take his mind out of gear and let it freewheel – at least, that was the theory, but the business with Frankie and the travellers had got him out of sorts.

Martin had spent the past fifteen years moving the family business forward, making it lower risk, higher profit, giving them legitimate fronts to cover their high income lifestyles. Christ, he'd even got Mickey to work with an accountant and file proper tax returns so that he didn't get busted for tax evasion! But this, this business with the travellers felt like a step backwards, like something that was going to unravel and unravel, like a thread pulled from a shirt that ended up undoing the whole damn thing. It felt, in a word, wrong.

Over the years, they had moved away from simply solving everything with violence and intimidation. Not that they didn't use that weapon when they had to, but, in the long run, Martin had found that it was more profitable to work with people than to simply beat the shit out of them at the first sign of trouble.

But this dispute with the travellers didn't have a good, clean solution. Neither violence nor money offered a way out. Despite Mickey's claims, you couldn't go to war with the travellers and win – it would be like fighting an octopus. There were so many of them, and most of them had no permanent home, so it was hard to take the fight to them. And as for solving the issue with money, well they had already seen where that got them.

The bottom line was that Big Frankie didn't want to move. Mickey had come on too hard in the first instance, had put Frankie's back up, and now it was a point of honour for him. He felt betrayed, and had dug his heels in.

Trying to drag his mind away from work, Martin glanced at the pan. The oil looked hot enough. Martin tossed the chicken into the wok, began stirring it, but despite his best efforts, his mind kept turning the matter over. How could they resolve this in a way that satisfied everyone? There were three elements to take into account – Mickey's anger, Big Frankie's honour, and Martin's desire to keep the business moving forward.

Martin idly moved the chicken around the wok, his mind elsewhere. Move the business forward? Was that what he wanted to do? Or, if they got this windfall, the money from the land in Stratford, did he have another plan? To get out all together?

His mind had been turning that way more and more often recently. He wasn't like Mickey, an adrenaline junkie who thrived on the power, the thrill, the kudos of being the big I Am. Martin had never felt the thrill that Mickey felt, never wanted to be seen and known as the Big Man. Truth was, many people, even in the business, still just thought of him as Mickey's little brother, had no idea how much of the business he ran. Whereas Mickey could barely set foot in the Dagenham area without being recognized, Martin could walk the length of the Heathway without a soul knowing who he was. He liked it that way.

For Martin, the reward wasn't being recognized, having people clap him on the back, buy him drinks. It was different for him. For Martin, it was first and foremost the sense of pride in helping the family. Helping Mickey stay alive by steering him away from the dodgy deals, the worst excesses that his temper would lead him into. And then providing businesses for Terri and Tommy that gave them a good income.

And for Martin, what was in it for him? It was all about the lifestyle. Living in Australia, building up his business there, for the first time in his life he'd had money. Not just a bit of cash in his pocket to flash around on a Saturday night and impress people, but real money. The kind of money that buys you a beach front apartment, a Ferrari, a Porsche. The kind of money that doesn't dribble away – that is always there when you need it.

If they sold the land in Stratford, they could all do that. They could bung a million each to Terri, Georgie, and Sharon – although it would probably go straight up Sharon's nose, thought Martin, just like the money from Bobby's diamonds – and still walk away with five million each for Martin and Mickey. Surely even Mickey would recognize that that was a perfect time to get out, to leave all the hassle behind, maybe even move to somewhere like Marbella. Mickey and Miranda already had a place down there, went there for holidays and long weekends. Would Mickey actually manage to retire while he was on top?

Like fuck would he! He was a Taylor, with everything that came with that name. And as that thought crossed his mind, Martin was suddenly taken back, to that night, that memory, that dark and dreadful nightmare that rose unbidden from the depths of his brain at the unlikeliest times.

Martin was in bed when Bobby came home, woke to violence, a huge hand grabbing his hair, dragging him out of the bed, along the hallway to his parents' room.

He felt a trickle of sweat roll down his back as the scene played out in his mind. It was strangely silent, he could feel his heart beating faster and faster as he saw himself as an eleven year old once again …

Martin felt a burning pain shoot through his head as he tumbled backwards and crashed onto the floor. He winced as Bobby, his dad, pulled harder, dragging him to his feet, twisting his head round by his hair so he was looking straight at him. Martin stared into those cold, callous eyes, not a trace of love or mercy in them. "Let's take you to see Mum, see if you can tell me what the fuck's been going on!" he snarled.

Bobby nudged him forward with a shove in the back that almost knocked him off his feet. He started to walk forwards, hurrying down the hall towards his mum's bedroom. His mouth gaped at the sight of what he saw. His mum, her nightgown ripped open, was on her knees at the foot of the bed.

Bobby shoved Martin hard so that he fell to his knees, then walked past him towards the bed. Martin's eyes went from his mother, her face tear-stained, mouth bleeding, to the bed, to the knife. The knife was about a foot long, with a sculptured edge, the metal glistening like diamonds.

Martin heard a whimpering in the corner, looked into the shadows, into the darkness, saw his sisters, Sharon and Terri, huddled in the corner, their hands tied behind their backs, mouths covered with duct tape. Their hair was stuck to their faces by tears and tape.

As Bobby picked up the knife, Lizzy, his mum, looked up in a state of fear, her face screwed up with tension, looking small and frail, helpless. Martin didn't know whether he wanted to run or fight. What should he do? What could he do? And where were Georgie and Mickey? They would sort it out if they were there, wouldn't they?

Martin knelt trembling by the side of his mum's bed, his breathing fast and shallow. He had to keep calm for his mum's sake. The knife flashed before his eyes, came to rest across Lizzie's throat, the cruel blade pressed to her flesh.

"Look at me, son, or I will kill her!" rasped Bobby.

Martin could hear her moaning and crying, watched helplessly as Bobby yanked Lizzie's hair to expose her neck further. He pulled so hard she screamed.

"Everything will be all right, just do what your dad says," gasped Lizzie.

Martin closed his eyes trying to stop the panic he was feeling inside. He felt like he was the passenger in his body rather than the driver.

"Who's been coming around here when I'm away!" screamed Bobby.

Martin had no idea what he meant, couldn't take his eyes from the knife. He imagined getting hold of the knife, what he would do to Bobby when he got hold of him, what he would do for putting his mum through this.

"Tell me!" yelled Bobby. "I know some other bastard is sticking his filthy cock in her when I'm not here!"

Martin could feel the knife in his hands, sliding the blade into Bobby's ribs, ramming it in until the knife came out the other side, sticking out his back. Then lifting him up by the handle so his feet were dangling, the blood oozing from his eyes, his nose, his mouth, his stomach, hearing him choking and gurgling on his own blood. Gouts of blood, bright splashes of it spilling down his shirt, the rasp of steel cutting through his throat.

"Are you listening to me!" screamed Bobby. His hand suddenly lashed out, a backhand slap that crashed into Martin's cheek and sent him flying across the room to crash into the wardrobe. His head hit hard and he flopped down, his head spinning.

"No!" Lizzie lunged towards Martin, trying to protect her youngest, and as she did so the knife cut into the flesh of her neck. She fell forward, crawled towards him, her throat bleeding, her frail arms reaching out to cradle him.

As she crawled towards him, blood streaming from her neck, Bobby standing over her, his sisters cowering in the background, Martin fixed the image in his mind. He knew that the blackness of that night would always be with him, watched the events as though it was someone else, like he was the passenger in a car, or watching a train that just won't stop, just keeps going by.

He looked around at the cool, brightly lit interior of his flat. He still couldn't sleep in the dark, still bore the memory of that night. Most of the time he felt untouched by what occurred, told himself that he was OK. Then out of the blue, like tonight, it would hit him with no warning. Sometimes it was when he was asleep, but it could just as easily be sitting at the traffic lights, in a meeting, playing golf, any time, any place. If he was in company he would quickly make an exit, make up some bullshit story that he had a migraine or something. No one could see him in that state, no one, not even Mickey.

That night, Martin had had a taste of the death and destruction that could be his destiny, a glimpse of a life of violence, of killing people. He had chosen to walk away, vanish and reinvent himself on the other side of the world, and had done it.

But when you were a Taylor you could never avoid it, never avoid the family, the blood. That was stronger than anything. That was why he had come back, why he had saved Mickey's life fifteen years ago, and that was why he was involved in Mickey's War right now. Once you committed, it was like Alice going down the rabbit hole. There was nowhere to go but deeper.

Martin took a deep breath, slid the chopped vegetables in with the chicken, stirred them around, then glanced up at the clock. Running late as usual. Why couldn't he ever pick the punctual ones? Sod it, he would eat alone if he had to, but he wasn't best

pleased about it. The whole point of having someone
else in your life was that they were there when you
needed them. Like now, at the end of a long day,
when you were tired out and just wanted to eat and
relax.

Martin pulled out two bowls, served the stir
fry into them, carried them to the elegant dining table,
already set for two with a bottle of wine. Just as he
set the bowls down, the doorbell rang.

"About bloody time!" murmured Martin, but
he was grinning.

He checked one more time to make sure the
table looked perfect, then headed for the door.

"You must have smelt the food!" he laughed
as he opened the door.

"You know me, always show up when there's
something good to eat!"

Graham pecked Martin on the cheek, headed
straight for the table. "Mmm, stir fry, smells yummy!"

Martin followed more slowly, watching
Graham as he peeled off his coat. He was in his
twenties, with a lithe athletic body, a head of straw-
coloured hair.

Graham tossed his coat on a chair, reached for
the wine.

"That's it?" challenged Martin, his eyes
sparkling with humour. "Straight to the wine without
even a kiss?"

Graham paused, looked at Martin for a moment as though considering, then carefully put down the bottle, walked slowly over to where Martin stood. "A kiss, huh?"

Martin nodded.

"Oh, all right!" Graham suddenly grabbed Martin, pulled him in close, kissed him passionately.

Martin melted in his arms, truly relaxing for the first time all day. This, thought Martin, this is what makes it all worthwhile.

The sharp ring of his phone cut through the quiet of their embrace.

Graham felt Martin stiffen in his arms. "Leave it," he whispered, "we've got more important things to do right now."

But Martin couldn't ignore it, much as he wanted to. He pulled himself free. "I have to answer that. It's my brother."

He disentangled himself from Graham's embrace, picked his phone up off the table. "What's up?"

"We've got a situation. We need a clean-up crew, and pronto."

Martin sighed, moved towards the kitchen counter, where he kept a notepad and a pen. "All right. Give me the details …"

Terri

Terri sat up, tried to focus. What day was it? Where was she? Her head was pounding with a fucker of a headache, she felt like a bag of shit. Just sitting up made her feel nauseous, she was tempted to lie back down again, close her eyes and drift back off to sleep, but something was nagging at her, something she needed to do. Christ, what was it?

She looked around the room. It was a tip, a left over pizza box on the table, cigarette stubs and a couple of dead roaches in the ashtray, two vodka bottles on the couch beside her. One was empty, the other had a little left in the bottom. Terri reached out for the bottle that still had some clear liquid in the bottom.

There was a glass on the table, but she didn't want to risk leaning forward that far – she'd probably just topple forward and smash her nose on the glass table top. With fumbling fingers, she picked up the bottle. Oh no, she must have had a drink last night.

That explained why she felt like a heap of shit, she had a hangover. Her arm shaking, she lifted the bottle, what the fuck had happened that sent her over the edge back to the booze.

As soon as the last drop hit her throat, she leaned back on the couch, tried to piece together what was going on. She definitely drank the vodka, her head told her that, but there was only glass on the table – so she'd been drinking alone. So far so good – the fags and roaches, they'd be hers too. But what about the pizza box? She didn't eat pizza. So who else was here – or had been here?

She looked down. She was wrapped in a pink fluffy dressing gown, but the legs that stuck out the bottom wore black stockings. What was that all about? Still puzzled, Terri slowly pulled the dressing gown open – she was wearing a tight black basque, her tits spilling out the top. Now why on earth would she be …

And then it all came back to her. Jimmy. The seduction. The gun.

Jesus fucking Christ! She had actually killed him! This was no booze fuelled dream. Terri had killed her husband then drunk herself into oblivion.

She looked around quickly as though expecting to see him there, screaming at her for being such a fat, lazy cow, for having the nerve to actually stand up to him, for daring to think that she could get rid of him.

But no, he wasn't there, he was … her eyes strayed upwards, up towards the bedroom. Holy shit – he was still there, wasn't he? She didn't remember doing anything with the body, and she certainly wasn't dressed as though she had gone anywhere or done anything.

He was still up there. His body still lay in their bed. Right where she had left him after shooting him in the face. Shit.

Terri felt herself beginning to shake, a wave of hysteria washing over her. She had to pull herself together! She had her husband's body upstairs – the last thing she could do was panic. She reached out a shaking hand towards the ashtray. One of the roaches wasn't finished, there were a few puffs there, enough to calm her nerves.

She picked up the roach, put it to her lips, found her lighter and got it alight at the second attempt. She pulled the smoke deep into her lungs, the familiar taste of the marijuana immediately relaxing her, even as the drug started to flow through her veins. Three more deep pulls, and the joint was down to a nub, but it was enough, enough to stop the shaking, enough to slow her breathing, enough to prepare her for what she had to do.

Slowly, carefully, she pushed herself to her feet. She still felt a bit hung over, no big surprise after two bottles of vodka, but she managed to get her feet moving, shuffled to the door, stepped out into the hall.

She paused at the bottom of the stairs, gazed upwards. He was up there. Cold and stiff and dead. Lying alone in the dark for Christ knows how long.

She flicked on the light, steeled herself, then began to climb the stairs, one weary step at a time, each one taking her closer. She didn't want to see him, but she had to. Had to for herself. Had to in order for the last, darkest, most fearful corner of her brain to finally accept that the bastard was gone, that the beatings, the insults, the abuse were all finally finished.

One weary leg at a time, Terri climbed the stairs, turned towards her bedroom door. The bedroom was in darkness, the door half open. She shuffled down the hallway, pushed the door open, looking down at her feet, not daring to look up.

Still looking down, she shuffled to the bed, eyes fixed on her feet, the black stockings, the red painted toe nails. Finally, she stopped by the bed. There was a heavy smell in the air that turned her stomach. How long had it been if he was already smelling a bit ripe? It was summer, the days heavy and hot, the nights close, claustrophobic. A body would start to turn pretty quickly in weather like that.

Still she stood by the bed, putting it off, not wanting to, but knowing she had to. Slowly, slowly, she raised her eyes.

She grimaced in disgust as she saw his naked, bloated body, still handcuffed to the bed. His skin was a mottled pink, some of the veins starting to show, the stomach distended, his limp prick looking small and harmless.

Her eyes traveled up to his head, still covered by the pillow she had used when she had shot him. The pillow was half-destroyed, blood had soaked through it, and two fat, lazy bluebottle flies were gorging themselves, their feet deep in the sticky red goo.

Terri looked away for a moment, fighting back the nausea. Everything that she had done, everything that she had said had come rushing back to her as she stood there, everything up to the moment when she put the gun to Jimmy's head and pulled the trigger. That she couldn't remember. Had she actually done that? The evidence was incontestable, the bloated, stinking body, the bloody pillow, but there was one more thing she had to do, one more thing she had to see.

Slowly, reluctantly, she reached out a shaking hand, gripped the corner of the bloody pillow, then whipped it away.

Terri's eyes were drawn irresistibly upwards to look at the face of her dead husband. It felt like time froze for a moment as she took it all in. Her breathing stopped, even her heart seemed to skip a beat. One eye was gone, blasted away by the gun shot, along with most of his left cheek, but the other stared up at her accusingly, unblinking, frozen forever in that moment of horror, that realisation that this wasn't a game, that he wasn't going to cajole or threaten or talk his way out of this, that the deep pool of hatred that Terri had built up was finally engulfing him.

Jimmy was dead.

The thought raced through Terri's mind over and over again, like kids racing around a room until something stopped them. And then that thought suddenly stopped, was replaced by something else, something bigger, darker, more powerful.

I killed my husband.

Jesus fucking Christ, I killed my husband!

Again Terri could feel the hysteria rising, threatening to overwhelm her, standing frozen above her husband's rotting corpse, above the body of the man she had killed. No, not killed. Murdered. She had murdered him in cold blood.

Premeditated.

Brutal.

Murder.

There was no doubt that any judge, any jury would find her guilty. She was guilty as charged, guilty as hell, going to spend the rest of her locked up for killing the fat, vicious, sadistic . . .

Terri's runaway thoughts were stopped short by the one sound that could cut through everything, bring her back to her senses with a gasp.

The front doorbell.

Terri froze, instantly sober, instantly on alert.

Who the fuck was that?

Again the doorbell rang.

What the hell was the time? She glanced up – night, it was dark outside, but she had no clue whether it was nine o'clock at night or three in the morning.

And yet again the bell rang.

Was it the police? Had someone heard the gunshots? No, wait, it had to be at least a day since she had killed Jimmy.

Then maybe it was the smell? Someone had complained about . . .

Terri froze. An even worse sound. A key in the lock, the front door opening.

Suddenly Terri found herself moving, running out of the bedroom, along the hallway, down the stairs, her stockinged feet slipping on the carpet as she raced downwards.

She was almost at the bottom of the stairs when the door burst open, and Mickey strode in, one arm around Georgie.

Mickey looked up as Terri skidded to a halt at the bottom of the stairs. "Sorry to come round so late," he began, then suddenly noticed the look on Terri's face. "Christ, Tel, you all right? You look like shit!"

Mickey kicked the door shut, glanced around. "Is that cunt of a husband around? We could really do with a bit of peace and quiet."

Terri gulped, fumbled for words. "No. He's …
I mean … he won't bother us."

Mickey didn't seem to notice her shocked
state. "Great. Let's get you in here." He half shoved,
half carried Georgie into the living room, Terri
trailing behind, plonked him down on the couch.
Georgie sat primly, adjusted his skirt, checked his
wig, seemingly oblivious to the huge bloodstain on
the front of his dress.

Terri gasped when she saw the blood, hurried
over to sit beside Georgie. She placed a protective
arm around him. "Georgie? You all right, love?"

Georgie blinked slowly, looked at Terri with
uncomprehending eyes. "All right?" repeated
Georgie vacantly.

"He's fine," said Mickey, picking up and
checking the two empty vodka bottles. His eyes took
in the rest of the room. "Been on a bit of a bender,
have you?"

Terri tore her eyes away from Georgie, met
Mickey's cold, calculating gaze. "Yeah, you know, I
was –"

Mickey cut her off. "Well, whatever you've
been up to, I need you now. Go make us all a cup of
tea, then we'll talk, figure out what to do with the
body."

Terri's eyes widened, her mouth half-open,
rigid with fear. "The body?" she gasped.

Mickey nodded towards Georgie. "Yeah.
Didn't think all that blood was Georgie's did ya? I

told you he was OK." Mickey leaned down, rummaged on the table and found a packet of cigarettes. He pulled one out for himself, gave one to Terri, shoved a third between Georgie's lips.

One by one he lit them, sucked the smoke deep into his lungs. He'd knocked smoking on the head a while back, but at times like this there was nothing better than a cigarette to calm him down, help him think straight. He pulled his phone out, looked down at Terri, still sitting frozen on the couch. Christ, he'd brought Georgie here so that Terri could look after him, but right now she looked as fucked up as Georgie. What the hell was going on with her?

"Oi, Terri? Are you going to make us that tea or what? I'm just going to give Marty a call, get him to take care of something for us." Still she didn't move. Didn't blink. Didn't do anything. Mickey peered at her. What was the fucking matter with the dozy bitch? "Oi! Terri! Chop, chop! We've got a bit of a situation here, and I need you to help me!"

Terri's eyes slowly came back into focus. Mickey was staring at her, eyebrows raised in expectation. She let out a deep breath, climbed wearily to her feet. "Got something I need to show you," she said slowly.

Mickey scowled. "Can't it wait?" He nodded to Georgie, still sitting gazing into space, lost in his own world. "This is fucking important! Georgie's killed some fucking geezer!"

Terri slowly nodded, reached out and gently took Mickey's hand. "He's not the only one," she said softly.

Mickey

Mickey didn't often drop into a pub in the morning unless it was on business, but after the night he'd had he needed a drink, somewhere quiet, somewhere where people wouldn't immediately know him, where he could sit quietly, sip his drink without questions, without demands, without stupid fucking family members killing someone and needing him to clear up the fucking body!

The Cross Keys was perfect. Mickey knew the owner, Sean Slattery, but went in there rarely enough that he was likely to able to sit and drink without anyone bothering him.

The pub was mercifully quiet when he arrived, just a couple of old men sitting in the corner with their half pints, noses buried in the Sporting Life as they made their selection for the day.

Mickey ordered his drink, double Scotch on the rocks, propped himself at the bar, and tried to unwind. Dean was an old geezer, white-haired, a bit shaky on his legs, but he was solid, an old school publican who knew when to talk, when to leave you alone, and most of all, when to turn a blind eye.

Mickey gave his drink an appreciative look. Just what he needed. He took a sip, his mind still full of the image of Jimmy's bloated body. That was a turn up for the books. He'd known Terri was unhappy with Jimmy – the bloke was a first rate cunt, but he'd never thought she'd have the bollocks to kill him. Fucking hell, he didn't realise how miserable and fucked off Terri was to do that . . . Something had tipped her over the edge. A few times Mickey had offered to sort him out, but she'd always declined, so Mickey had figured that underneath it all she still loved him, not that she was waiting for the opportunity to do it herself.

Still, Mickey could relate to that. It was a Taylor family trait; none of them liked other people to do their dirty work, they all dealt with things themselves. But murder? Terri? That was one he'd never seen coming.

Mickey sipped his drink, gazed around the pub in a distracted way. One of the reasons Mickey had chosen the Cross Keys today was that it was so wonderfully old-fashioned. Turning the pub into a teenage hangout with loud music and games machines was not for Sean. No massive TV screens showing sports 24/7. No, Sean was old school, thought a pub should be a comfy place for men to come and have a drink and chat with their mates in peace and quiet.

The décor was as old as Sean himself, which was to say it hadn't changed in all the years Mickey had been coming there. Small windows letting in very little light, dark flocked wallpaper, red velour benches along the walls, sturdy oak tables and chairs, and on the walls, old paintings of fox hunting and horse brasses.

Mickey grinned; he couldn't remember the last time he'd seen a pub that still had horse brasses on the walls! And above the mantelpiece, Sean's pride and joy, a pair of old crossed swords. They were dusty, the metal tarnished and, like everything else in the pub, stained from the years and years of smoking.

Though the law had changed, the pub hadn't, and there was still a heavy smell of smoke permeating everything. It was well-known in the area that there was regular lock-ins at the Cross Keys where smoking was allowed. Mickey had been once or twice, they were real men's events with 70s music, a couple of dodgy strippers, and at least one good fight every time. A proper night out!

He sipped his Scotch, took a deep breath, slowly relaxing. It had been a rough few weeks, from Charlie and Del's death to the raid on the Vietnamese and the row with the travellers, and now Georgie and Terri pulling their stupid fucking stunts.

Mickey knew what he was going to do with the pair of them, and it would serve them both right. They had always been close, Georgie and Terri, always talked to each other and seemed to understand each other. Well, if that was the case, and they were pulling shit like this, there was one simple solution – they could fucking live with each other.

They would whinge and moan about it of course, but ultimately it was the best solution for everyone. Terri's kids were grown, Jimmy's bastard offspring lived with their mother, and Mickey knew for a fact that Terri hated them.

Georgie had a big flat all to himself with plenty of room for Terri, she could move in with him and flog her place. They were a pair of old hens, it would give them both someone to look after, and a babysitter each to keep them out of trouble. Perfect!

Mickey nodded to himself. Problem sorted. That would give him one less headache to deal with. Another tiny sip of his drink. It was almost gone. When he was finished it would be back to work. He knew people would be looking for him, wanting him to sort stuff out, what to do with this, what to do with that, but he'd turned his phone to silent, promised himself that as long as this drink lasted he was off the clock.

One of the old men stood up, nodded to his mate. "See you, Norris. Cheers, Sean!" He pulled his coat around him – even though it was midsummer – and tottered out of the pub.

Mickey lifted his drink.

Last sip.

Almost time.

Then suddenly he froze. Norris? Why did that name ring a bell? Mickey paused, the glass halfway to his mouth, his brain suddenly back at full speed. Norris. Fucking unusual name that. Why did it stick in his mind? Something from a long, long time ago, something about Norris from way back in the past, way back when Bobby was alive, Norris, Norris … Mickey fumbled in his mind for the name, the connection. And then suddenly there it was. Suddenly he knew exactly who the old man was, knew exactly what he needed to do.

Mickey drained his glass, set it down firmly on the counter, turned around Norris Attley?"

The old man looked up, a challenging look on his face. This was a bloke who had seen his share of fights and trouble, with a hard face, a large purple nose, narrow eyes. Even in old age he still had a belligerent way about him. "Who's asking?" challenged Norris

Mickey adjusted his cuffs, smoothed back his hair, buttoned his jacket. When you have waited this long for something, there's no need to rush it. He could feel the adrenaline surging through him, feel forty years of vengeance flushing through his system as he strode forward. "Mickey Taylor!"

If Mickey had harbored any doubts that this was the bloke, the one he had been looking for, for so long, the expression on the old man's face blew them all away. It was a look of fear, of recognition, the look of a hunted animal that thinks it has escaped, only to find the hunter suddenly right behind it.

"Mickey, I …I …"

Mickey's movements were sure, certain, decisive. Without even breaking stride, he grabbed one of the swords from the mantelpiece, pulled it free from its bracket, and in one smooth movement buried it in Norris Attley's belly.

The old man's eyes shot wide open in shock, then immediately started to droop as his guts spilled out and his life blood began to drain away.

Mickey let go of the sword, still buried deep in the old man's guts, stood watching as he died in front of him. Forty fucking years he had waited for this, and he was determined to enjoy every fucking second. "You should have stayed away," he told the old man.

Norris looked up, his eyes already clouding over. "I thought you might have forgotten," he whispered, blood bubbling from his mouth. "I thought …"

He never finished his sentence. And just like that he died. Just like that forty years of brooding and plotting, hope and frustration were at an end.

Attley's head drooped forward, but he still sat bolt upright, pinned to the bench by the sword.

Mickey was calmness personified as he marched to the doors of the pub, bolted them shut, then returned to the bar, where Sean stood, white-faced, open mouthed. "Another double Scotch," Mickey ordered. "And it looks like the pub's closed for remodelling."

As Sean fumbled to get his drink, Mickey looked around at the smoky, dreary interior. Suddenly it no longer looked warm and inviting, no longer looked cosy and traditional, it just looked dirty. Dirty, old and tired. "It's about fucking time this place got a face lift," Mickey told Sean as he handed Mickey his drink.

Sean was still staring wide-eyed at Norris's body, sitting in the corner. Apart from the sword buried in his stomach, the pool of blood staining the carpet, he looked like an old man who had dozed off down at his local. Sean licked his lips, finally found his voice. "Jesus Christ, Mickey!" A deep breath. "I mean, what the fuck?"

Mickey took a long drink, met Sean's eyes. "You got a problem?"

"No, no, but …" He glanced over at the dead body. "And I can't afford a remodel, can't afford to be closed for –"

"The remodel will be paid for. You'll be paid the whole time you're closed. Five grand a week do it?"

Sean nodded. "Yeah, yeah, of course, Mickey ..."

Mickey was certain that Sean didn't make five grand in a good month. It would be money well spent.

Sean tried to look at Mickey, but his eyes kept straying back to the old man in the corner, the sword through his guts.

Mickey glanced back at Norris, then returned his gaze to Sean. "You're wondering about the old geezer? What he ever did to me?"

Sean nodded.

Mickey gazed at his glass for a moment. He didn't usually explain himself to anybody, but Sean was an old family friend, he deserved an explanation. "You know I used to be a pretty handy boxer?" he said suddenly.

Sean nodded. "Yeah, but–"

"When I was eighteen," continued Mickey, "I was one of the favourites for the ABA junior middleweight title. Christ, I loved it. Nothing was gonna stop me. Trained my bleeding arse off, et right, massages and warm baths after training to relax the muscles, I did fucking everything I could to be ready." Mickey paused, reflexively rubbed his elbow, his forearm.

Sean's eyes were now glued to Mickey. "What happened?"

Mickey turned, eyes like chips of fiery venom. "That cunt. That's what happened!"

Mickey felt great, at the top of his game. There was a swagger to his walk, his skin glowed with health and energy, he was like a coiled spring, counting down the days to the big fight, slowly reducing his training so that come the day he would be fresh, fired up, ready to unload on the unfortunate bastard that stepped into the ring with him.

His sparring partners at the gym couldn't wait for the championships, couldn't wait for Mickey to have a real opponent to pound on. Even though he had been holding back, he'd beaten them black and blue. He was ready.

He strolled down the Heathway towards his house, his gym bag over his shoulder, oblivious to the light rain, oblivious too to the car that stalked him, hanging fifty yards back, waiting for the moment when the road was clear, when nobody would see the accident that was about to occur.

Steak and chips, that was what his mum had promised him, a slap-up treat to celebrate his last night of training before he headed up to Nottingham the next day for the championship. He was going up there as a contender, but would come back as a champion, as a real somebody.

So consumed was Mickey by his daydreaming that he didn't see it coming, only barely registered the sound at the last minute as the car smashed into him, flinging him in the air and leaving him sprawled and bleeding on the pavement in a pile of blood and broken glass ...

"It was my old man," Mickey told Sean. "That cunt Bobby paid for the hit."

Sean stared in disbelief. "Your own dad had you knocked down, wanted you dead?"

Mickey nodded. "Couldn't stand that people were all talking about me. Mickey this and Mickey that, Mickey's going to win the ABA, he'll be the most famous bloke in Dagenham, all that shit. So he hired someone to run me over, kill me." Mickey turned and looked over at Norris, slumped in the corner. "Hired that cunt, Norris."

Mickey drained his glass, held it out for another. "Not to kill me, just to fuck me up."

Sean quickly refilled Mickey's glass.

"He did a perfect job on ending my boxing career though." Mickey shook his head. "It was several years before I even knew Attley's name, and by then he'd long since left the area." Mickey contemplated the glass for a moment. "Must have thought it had been long enough – that I would have forgotten by now." Mickey's hand tightened around the glass, his eyes darkened. "But that's one thing people should know about the Taylors. We never, ever forget."

Mickey stood up, drained his glass and set it on the counter. "Gimme your keys, Sean."

Sean turned quickly, rummaged in the cash drawer, came up with a big bunch of keys.

"Good man. So here's what happens. Is there somewhere you've always fancied going on holiday but never been?"

"Egypt," said Sean quickly. "I've always wanted to see the pyramids before I die."

"Lovely. Egypt's lovely." Mickey gestured for Sean to come out from behind the bar. He moved slowly on arthritic legs, tottered out to stand beside Mickey, who put a heavy arm across his shoulder. "You go home, put your feet up, watch a bit of daytime TV. Maybe the racing, something like that?"

Sean nodded.

"Later this afternoon, someone will come round to see you. They'll sort you out financially, pay for your holiday in Egypt – a couple of weeks sound good? Perfect. Then you go off on your hols, and when you come back, the pub will be all fixed up and ready for its grand reopening."

They had reached the door. Sean looked up at Mickey. "That's very kind of you, Mickey." He hesitated, glanced back at Norris. "But what about him?"

"He came in today, had a drink, looked at the Sporting News. End of story."

Sean nodded. "And the body?"

Mickey held the door open for Sean. "Enjoy Egypt, Sean."

Sean met Mickey's eyes, then with a last glance back tottered out into the bright, sunny street.

Mickey slowly closed the doors, slammed the bolts into place, pulled his phone from his pocket, dialed. He glanced across at Norris slumped body as the phone rang, and a smile creased the corners of his eyes. "Marty? Listen, mate, you'll never guess who I crossed swords with today ..."

Tommy

"We shouldn't be doing this." Tommy looked around nervously as they strolled into the pub. It was quiet, a Tuesday evening, just a handful of punters propping up the bar. As usual, Tommy and Jeanette had driven out to a country pub, hopefully far away from any familiar faces. But still, with Jeanette, you never knew.

Jeanette was her usual carefree self. She squeezed Tommy's hand, smiled the smile that melted his worries. "Relax. You get the drinks, and I'll find us a table outside."

Tommy watched her as she walked away. Christ, she had a walk that could start a war, wearing a micro miniskirt that clung to her bum, revealing every gorgeous curve. Even the old men at the bar, old geezers who probably hadn't had a hard on in twenty years, even they followed her with their eyes as she headed for the beer garden.

Tommy tore his eyes way from Jeanette, ordered their drinks. He had to be careful how he approached this. He didn't want to piss Jeanette off, send her scurrying back to her old man, but he sensed that she was as fed up with all of this as he was. If he could just get her to agree to work together on all this shit going on, then maybe they had a chance. Well, it could end up making Tommy a right fucking hero. Bet his dad wouldn't see that coming!

Mickey was sharp, no doubt about that, and Tommy knew not to underestimate him. He had more contacts and informers than the fucking KGB, which was one reason Tommy was so paranoid about being out in public with Jeanette. The other, of course, was Jeanette's family. They made Mickey's network seem like a handful of schoolboys spying on the girls' shower room. Tommy felt certain that everywhere they went, someone would be there who recognized her, and who would immediately report it back to her family. If that happened, the shit would really hit the fan.

Tommy grabbed the drinks, headed outside. Jeanette was sitting at a bench on the far side of the garden, a young bloke leaning over her, clearly chatting her up. Tommy's eyes narrowed as he approached.

"Oi! Fuck off!"

The bloke looked up. He was well built, probably a bit taller than Tommy, but there was something in Tommy's eyes, the way he stood, that made the bloke back away. "All right, geezer, no harm, just saying hello."

Tommy set the drinks on the table, turned to the bloke. "Yeah, well now it's time to say goodbye!"

The bloke looked over at his two mates, sitting at another bench watching, then decided against doing anything. Sometimes it was better to just walk away. "All right, keep your knickers on …" He backed away, hands up.

Tommy watched him all the way back to his mates, then finally sat down beside Jeanette.

She grinned at Tommy, her eyes gleaming. "There are times I almost forget that you're a Taylor," she cooed, sipping her drink. "Then you react like that, remind me exactly who your dad is!"

Tommy finally tore his eyes away from the three blokes, turned back to Jeanette. "I don't like people taking liberties, that's all." He wrapped a possessive arm around her shoulders, his thumb stroking the soft skin of her shoulder.

She snuggled into him. "Don't worry, I'm not looking to trade you in yet!"

Tommy grinned. That was one of the things he loved about Jeanette; she had a sense of humor, kept him on his toes.

He gave her a quick kiss, then turned to face her. "Listen, there's something I wanted to talk to you about."

She smiled. "Oooh, you're getting all serious. You're not about to propose to me, are you? Because I don't know if you remember, but you're married!"

Tommy laughed. "No. I'm not about to propose to you."

She pretended to pout.

"It's about this shit with your dad, with my dad."

Instantly her face turned serious. "We agreed not to talk about our families, Tommy."

"I know, I know. But I don't think we can avoid it anymore. I mean, if they don't sort out this thing with this piece of fucking land soon, it's going to wind up in a fucking war between the Taylors and the travellers!"

Jeanette looked away, gazing at a wild rose bush that had emerged from the hedge at the end of the pub garden, its pale yellow flowers seemingly too fragile to possibly survive amidst such a tangle of greenery. "You spend your whole bleeding life trying to get away from your family," she sighed, "trying to pretend you're not one of them – that you're different, but you can't." She turned to meet his adoring gaze. "You can't outrun them, can't get away from them, can't get away from who you are."

"Tell me about it," muttered Tommy.

"I hate all of this, we will always be caught up in this secrecy, me and you creeping around hoping no one will recognise us. I can't handle this for much longer. What are we going to do about it all Tommy? I'm just so scared if we don't do something this will end in heartbreak for us both. We will never be together. I don't want any part of that, yet here I am with you, being pulled right back into it."

"But don't you see, love, that's exactly why we can do something here! Because we're not caught up in it. Not caught up in the bullshit, the emotion." Tommy took her hand, made her turn and look at him. "We are the only ones who can resolve this without a long, bloody war."

Jeanette met his eyes. "I love you, Tommy."

He softly kissed her. "I love you too ..."

The kiss was long, passionate. When they finally parted, her cheeks were flushed, her eyes bright. "OK. So what are you thinking?"

"We have got to sort this out so our families can be friends again ..." Tommy paused, looked away.

"What? Tell me Tommy, what are you thinking?"

"Well, maybe, only if you wanted, I could think about getting a divorce ..."

Jeanette gasped, put her hand to her mouth. "Are you serious?"

Tommy shrugged. "I don't know. It's always seemed so impossible for us, but you know, if we can do this, get everyone in the families happy again ..."

She nodded, her face serious. "So what do you need me to do?"

"Somehow, you've got to get into Big Frankie's mind. Your granddad is the one who has to agree to anything if we're gonna solve this, but we just don't know what he's thinking. It ain't money … so what does he want?"

Jeanette grasped his hand. "He's a tough old bastard, but he has a soft spot for me." She smiled. "I'll see if I can get him to talk."

Tommy grinned, kissed her. "You're a bleeding angel you are!"

Mickey

Mickey sat on the bonnet of his car, waiting. He was dying for a cigarette. Even though he'd quit twenty years ago, he still craved it at times like this, when he was under stress, when shit was going on, when he was doing nothing, just sitting, waiting. He knew he had been right to quit, had no illusions about what it had been doing to him, but it was hard to get out of his system, he'd done it for so long. Christ, he was barely ten years old when he started, that meant he'd smoked for almost thirty years. There were times when it was still tough not to do it, so many people around him smoked, but Miranda hated it, complained when he came home from a night out with the boys stinking of smoke.

He glanced at his watch. Talking of Miranda, where was she? It wasn't like her to be late, ran her life like a sergeant major she did, with a fully booked schedule of meetings with friends, yoga, classes, trips to the hairdresser, manicurist, beauticians. Her schedule made your average businessman's life look relaxed and uncomplicated.

Not that Mickey wasn't grateful. Even pushing sixty, she still looked like a million dollars, regularly got hit on by blokes half her age, but it was a full time bloody job looking that way, that was for sure.

Still, at night, with the lights low, when she came slinking her way to bed in some sexy lingerie, those long legs encased in sheer black stockings, she still looked like a supermodel. And the things she did. Well let's just say that their life in the bedroom hadn't calmed down from the days of their frantic first couplings, just after Mickey had got out of prison.

Mickey gave an involuntary shiver as he thought of prison. It was a long time ago now, over fifteen years, but there wasn't a day went by that he didn't think about it, that it didn't intrude its way into his thoughts. It was like a dark nightmare that was always lurking at the back of your mind, waiting for the moment when you fell asleep to creep up on you and wrap its tentacles around you.

Odd things would trigger it – the sound of a metal door slamming, a smell, or maybe a shout – and then it all came rushing back into his mind as though it were yesterday. No, worse than that, as though it were today, as though everything that Mickey had done in the past fifteen years was just a dream, and prison was the reality, the reality he was about to wake up to.

He'd thought when he got out that he would soon forget it, that being back out in the real world, having all those things he'd missed while he was inside would drive the memories away. He'd been dead wrong on that score. And Mickey was one of the lucky ones. Because of who he was, his reputation, his connections, he'd never had to fear for his life in there. Never had to worry about being raped in the showers, or getting a beating, or having his stuff nicked. The other cons made way when Mickey walked by; even the guards had treated him well, aware of the influence someone like Mickey could wield, even from behind bars.

Still, he'd hated every last, miserable minute of it, and had vowed never to go back. It was easy to say, but Mickey meant it when he said he would rather die than go back inside. That was why he was so grateful to Marty, for steering the business down legitimate paths, for putting a lid on Mickey's worst excesses, for calming him down when his hot temper threatened to get out of hand.

"Nice motor, mate!"

Mickey looked up. Two little tarts, couldn't have been more than sixteen, were eyeing up him and the car. Short skirts, bleached blonde hair, a right pair of Essex slappers. Mickey grinned. "Like it do ya?" He had the convertible Aston Martin tonight, his date car Miranda called it – he always drove it when they were going out, like tonight.

"Gorgeous it is!" One of the little tarts ran her hand seductively along the side of the car.

"Like a ride, I'll bet?"

"Cor yeah!"

Mickey's eyes were sparkling. "And what will you do for me in return?"

The girl got closer, ran a hand down Mickey's arm. "Anything you fucking want, mate …"

Mickey suddenly pushed her away. "You should be ashamed of yourselves!" he snapped at them. "Acting like fucking prozzies just for a ride in a fancy motor. You don't know who I am, what I might have done to you!"

The girls stepped back, gave Mickey a look that was full of attitude. "All right, granddad, keep your shirt on!"

They looked at each other, turned and strolled away. "Your loss!" one of them called back over her shoulder.

Mickey shook his head in disgust and amazement as he watched them stroll away. What was the world coming to? They were still almost kids, yet they were prepared to put out in exchange for a ride in a flash motor. Mickey checked his watch again … over half an hour late she was, he was getting the hump.

Mickey pulled out his phone, dialled Miranda again. It was the fourth or fifth time he called her in the past half hour, but just like every other time there was no reply, and he wound up getting her voice mail.

"Where are you, you dozy cow!" he snapped. "I'm still outside the restaurant. Fellini's, remember? Eight thirty? Our anniversary? Christ, it's the bloke who's supposed to forget, not the woman. Where the fuck are you?"

But by the time nine o'clock rolled around, Mickey's annoyance had turned to concern. His next call wasn't to Miranda, but Martin. "Marty. We've got a situation. Miranda's gone missing, isn't answering her phone."

One of the things Mickey loved about his brother was that when the shit hit the fan, you never had to explain anything to him, he never panicked, he just took control. "I'll call Sid, see where she is. There's probably a simple explanation." Sid had been watching Miranda ever since the situation with the travellers kicked off. He was discrete, reliable.

Mickey scowled. "I dunno, Marty, it feels wrong."

"All right. Just in case, I'll send Darren by the house; he's closest and get the boys together. We'll meet you at the club in fifteen minutes?"

"Yeah, yeah, that's good." Mickey let out a deep sigh of relief. "Thanks, Marty."

He climbed in the car, cranked the motor. It roared into life, and Mickey pulled away in a squeal of tyres. Thank God for Marty indeed. Calm as Mickey could be in almost any other circumstance – if Miranda really were missing – if anyone had done anything to her, he wouldn't be able to think straight.

Even now, as he drove at breakneck speed towards the club, he could think of nothing else. His mind was already filled with horrific images. Miranda dead with her throat cut. Miranda bound and gagged. Miranda shoved in the boot of a car somewhere.

It was those fucking pikeys! thought Mickey. They've gone and taken this too far. Not content with fucking with Mickey's business, they'd made it personal. He would show them personal! If they wanted to take it to this level, he would make it his mission to kidnap and kill every fucking one of Big Frankie's family. He would torture them, rape them, beat them, kill them! And if they had hurt her, or, God forbid, killed her, then there would be no end to his vengeance. He would spend the rest of his life hunting down and killing every fucking pikey in the country!

The car had barely stopped before Mickey was out the door, running into the gym, quiet at this time of night, straight to the office. Martin was already there, Brick too, and a couple of the other boys they used on rough jobs.

"Have you heard from Sid?"

Martin shook his head. "He's not answering."

"Fuck!" Mickey felt his heart sink. "What about Darren?"

"He's on his way, should be there any minute now."

"Did you tell him where the key was?"

"And the alarm code."

Mickey slumped in his chair, grabbed the Scotch that one of the lads offered him. He downed it in one go, held the glass out for a refill. "I will fucking kill Big Frankie with my own hands!"

"We don't know that it's them, don't even know if anything's happened to her yet," reasoned Martin.

Mickey shook his head. "They've got her Marty, I can just feel it. If Sid isn't answering, and Miranda's gone missing, that's bad fucking news!"

Martin looked at his brother, recognized the cold, mad look in his eyes. Christ – if anything happened to Miranda – if someone had done something to her, hell was going to break loose. He had seen Mickey like this a few times before, and it was never a pretty sight. People tended to wind up beaten to death in a storm of indiscriminate violence that made even Martin nervous.

They heard the door to the gym bang shut, and several more boys strolled in. Brick hurried out of the office to meet them, update them on what was happening without disturbing Mickey.

"I remember the first time I saw her," said Mickey suddenly.

Martin gestured to the other two lads to leave the office. They didn't need to be told twice.

"Fucking jail bait she was then, Marty. Couldn't have been more than thirteen or fourteen, so I would have been about eighteen, but Jesus Christ, to see her was to want her. She had those long legs already, great tits, those kiss me lips. Looked fucking outrageous in her school uniform she did, that tiny skirt, tight blouse ..." Mickey rubbed his forehead, sipped his drink. "I didn't touch her, even though she flirted with me something rotten. She was Sharon's best mate, and Christ knows Sharon needed a best friend, so I stayed away. Then I met Mandy, got married, went inside, that was it." He looked over at Martin. "She'd come on to me several times after I was married, and by then she was old enough, but for the first few years I was trying to be faithful to Mandy, and Miranda was a bit too close to home, if you know what I mean? But I never forgot her, even when I was inside. For some reason she stuck in my head, the one that got away."

He glanced out the office window at the boys gathered in the gym. Several were perched on the edge of the boxing ring, smoking, talking in hushed voices. "They're a good crew," he told Martin, "but they have no idea what is about to happen."

"We don't know that," repeated Martin. "She might have got sick, been in an accident; there's a thousand other explanations."

"And Sid?"

Martin had no answer for that.

Mickey stood up, paced the room, stopped in front of Martin. "They've got her. I just know it."

As Martin started to reply, his mobile rang. He snatched it up before Mickey could answer it. "It's Darren," he hissed to Mickey. "What have you got? Are you in the house?"

Darren's voice sounded strained, emotional. "I'm inside. You need to get over here right now!"

Mickey could see it was bad news from the expression on Martin's face. Hard as he tried to keep it in, he couldn't stop the clenching of his jaw, the tightening around his eyes. "What? What is it? Is she there? Is she OK?" Mickey stumbled towards Martin, reached for the phone. "Let me talk to him!"

Martin put his desk between himself and his brother, spoke calmly to Darren. "Darren? You have to tell me. Is she dead?"

Mickey's eyes were like chips of rock, cold, hard, unmoving as he stared at his brother, waited for the reply.

"She's dead," said Darren softly.

"We'll be there soon," said Martin, his voice clipped and cold. "Don't touch anything."

Mickey didn't need to hear the answer to know what it was. He felt the blood drain from his face, his legs go weak, stumbled backwards to collapse in a chair, buried his face in his hands.

"I'm sorry, Mickey," said Martin softly.

The sound that escaped from Mickey's mouth was an animal roar of pure anguish. It filled the small office, echoed out into the gym, where the men all stopped their conversation, turned towards the source of the sound.

Brick looked up, made eye contact with Martin through the glass, ran a finger across his neck. Is she dead?

Martin gave a brief nod, then turned to his brother. What do you say to your brother when he has just found out that his wife has been murdered? There are no right words for a situation like that, nothing you can say that will make it any better. So Martin did the only thing he could, crouched down beside the chair, wrapped his arm around Mickey's shoulders and leaned his head in against this brother.

For several minutes they stayed like that. Mickey was silent, unmoving, head in hands. The only thing Martin could feel, the only sign of life, was his breathing. Rapid and shallow at first, Mickey gradually brought it under control, slower and deeper with each breath. Finally he sat up, turned to Martin.

Martin felt a chill run down his back. He had seen Mickey angry before. He had seen him cold and calculating. Seen him kill people. But he had never seen him like this. His face was flat, expressionless, unreadable. Even his eyes – so expressive usually – were flat, as though he had willed himself to show no emotion. "Let's go to the house," he said quietly.

Martin stood up. "Are you sure you want to –"

"– the house! Now."

Martin nodded. "I'll drive, OK?"

Mickey nodded.

"What about the boys?"

Mickey glanced out into the gym, to where their men were huddled, silent, still, looking anywhere but towards the office, towards Mickey. "Tell Brick to have two of them follow us, just in case," replied Mickey, his voice barely a whisper. "Brick can wait here with the rest of them in case they decide to hit us here."

"Got it."

The drive to Mickey's house was the longest thirty minutes of Martin's life. He wanted to reach out, say or do something to ease his brother's pain, but Mickey sat silent and rigid the whole way there. Martin wondered if he would even hear anything if he did speak. He seemed completely locked inside himself, sitting totally still, hands clasped together in his lap, staring straight ahead with unseeing eyes.

Not once in the entire journey did Mickey move, adjust his position, move his head, his hands, anything. He was like a statue, frozen, carved from granite, a hard, impervious, unmoving object.

That was creepy enough, but what worried Martin even more was what would happen when they got there. It was all very well holding it inside, but how would Mickey react when he saw Miranda's body? Because make no mistake, that was what they were going to see, and though Darren hadn't said much, it was clear from his voice that whatever had been done to Miranda, it wasn't going to be a pretty sight.

Would he stay calm, or would he lose it? Mickey out of control wasn't a pretty sight. People would get hurt. Badly hurt. Lots of them. Shit hitting the fan didn't even begin to describe what happened when Mickey got out of control.

They turned off the main road, Martin easing his way through the quiet suburbs of Upminster towards Mickey's house. "Mickey?" he said softly.

No reply. No indication that he had even heard Martin.

"When we get there, I was thinking I should go in first, see what –"

"– I'm coming in with you."

"But what if –"

"– they killed her, Marty. I get that."

"Do you really want to see that? I won't be –"

"– I'm coming in, Marty." He finally moved, turned his head to look at his brother. "They murdered her in cold blood. It will be bloody. I get that. Horrific. I get that too. But I have to see. Have to say goodbye."

Martin turned on to Mickey's street, made one last attempt. "Do you really want that image – of Miranda dead – to be the last memory of her?"

The car came to a halt on Mickey's driveway. Mickey reached for the door handle. "Nothing will ever change the memories I have of her. But I need to see what the fuckers did, need to have that image in my head as I gut them pikeys one by one and watch them slowly die."

Darren was waiting for them, opened the door as they came up the drive. He caught Martin's eye, then held up a hand to try and stop Mickey. "Guv'nor, I really don't think you should –"

Mickey pushed past him, wordless, Martin following right behind. "Thanks, Darren," he said. "Where is she?"

"Upstairs."

"You wait here, keep an eye out?"

Darren nodded, slowly closed the door behind them.

Mickey took the stairs slowly, steadily. He felt out of control, as though someone else was in charge of his body. Although his legs felt heavy, each step was a huge physical effort, he was powerless to stop the steady tread upwards. Step, step, step, each stair he climbed brought him closer to seeing the one thing in all the world he didn't want to see, his body fighting itself as he continued the relentless climb.

What he'd said to Martin in the car was true – he needed to fix the image in his mind as a way to steel himself for the carnage that was going to come. What he planned to do was going to be, even by Mickey's standards, horrific. He'd killed people before – more than he really cared to count – but never with the icy cold, slow deliberateness that he had in mind for Miranda's killers. He would wipe out Big Frankie's whole family, no question there, but most important of all was knowing who had actually done it.

For the actual killers he had a long, excruciating death planned. It wasn't going to be quick. It was going to be the longest, most gruesome death he could manage to come up with. It would be days, weeks, months even of pain and torture and misery, and he planned to see every last minute of it. This wasn't going to be a time to delegate, to have the boys do the dirty work. Mickey wanted to get blood on his hands, to bathe in it.

Mickey reached the top of the stairs, turned instinctively to the right, towards the master bedroom. He knew that's where they would have done it, where they would have left the body. It was what he would have done if he had wanted to leave a message, if he had wanted someone to know exactly what he had done.

There were many options in a situation like this; Mickey had used many of them himself in the past. You could kidnap the person and say nothing, let their loved ones wonder where they were, fear the worst. That was cruel because it allowed hope to build.

Or you could seize them and tell the other party, let them wonder and fear what you were doing to them. Would you let them live? Would you kill them? Were you torturing them? Would they ever see them again?

Or finally, you could simply kill them. Do it somewhere – like their own house – that left no doubt about the message. This is war. We are coming for you. We will stop at nothing, we will hit you where it hurts, where you are most vulnerable.

That was what they had chosen, and Mickey was ready for it.

He stopped outside the bedroom door, took a deep breath. He could feel Martin beside him, looking at him, imploring him with his eyes not to do this, but Mickey couldn't stop now. He had to see what they had done, see his beautiful Miranda one last time, so that he could say goodbye to her.

He reached out, his hand shaking, grabbed the handle. His hand was sweating as his fingers wrapped around the cold metal, it seemed to take an age just to perform the simple act of closing his hand around it. He stared at his shaking arm, his fingers, pale as they gripped the handle tight. They seemed like someone else's fingers, someone else's hand as he stared and stared, slowing his breath, preparing himself to do the unthinkable.

He could feel Martin right behind him, sense his fear, his emotion. Mickey knew if he hesitated any longer Martin would try and talk him out of it, try and stop Mickey from going in. He had to do it now before he lost the nerve, before his knees collapsed beneath him.

This was it.

He was ready.

He turned the handle, pushed the door open.

"Oh, sweet Jesus Christ!" Martin gazed at Miranda's mutilated body for a second, before tearing his eyes away, catching Mickey as he fell to his knees.

Mickey was sobbing, gasping, his heart barely beating, great rasping sounds coming from his mouth as he fought for breath, fought for life, fought for a way to continue after what he had seen.

He curled up into a ball on his knees, his face pressed to the thick carpet, arms around his head as though warding off a blow, but it was too late, the blow had already been struck, he had seen what they had done to Miranda.

Martin wrapped his arms around him, held him, listened as the gasping turned to a wail of anguish, as he tried desperately to articulate something, crying, sobbing, moaning.

Somehow Martin pulled him to his feet, turned him away from the bed, shoved him out the door, down the hallway, Mickey stumbling, tears and snot and saliva streaking his face.

Martin shoved him into the bathroom, kicked the door shut behind them. Mickey turned and buried his face into his brother's shoulder, still sobbing desperately while Martin hugged him, felt his body heave with great intakes of breath, Mickey's hands gripping Martin's arms tight.

"Why, Marty? Why?" he finally managed to gasp. "I knew she was dead, but why did they have to do that to her?"

Martin stared at his own reflection in the mirror, his eyes cold, his expression set and hard. His own face stared back at him, but what he saw still was Miranda's blood-covered body.

She was spread-eagled on the bed. Her throat had been cut, that was what had killed her, hopefully, but they had also sliced up her face, cut off her breasts. She had also bled profusely from between her legs. Martin shuddered to think what had caused that, prayed that all of the abuse and mutilation had happened after she was dead.

The entire bed was covered in blood; the whole room smelt of it. Martin doubted that he would ever get that smell, the sight of Miranda out of his mind.

He felt Mickey stiffen against him, pull himself upright, his breathing returning to normal. He turned away from Martin, turned on the cold tap, buried his face in the sink. He splashed cold water on his face for a moment, then grabbed the hand towel and fiercely dried his face.

When he turned back to Martin, it was almost as though it had never happened. Apart from some redness around his eyes, he looked normal. Normal for Mickey, that was. He met Martin's gaze, his eyes narrowed to chips of granite, his jaw muscles tight. "Organize a clean up here. Get Doc Waters to deal with the necessities. She had a heart attack or something, whatever he thinks will sound convincing."

Martin started to say something, to offer some comfort, some words of solace, but Mickey was already past that – had locked away his emotions, his feelings. All that remained in Mickey's heart was revenge. As Martin met his brother's eyes, the look in Mickey's eyes left no room for doubt, for disagreement, for discussion. Martin nodded. "I'll get it done."

Mickey pushed past his brother, opened the bathroom door. "Then get the rest of the boys together. Everyone we can trust, everyone who owes us, everyone who can get the job done, have them meet us at the gym." He paused in the doorway, took a final deep breath before going back out into the world. "It's payback time!" he rasped as he stalked out.

Mickey

It was dark by the time Mickey and Martin pulled up outside the gates of the scrap metal merchants. The high gates were locked tight, the glow of a bonfire lighting up the sky behind the gates.

Martin cut the engine, turned to his brother. "This is not the way to do this, Mickey. We need a plan, a strategy. We can't just crash through the gates and start killing everyone inside."

Mickey stared straight ahead. "Why not?"

"Because we have no fucking idea what is the other side of those gates!" snapped Martin. He had tried several times to talk Mickey down, to get him to figure out another way to do this, but Mickey wasn't listening, wasn't interested in anything but pure, naked revenge. He wanted it to be bloody and violent, and he wanted it to be now. "Have you even thought about how we're going to get in there?" asked Martin, desperately.

"I told Brick to bring something big. We'll just blast right through those fucking gates, scare the fucking shit out of them."

Martin shook his head. "It will be a bloodbath."

"That's what I want."

"With us getting killed?"

Mickey turned and looked at him sharply, started to say something, but Martin cut him off. "Think about it," begged Martin. "You declared war on them. They've struck back. You think they're not expecting us to come after them? They'd have to be fucking soft in the head not to have someone keeping an eye out, especially after we set that fire bomb off inside their place before."

Mickey leaned forward, peered down the end of the street at the gates. It was quiet – really quiet – no one visible. "What. You think they're watching us right now?"

"I'd lay good fucking money on it!" asserted Martin. "They may be murdering cunts, but they're not fucking morons!"

Mickey looked thoughtful for a moment. "Then I guess we'd better get the fuck on with it! Before they call in their reinforcements!"

"Jesus, Mickey, take a moment to think before you do this! We don't know for certain that they killed Miranda, and even if they did, we have no idea who's in there right now. Maybe Big Frankie and his family have buggered off back to Ireland? Maybe there's just a bunch of blokes with shotguns waiting the other side of those gates. What about that?"

Mickey respected Martin, respected his brain, his strategy. He wanted to listen to him; half knew that Martin was right. But the other half of his brain refused to let him think logically. The other half of his brain was filled with the brief, horrific glimpse of Miranda that he'd had, was filled with one simple, primal thought. Revenge. Kill every fucker who had been even distantly related to her death. And he was convinced that whoever had perpetrated that killing was lurking on the other side of those gates.

"He's in there," he said finally, in a low voice. "Big Frankie. He's in there." He glowered towards the gates, the dancing flames of the bonfire lighting the sky with flickering tongues of orange, a column of dark smoke rising up into the clear, starry sky. He glanced in the mirror as a set of lights rolled up behind them. "Here's Brick."

Mickey threw the door open, climbed out, breathing in the warm summer air, gave an approving nod as Brick jumped out the cab of an artic.

"Big enough?"

Mickey looked towards the gates, then back at the truck. "Perfect. You up for this?"

"Yeah, I'll drive it."

Martin had climbed out too, was looking in disbelief at the artic.

"Tell all the boys to be ready," ordered Mickey. "Safeties off. We go in firing, shoot anything that moves. I don't care if it's a cat, a rat, a fucking ant. If it moves in there, kill it."

Brick nodded.

"Let's do it!"

As Mickey turned back to his car, he froze. There was a rattle of chains coming from the gates. Someone was opening them!

Tommy slid his car through the turn, driving with one hand, his phone clamped to his ear. "OK, OK, slow down. They're outside the gates right now? Well how the fuck should I know what they are doing there?"

Jeanette had called Tommy just a few minutes ago, frantic. Tommy had told her that Miranda was dead, but now she said that Mickey and his boys were outside the gates of the scrapyard. The war was escalating to a new level.

He sped towards a red light, a quick look right and left, and he raced through it, the telltale flash of light telling him that he'd been caught on camera. Sod it, let Sol deal with that problem later.

"OK, slow down, slow down, take a deep breath and think," he told her. "What would solve this? What would satisfy your grandfather and get everyone to step back from the brink?"

The traffic slowed ahead of him. Tommy didn't have time for this. He pulled into the other lane, flashing his lights at the oncoming traffic. Startled drivers pulled over, or ground to a halt, and he weaved from side to side until he could pull back into his own lane, partially dazzled by the lights being flashed at him. "Something, anything!" he implored.

A left turn loomed ahead. He cut the wheel hard, forcing the tyres to fight for traction as he slid round the turn. For a second, he thought the car wasn't going to make it, then the rubber gripped and he was round, tearing down the narrow side street at sixty miles an hour, praying that no one pulled out in front of him.

"Yeah, yeah. Course I've heard of that. You think it will work?"

The car hit a pothole, jerked sideways, but he held it, tore round a tight curve.

"OK, I'll give it a try. Stay safe! Stay inside! I'll be there in five minutes!"

Mickey stood in the middle of the street, a shotgun across his arm, Martin beside him. Behind him were gathered his crew, a dozen or so of London's most vicious hard men, all armed, ready for battle.

Slowly, inch by inch, the gates opened. The bonfire blazed behind it, casting a garish light on the scrapyard, the piles of crushed cars towering high above the small office.

A solitary figure stepped forward, backlit by the flames, like a figure stepping out of hell itself. Even though he could just see a silhouette, Mickey could tell that it was Big Frankie.

Mickey stepped forward to meet him.

"It doesn't have to come to this, Mickey!" the old man shouted.

Mickey still had his shotgun over his arm as he marched forward. Despite his anger, he was in a cold, calculating mood, his eyes scanning the shadows of the junkyard, looking for anyone hiding there. When the shit hit the fan, he wanted to know what they were up against.

"You brought this on us all!" shouted Mickey. "You made it personal!"

Big Frankie moved slowly forwards, keeping the fire behind him. "We had an agreement, your father and me."

The two men stopped, ten yards apart. "Who gives a fuck about that now?" snarled Mickey. "You've messed with my family, there's only one way this ends!"

Mickey, staring towards the blazing bonfire, couldn't see Frankie's face, but he could hear the puzzlement in the old man's voice. "Family? I've done nothing to your family!"

"Don't lie to me, Frankie! I've just come from my house, seen my wife's bloody body lying in my bed. I'm going to wipe you and your family from the face of the Earth!"

Frankie took another step forwards. "Your wife? We didn't touch your wife, Mickey. We would never do that!"

"Don't fucking lie to me!"

"I'm not lying!" He stepped forward again, closer now, allowed Mickey to see his face. They were about five yards apart, the flames giving Mickey's face an orange glow, but he could see genuine concern in the old man's expression. "I would never touch your family."

"Well if you didn't, some of your fucking boy's did, coz my wife's fucking dead, and I aim to kill the bastards who did it!" Mickey struggled – but failed – to keep the emotion out of his voice.

Big Frankie turned, gazed back into the darkness. "Is this something I should know about?"

There was a moment's silence, then Frankie Junior emerged from the shadows. Like Mickey, he had a shotgun slung casually across one arm, his hands in his pockets. He walked slowly over to stand beside his father. "Nothing to do with us, Fa. I'd swear to it."

Mickey scowled. "You're a bunch of fucking liars!" he snapped. "You've fucked with my business, killed my fucking wife!" He suddenly raised the shotgun, aimed it directly at Big Frankie. At this distance it would blow him apart. "It's time to settle this!"

In an instant Frankie Junior had also raised his shotgun, aimed it at Mickey.

Big Frankie seemed to be the only one who was staying calm. "Mickey. I'm sorry for your loss. But think about it. You've known me –" he motioned with his arms "– known us, for a long time. Have you ever heard of us doing something like that? Family is sacred to us, you know that."

Mickey held the shotgun level, his hands steady, his finger resting lightly on the trigger. One gentle squeeze, that was all it would take. One little squeeze of his finger, and the old man would be dead. He might not have been the one to actually kill Miranda – he almost certainly wasn't – but it would have been on his orders. Of course, Mickey would die too. Frankie Junior would see to that. And then a huge fucking battle would break out, ending this matter once and for all. Would that be so bad? Miranda was dead – what the fuck did Mickey care about anything else? Miranda was dead …

"We didn't do it, Mickey," Frankie Junior repeated.

Mickey blinked away the tears that were prickling the corners of his eyes, turned his focus to Frankie Junior. "You're a fucking liar!" he shouted. "You're all fucking liars!"

Frankie Junior raised his shotgun slightly. "Nobody calls me a liar!"

They stared at each other, eyeball to eyeball down the barrels of their shotguns. "Well I did! I just called you a liar! A dirty, fucking pikey liar! What are you going to fucking do about it?"

If Mickey shot first, he could kill Frankie Junior with his first shot, put the old man down with his second. There were almost certainly guns trained on him right now, but if he'd put both of them down, who cared? Marty and the boys would take care of the rest, they would get the land back, and the Taylor family would all live happily ever after on the money. And Miranda would be avenged.

"Don't call me a liar Mickey! We didn't touch your wife!"

"Liar!!"

Mickey tightened his finger, squeezing gently the way he'd been taught, almost caressing it as he slowly increased the pressure. Soon it would be over, soon he would . . .

There was a squeal of tyres behind him. Mickey released the pressure on the trigger, turned to see the source of the noise.

A car came screaming down the road towards them, scattering Martin and the boys out the way, screeched to a halt just behind Mickey. He squinted into the lights, couldn't see who it was. The door flew open, and to his amazement, Tommy climbed out.

"Tommy? What the fuck are you doing here?"

Tommy ran past his dad, stopped midway between him and Big Frankie. "They didn't do it! They didn't kill Miranda!" He held his hand up to stop his father, who had started forwards, turned to Big Frankie and his son. "Tell him!"

Frankie Junior glared at him. "Who the fuck are you?"

Mickey was still confused by Tommy's sudden appearance. "He's my son …" he muttered.

Frankie Junior shrugged. "I already told him. He called us liars!"

Mickey started to raise his shotgun again, but Tommy strode towards him, pushed the gun back down. "No guns!"

Mickey glared at him, confused, angry. "Tommy, what the fuck are you doing? This is none of your busin –"

"This is none of my business?" snapped Tommy. "This is none of my fucking business!" He looked around. "You are standing here about to get yourself killed, Uncle Martin's here too, and you say this is none of my business! This is absolutely my fucking business!"

To Mickey's amazement, Tommy suddenly wrenched the shotgun from Mickey's hands, threw it on the ground. Mickey was so surprised that he let him do it.

Tommy turned back to Frankie Junior. "You too!"

Frankie Junior started to say something, but the old man did the same as Tommy, wrenched the shotgun from his son's hands, threw it on the ground. "Let's hear what the boy has to say," growled the old man. "He seems to be the only one here talking any sense!"

Tommy took a deep breath, feeling the eyes upon him. "Our families have a long history," he began, his voice suddenly croaky. He'd got their attention, now he needed to make sure this thing ended the right way. He cleared his throat, continued. "We've been friends a long time."

"None of that matters now," began Mickey.

Tommy turned on him. "Shut it!"

He turned back towards the others. "The land is ours, there's no doubt of that." Frankie Junior bristled at this, but said nothing. "But Frankie's family has been here a long time, have settled here."

He took another deep breath, looked back and forth between them. "You're both right. And you're both being a bunch of stubborn, pig-headed wankers!" Everyone was watching him, wondering where this was going. "I know the lawyers think it's all about the money, about agreeing an amount that both parties can accept, but it was never about the money. It's about pride. Right?" He looked back and forth between them. No one was arguing with him. "This is about the Taylors," he continued. "This is about Frankie's mob. And we all know that neither side is going to back down. So there's only one way to resolve this!"

You could hear a pin drop.

No one said a word.

The traffic rumbled in the background.

The bonfire crackled.

Tommy took another deep breath, forced his voice out despite the nervousness he felt. "We do it the old way. In the ring. Bare knuckle."

Still no one said anything.

For a moment, Tommy thought they hadn't heard him, or were about to laugh out loud. Then Old Frankie spoke. "What are the terms?"

Tommy had to fight to keep a smile from his face. It was working! It was fucking working! "If we win, you walk away, leave here," he told Frankie. He turned to look at his father. "If you win, the land is yours. You can stay and fight the government, or you can sell it, your choice."

Old Frankie nodded. "And you stop the accusations? We didn't touch your family, never would. I swear that on my soul."

Mickey stared back at Tommy, eyebrows furrowed, scowling. "We give them the fucking land?"

Tommy turned on him, eyes blazing. "Yes! If we lose, that's what happens!"

Big Frankie nodded. "We accept."

Tommy turned to Mickey. "Well?"

Mickey's cold eyes glared back at Tommy. He glanced at Big Frankie for a moment, his huge, craggy figure silhouetted by the flames, then finally nodded. "We fight."

Tommy felt a huge wave of relief wash over him, wanted to jump up and down with joy, but knew it wasn't yet time to celebrate.

"So who fights?" asked Big Frankie.

"I'll fight for our family," said Frankie Junior quickly.

The old man nodded.

"And I'll fight for the Taylors!" answered Tommy.

"No fucking way!" Mickey stepped forward, shoved Tommy aside. "I fight for the Taylors!" Tommy started to say something, but Mickey stopped him, gently touched his shoulder. "You've done good, son, you've brought us this far. But this is my fight. Mine to win or to lose."

Tommy nodded. He wanted desperately to be the one, the one to fight for the family, to finally gain the acceptance he so desperately craved, but he knew deep down that he would never get his father to agree to it. "OK," he said slowly.

"Where and when?" demanded Big Frankie.

Mickey grinned. "Taylor's gym, midnight!"

Big Frankie nodded. "We'll be there!"

Mickey

The gym had never been so full. Tommy and Big Frankie had sorted the details, agreeing that each of them could have fifty supporters. Of course, in the event, many more had shown up, and now the club was packed to the rafters, a haze of blue smoke curling up to the ceiling to hover round the lights, diffusing and softening the usually harsh fluorescents.

Mickey sat on his desk, stripped to just his shorts, taking a last sip of water before the fight. Tommy and Martin had wanted to be with him, to help him in some way, but Mickey told them to leave, wanted time to himself, knew there was nothing anyone could do at this point to help him. He needed to be alone with his thoughts.

His thoughts. Christ, for most men, under the circumstances, the last thing they would want would be to have time alone to brood and reflect. In the past few days he had found out that his brother was going out dressed as a tranny giving blow jobs and had killed someone, his sister had offed her nonce of a husband, his wife had been brutally murdered in their own home, and now he was going to have to fight for his family's honour, not to mention a plot of land worth millions.

Most men would have been crushed and beaten already by that succession of hammer blows. Most men would have broken down long ago, burst into tears, lost themselves in booze, or drugs. Most men.

But Mickey Taylor wasn't most men. Mickey Taylor had survived his dad and the endless years of beatings and abuse. He had survived prison. He had survived kidnapping, torture, anything and everything that his brutal lifestyle had thrown at him.

He wasn't most men.

He was Mickey fucking Taylor.

He was The Man.

He was Dangerous.

Mickey rolled his shoulders, his neck, clenched and unclenched his fists. It somehow felt that his whole life had been building to this. From the moment he had first scrunched his ten-year-old hands into tight fists and battered the shit out of a bunch of bullies who had been picking on him for years, he had known that this was what he was good at. That when other men had doubts or fears, when other men were faced by a bigger, tougher opponent, felt that cold chill in their stomachs, that was when Mickey came into his own.

He would take on anyone one on one, no matter how big, how good, how much younger than him, he would take them on, and he would expect to win.

Why?

Because he was Mickey Taylor.

A roar from outside broke through Mickey's thoughts. He glanced out the window. The travellers were all cheering, greeting their boy. Young Frankie might be his name, but he was no kid, thought Mickey as his opponent walked calmly towards the ring, pushing his way through, his family, friends and supporters slapping him on the back and loudly cheering him.

He was a big fucking boy was Young Frankie. He was lean and muscular, with a long-limbed, raw-boned look about him, like a farm boy, or a labourer whose muscles had been honed by years of hard work.

Mickey already knew of him by reputation – he'd won the big fight up at the Appleby horse fair six years running, was known as a bruising, relentless fighter, a skilled boxer too.

Mickey watched him all the way to the ring, looking for any sign of weakness in his movement, his face, his body language.

There was nothing.

He was calm, confident, had a faraway look to his eyes that Mickey recognized as that of someone who was in the zone, someone completely focused on what he was about to do.

Mickey looked away, and just like that, he shut himself into his own world, his own zone. He closed his eyes, took several deep breaths, shut out the noise, the shouts, the chatter, everything suddenly gone as Mickey got himself into the frame of mind he needed to win the fight. Sometimes it could be hard, hard to find that seed, that spark of cold hard anger that Mickey thrived on, but today it was easy, today it was different. Today he had Miranda to fight for.

Eyes still closed, he pictured her as he'd known her, as he'd loved her.

Smiling and laughing at him.

Correcting him on his manners.

Excitedly showing him what she'd bought on her latest shopping trip.

Moving beneath him, her perfect body covered in a sheen of fine perspiration, her eyes gazing up at him with adoration and wonder as they made love.

And then finally Miranda dead.

Miranda's beautiful body desecrated and bloodied in the very bed in which they had spent so many happy hours together.

There was a sharp rap on the door. "It's time, Mickey."

Mickey let out a long, deep breath, rolled his shoulders one more time, then opened his eyes.

And when he did, the look was there. The mad, murderous, cold-eyed look that people knew and feared. The look that meant that Mickey was ready. That Mickey was Dangerous.

It was game time.

Mickey stepped out of his office, and the crowd fell silent for a moment. Like a Roman Emperor among the populous, Mickey looked neither left nor right, walking to the ring with calm, measured steps, a look of absolute calm on his face as the crowd parted like the Red Sea to let him through. So powerful was the aura that surrounded him that the few people who reached out to slap him on the back quickly stopped, thought better of it, watched him pass in reverential silence.

The strange calm lasted until Mickey climbed up and then ducked through the ropes and into the ring, at which point an absolute roar broke out from both sides.

The two men moved forwards to meet in the middle, dwarfing Harry Foster, a local boxing referee who had been drafted in at short notice for the occasion.

Harry looked nervously from one to the other, then held up his hand for quiet.

The gym gradually fell silent.

Harry made eye contact with the fighters. Mickey, stocky, powerful, wound tight and ready to explode, with his mad, murderous, cold-eyed stare.

Young Frankie, several inches taller than Mickey, loose-limbed and rangy, with a look of utter clarity and determination on his handsome face.

"Rules are simple," announced Harry. "No kicking, kneeing, gouging, biting, butting or elbows. Rounds last two minutes, with a minute break between each round. If you hit a man when he's down, it's an automatic disqualification." He took a deep breath. "We fight until one of you is knocked down and doesn't get up."

He looked to both of them for their assent, was rewarded with a barely perceptible nod from Frankie Junior, nothing from Mickey. It was as though Mickey was locked in his own private world, oblivious to everything but his own body, nothing penetrating his shell.

Harry nodded to the bellman. "May the best man win!" He stepped back. "Fight!" The sound of the bell was drowned out by the roar of the crowd as the fight began.

From the start it was clear what the tactics were. Mickey advanced with relentless intent, keeping his head down, his elbows in close, aimed a barrage of thunderous blows at Frankie's ribs.

Frankie was taller, more of a boxer, worked hard to keep Mickey at bay with good footwork and a rangy right jab.

After their initial roar the audience held their breath, watching to see how it would unfold, occasional cheers of "Come on, Mickey!" or "Nice shot, Frankie!" punctuating the room.

The first round was Frankie's, landing more punches, mostly staying out of range of Mickey's savage body blows, picking him off with jabs, though most of them hit his arms, or the top of his head. Like an elephant being bitten by mosquitoes, Mickey seemed oblivious to them, kept coming forward relentlessly, his thick arms held close to his body, then suddenly darting out to slam his fist into Frankie's ribs. And each time he did there was a little grunt from Frankie as the wind was hammered out of him.

As they returned to their corners at the end of the first round, both men were already bathed in sweat – the combination of the overhead lights and the mass of bodies had made the gym like a sauna, so even the spectators were sweating. For the two fighters, it was brutal.

Mickey leaned against the ropes as Tommy toweled him off, Martin held a water bottle to his mouth.

"He's picking you off too easily!" barked Martin. "You've got the strength, but he's got the range. If some of those jabs or hooks really connect, you're going to be in trouble."

Tommy dropped the towel, massaged Mickey's shoulders. "I've seen you fight plenty of times!" he shouted above the hubbub of the crowd, "your footwork's better than that! Move around a bit more!"

Mickey's eyes were closed, locked in his zone, picturing Miranda's violated, bloody body over and over again.

"Can you hear me, Mickey?" shouted Martin, peering at his brother's face. "You've got to –"

Mickey suddenly stepped forward, almost knocking Martin over. "I know what I'm doing!" he growled, pushing the two of them away and striding to the centre of the ring.

The second round followed the pattern of the first. This was brutal fighting, little finesse, though both men were good boxers. Mickey stalked Frankie Junior like a robot with just one program while Frankie danced and skipped and jabbed, picking Mickey off at will while mostly avoiding Mickey's stamina sapping punches. But every now and then one slipped through his guard, and the whole crowd groaned at the sound of the punch, a solid, meaty thump that made experienced fighters wince in shared pain.

Through rounds three, four, five and six Mickey kept up his relentless plod forwards, Frankie still dancing and jabbing, but it was clear that the pace was taking its toll on both men. While they were both in shape, neither had trained for the relentless pace of an actual fight such as this, especially one that carried such an emotional burden for both men.

Mickey leaned heavily on the ropes at the end of the sixth round, his chest heaving as he fought to control his breathing. The side of his head was bruised and slightly bloodied from the blows he had taken, but as he looked across the ring a grin played at the corner of his eyes.

Frankie's seconds were holding his hands in a bucket of water. Tommy followed his gaze, grinned. "Must be fucking killing him, keep hitting that hard head of yours, eh?"

Mickey nodded. "His speed is good, but he's tiring," he said softly. He looked over, met Martin's gaze. "Reckon it's time?"

Martin sucked his teeth, thoughtful. "Give him one more round, then I think he'll be ready."

Mickey nodded, took another sip of water, headed back out.

As they two men re-engaged, a little slower this time, Tommy turned to Martin. "What are you two cooking up?"

Martin grinned, nodded towards the ring. "Just wait and see."

The seventh round was a slow motion version of what had gone before. Mickey was still the aggressor, but his forward march had slowed to a plod, his arms looked heavy, he was having trouble holding them up, and Frankie managed to get a few more jabs through, even a right hook that crashed into the top of Mickey's head.

As the bell sounded for the end of the seventh round, Mickey tottered back to the corner. He looked beat.

Tommy looked concerned, couldn't help notice that Frankie's seconds were looking over at Mickey, pointing and whispering in Frankie's ear. "Dad, are you all right?" he said as he rubbed Mickey's shoulders. Mickey's arms hung by his side, his face was slack jawed as he sucked great lungs full of air down into his aching lungs. "Dad?"

Mickey didn't respond, seemed not to have heard Tommy, his eyes fixed on the floor in front of him.

The sound of the bell to signal the start of round eight came far too soon for Tommy's liking. He was watching his dad wilt before his eyes. The great, unbeatable, indestructible Mickey Taylor was finally in trouble, his sixty plus years catching up with him as he tried desperately to defeat a skilled fighter twenty five years his junior.

Frankie Junior had seen it too. His punches suddenly had more snap, his jabs flicking out with a verve they hadn't had for several rounds, catching Mickey again and again.

Suddenly he could see an end to the fight, could see the finish line. For the first time he was on the front foot, for the first time in the fight Mickey took a step backwards.

Frankie pressed forward, a three-punch combination rocking Mickey, sending him back into the ropes where he cowered like a wounded animal. A few more big punches and it would be over, Mickey would be on the canvas.

Frankie took his time, bobbing and weaving, looking for the opening, then flicking out a jab, opening Mickey up before following it with a cross or a hook.

Each punch that he landed seemed to diminish Mickey. Second by second he looked older, more tired, his arms dropping constantly as he tried to stop the onslaught.

When the bell finally came, Mickey looked out on his feet, barely making it back to his corner before slumping down. Tommy quickly wiped him down with a wet towel, started drying him off. He looked between the two of them. "This is your fucking master plan? Getting the shit beaten out of yourself?"

Mickey said nothing, just sucked on the water bottle that Martin held to his mouth, looked across the ring at Frankie, hands in a water bucket, bobbing and moving right through the break.

As the bell rang he turned quickly to Tommy. "Watch and learn, son!"

Frankie could not have been more surprised if Mickey had suddenly sprouted wings. He raced to the middle of the ring, stood there, hands to his sides, chin out, challenging Frankie to hit him.

Frankie hesitated for a minute, then unleashed a huge left hook, aiming to finish the fight in one blow. It was what Mickey had been waiting for.

He ducked as the blow came in, and at the same time launched a thunderous left at Frankie's exposed ribs.

Frankie's punch glanced off the top of Mickey's head, but Mickey's fist found its target, his balled up knuckles slamming into Frankie's ribs. The crack of bone could be heard throughout the gym, as could Frankie's groan of pain.

He staggered back, tried to cover up, to protect himself, but he was grimacing, his face a mask of pain.

Mickey went straight for the kill, no attempt to even cover up or defend, he just attacked Frankie like he would a heavy punchbag, blow after crushing blow aimed at his opponent's mid-section.

As good as Frankie Junior was, as well as he defended, Mickey's punches were too hard, too fast, and for every three punches that Frankie blocked, one got through.

It didn't take long. Another heavy punch slammed into Frankie's broken ribs, and as his body folded in on itself, Mickey threw everything into a savage uppercut, ducking down to power it upwards into Frankie's sternum.

The blow almost lifted him off his feet, sent him flying backwards into the ropes. He bounced off the taut ropes, almost curled up into a ball, straight into Mickey's path. As Frankie tottered towards him, Mickey aimed a clubbing right to the side of his face, smashing his cheekbone and sending him tumbling to the canvas.

The roar of the crowd filled the room. There was no coming back from that barrage, everyone knew it. Frankie lay curled in a ball, gasping, blood flowing from his open mouth while Mickey stood over him.

Harry jumped forward quickly. He'd had little to do in the fight, but he could at least preside over the last rights. "One, two!" He started to count, but struggled to be heard over the din. "Shit!" he shouted, "he ain't getting back up!" He grabbed Mickey's arm, held it aloft. "The winner by a knockout! Mickey Taylor!"

Mickey had been almost in a trance since the fight started. No matter that Big Frankie had denied any part in Miranda's death, Mickey couldn't get the image of her body out of his mind, had used that as a motivation. Cocooned inside his armour, he had barely felt Frankie's repeated blows to his head, his arms. Each time a punch landed, he had imagined it making him stronger, feeding him, feeding his fury, his anger, his desire to seriously hurt someone for what had been done to his wife. And when the chance had come, when he had had the opportunity to inflict pain on Frankie, he had delivered the blows with savage delight.

In truth, he hadn't wanted the fight to end. Who cared about the land, about anything? Miranda was dead. Miranda was dead, and Mickey was doing the only thing he could do to salve his wound – inflict pain on someone else. As long as the fight continued, Mickey could avoid the aftermath, could avoid going home to his empty house, to the memory of what had happened there, of what he had lost. As long as the fight lasted he could bury his grief in a sea of violence.

As the crowd washed over him, cheering, celebrating, Mickey simply felt numb. It was done. He had fought. He had won. Now he had to live the rest of his life without his one true love. How did you do that?

He was lifted high by his friends and family, carried round the ring like a heavyweight champion, a sixty year old man with nothing to live for being feted as though he had just claimed the whole world for his domain.

Finally the noise subsided a bit, Mickey was set back down on his feet. Martin hugged him from one side, Tommy from the other. Together they steered him towards the centre of the ring, where Big Frankie waited.

Mickey slowly pulled himself out of his trance. Life had to go on. The family needed him. And when all was said and done, he was still a Taylor, still the head of the family.

Big Frankie nodded slowly as his eyes met Mickey's. "You're one hell of a fucking fighter, Mickey Taylor." He held out his hand. Mickey reached out a weary arm, shook Frankie's huge hand. "I'd be proud to have you as my own son."

Mickey nodded. "Thanks."

"We'll be off the land in a few weeks," he continued. He looked tired, beaten.

Mickey glanced quickly at Martin, who nodded. "When we sell the land," said Mickey quickly, "we'll give you your cut. Two million."

Frankie paused. For a moment, Mickey thought he was going to refuse, but he finally nodded. "Thank you." He reached a hand out, touched Mickey's arm. "And please believe me, we had nothing to do with your wife's death."

"I know."

Epilogue

The Cross Keys had been the scene of many Taylor family celebrations, but few had ever been this big. Mickey had won the fight – that was cause for a celebration – and at the same time, it was a chance to drink to Miranda, honour her memory while trying to figure out who had killed her.

Mickey stood at one end of the bar, battered but unbowed, his face swollen and grazed, his hands gnarled, stiff. He had trouble holding his glass of Scotch, had to concentrate to wrap his fingers around it, but it felt good as the cool, fiery liquid slid down his throat.

A stream of well-wishers and hangers on came by to congratulate him and wish him well.

"Never had a moment's doubt!" they told him.

Or, "You fucking nailed him, Dangerous, fucking nailed him!"

Mickey forced a grin through his swollen lips, nodded his thanks, wishing he were anywhere but there. Wanting to be home, in his bed, relaxing, sleeping … but then, as soon as he thought of home, he pictured Miranda, as he'd last seen her, on their bed, the blood-soaked covers …

He knew the boys would have done a total clean-up, there wouldn't be a trace of anything when he got home, but he also knew that Miranda wouldn't be there when he got home. And so he sipped his drink, kept nodding and smiling, doing anything to prolong the evening, to drink himself into oblivion, so that he could finally fall asleep and forget.

"All right, Mickey?"

Mickey blinked, looked up and met Martin's gaze. "Yeah, yeah, Marty. Just a bit tired, that's all." But simply speaking the lie was enough to bring the feelings to the surface. Mickey suddenly clutched his brother's arm, felt the hot tears sting his cheeks as he turned away, gasped. "She's gone, Marty! She's fucking gone!"

Martin's arms held him in a death grip as he shielded Mickey from any prying eyes who might see his tears, his moment of weakness. "I'm sorry, mate," whispered Martin. "We'll find them, Mickey. Whoever the fuck did it, we'll find them and fucking string 'em up by their balls!"

Mickey swallowed deeply. He couldn't do this, not now, not here. There would be a time for grieving, a time for tears, but this wasn't it. He wiped a

battered hand across his face then straightened up, looked Martin in the eyes. "OK, OK, I'm all right."

Martin gave him a searching look. "Sure?"

Mickey nodded.

Martin let him go, glanced around the pub. No one seemed to have noticed Mickey's moment of weakness; they were all still chatting, drinking, some of them reliving moments of the fight with dodges, feints and uppercuts mimicking what they had seen.

Mickey looked at his brother. Martin was a fucking rock. He looked happy right now, and why not? He was the one in charge of the family's finances, and today had turned out really good for all of them. Once the travellers were gone and the land was sold, they were all going to be very rich.

Martin glanced back at Mickey, the tiredness and sorrow in his face impossible to hide despite his best efforts. "Why don't you sleep over at my place tonight?" he offered.

For a moment Mickey was tempted. Not having to face it, not having to walk in the house, that would be nice. But if not today, when? How long could he keep putting it off? Martin had already suggested that if Mickey wanted, they could sell the house, clear his stuff out for him, and he would never even have to go back there. But Mickey wanted to go back there. That was his house – his and Miranda's – and it held a million happy memories. He didn't want to lose those. "Let me think about it," he said

diplomatically, not wanting to refuse Martin. He downed his drink. "Right now, I need a piss!"

Martin gave him a sad smile. "As long as you're all right?"

Mickey forced the fake smile to his battered face. "Course I'm all right!" He pushed away from the bar, made his way through the crowd towards the toilets, followed by shouts and cheers of "Dangerous!" or, "Mickey!"

Mickey pushed open the door to the bathroom. It was mercifully deserted. It was a relief to be alone, to not have to smile, answer inane comments.

He stood at the urinal, one hand on the wall to support his tired body as he pissed.

The door opened. Mickey glanced over, hoping it wasn't someone else wanting to congratulate him, shake his hand, but it was just some Asian guy. He strolled in, a cocky look on his face, came and stood next to Mickey.

Something about the way he came and stood there made Mickey uncomfortable. Why wasn't he pissing? Suddenly Mickey's nerves were on high alert. There was something wrong …

Before Mickey could react, do anything, the door to the cubicle behind him flew open, and two more Asian guys swarmed out.

Mickey still had his dick in his hand as a garrote slipped over his head, tightened round his neck.

He tried to reach up to pull it free, tried to grab the guy behind him, but as he did so, the lad next to him slammed a long thin blade into Mickey's ribs.

The pain seared through him, he gasped, tried to draw breath, but couldn't. The garrote was tight around his throat, the knife had punctured his lung.

Another thrust, this time to his stomach, and Mickey collapsed, dragging the guy with the garrote down with him.

His vision started to cloud.

He was dying.

How was this possible? He had just fought the greatest battle of his life and won. How could this happen now?

Mickey lay on the floor, flailing and squirming like a dying fish, blood flowing from his stomach where the blade had severed his aorta.

He could feel himself slipping, feel his life ebbing away.

As darkness took hold of him, a hand gripped his face, forced him to look up. He opened his eyes, stared into the face of an older Asian man. "Mickey Taylor!" he sneered. "They told me you were dangerous!" He snorted in derision. "But you are just a local thug, couldn't even protect your wife from us! You couldn't possibly have thought you could beat us?"

The man stood up, adjusted his cuffs, his tie, nodded to the man with the garrote, who released his grip, stood up. The three of them turned to go.

"Wait!" Mickey's voice was a barely audible whisper as he gazed up at them.

The older man paused, looked down at Mickey, his battered face pale and drained of blood, lying bleeding to death on a urine soaked floor. "Who the fuck are you?" gasped Mickey.

The old man regarded him for a moment, watched as the last life drained from Mickey Taylor's eyes, his head slumped back onto the dirty floor, then turned and walked out.

Martin stood at the bar, sipped his gin and tonic. It had been a good day. Mickey had upheld the family honor and secured their financial future. He looked around the pub. There were times when he doubted his brother, his violent, impulsive ways, but when the chips were down, you could count on him. As long as Mickey was around, the Taylors would never have anything to fear.

Tommy came up to him, slightly drunk, his eyes sparkling.

"Proud of your old man?" asked Martin.

"Hey, less of the old," Tommy laughed. "He fucking schooled Young Frankie today!"

"That he fucking did!" agreed Martin.

Tommy leaned in close, the beer on his breath strong in Martin's nostrils. "You know, when he started down this whole path, fighting with the travellers about this land, I thought he was dead wrong."

"Me too."

"But if there's one thing I've learned," Tommy concluded, "it's that when my dad goes to war, he always fucking wins!"

Martin nodded.

Tommy held up his glass. "Here's to Mickey's fucking war!"

Martin lifted his glass, clinked it against Tommy's. "To Mickey's War!" He drained his glass, set it on the bar. "Now where is the old bastard? He can't still be pissing! It's time to get him home before he gets himself into more trouble!"

The End

Books by Sandra Prior

Dangerous – published 2012

Diamond Geezer – published 2014

www.SandraPrior.co.uk

http://www.facebook.com/sandrapriorauthor

http://twitter.com/Sandra_Prior

About the Author Sandra Prior

Most new authors are told to "write what you know", but Sandra Prior did just the opposite! She fulfilled her dream of becoming a crime novelist by creating the Taylors -- a family that couldn't be more different from her own.

Growing up in Dagenham, Sandra was surrounded by four sisters, a brother, and loving parents. She describes her childhood as "sunny and safe", and when she got older, she headed off to other safe places -- the Open University and the University of East London, to be exact, where she graduated with a degree in Cultural Studies. All are a far cry from the mean streets where Dangerous, Diamond Geezer, and Mickey's War take place!

By 1998, Sandra was a successful business owner, but she couldn't ignore the calling she felt from within. She had wanted to be a writer for as long as she could re-member, but in those days, it was simply a nice dream to have. It wasn't something that she actually thought she could go out and do.

Everything changed, though, when Sandra read about a life coach named Anthony Robbins. She went to one

of his London seminars and actually walked across a 15-foot bed of hot coals!

After that, she decided to "keep walking"…

Sandra started writing Dangerous, and even though there were plenty of times when she thought about throwing the half-written manuscript in the trash, she refused to give up on her dream. She stuck with the Taylors, and now the entire trilogy is proof that Sandra's dream has indeed become reality.

Today, Sandra lives in Clacton with her partner, her youngest son, and her dog -- who lets her write in peace as long as she takes him for walks on the beach when she's done!

www.SandraPrior.co.uk

http://www.facebook.com/sandrapriorauthor

http://twitter.com/Sandra_Prior